INVADERS FROM THE NORTH BEWARE!

Rounding the corner to the entrance of the house, I saw a terrible battle taking place. My mother's men were fighting a crowd of strange, pale-skinned warriors I had never seen before, speaking a language that was equally unfamiliar. I saw Teta, the leader of the Port House guard, fighting valiantly against four of them, while several of his guards went down before the large mass of foreign warriors.

With strange round shields and long swords of a make I had never seen, the men were vicious and gave no quarter. No one had yet noticed me as I stood before the house, looking desperately for my mother and sister, trying to decide what to do. Then I spotted Meri-Ta, my mother, surrounded by four of her faithful warriors. They were hopelessly struggling to protect her against the imposing wave of attackers.

My mind was then made up. Springing forward, I seized the sword-arm of one of the aggressors, striking him in the belly until he let go of his weapon. Then several of the strange warriors turned towards me...

SHADES OF MEMNON

Memnon and two other Ethiopians. Greek vase, 700 BC

SHADES OF MEMNON
BOOK ONE

BROTHER G

SHADES OF MEMNON

SHADES OF MEMNON

SHADES OF MEMNON
THE AFRICAN HERO OF THE TROJAN WAR AND THE KEYS TO ANCIENT WORLD CIVILIZATION
BOOK ONE

Copyright © 1999 by Gregory L. Walker (Brother G)

Published by Seker Nefer Press, a division of  Seker Nefer Group. www.memnon.com.

First Printing 1999.

This novel is a work of historical fantasy fiction based
on the legends and myths of the great African hero Memnon.

Book cover artist credit: Darryl Spicey
Book cover design: Courtney Jolliff / Direct Effect and the Ancestors
Library of Congress Cataloging-in-Publication Data:
Walker, Gregory Lyle
Shades Of Memnon: The African Hero Of The Trojan
War And The Keys To Ancient World Civilization
ISBN 0-9662374-0-4 (Original 1999 Softcover Edition)
1, Mythology. 2, Historical Fantasy Fiction.
3, African Studies. 4, Martial Arts. 5, Spirituality.
I Title
Library of Congress Catalog Card Number: 98-83244

BROTHER G

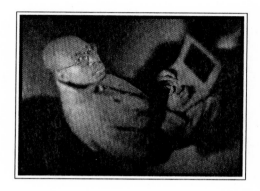

Brother G (Gregory L. Walker) is a Chicago based journalist, poet, historian and author. While working part-time for the Associated Press, Brother G spent 10 years conducting research for the African Legends genre, writing "Shades Of Memnon," and developing contacts in archeology, anthropology and linguistics worldwide. He has also written columns on comic books and graphic novels for the American Library Association, contributed to the national news publication "In These Times" and is one of a popular group of Chicago poets who inspired the motion picture "Love Jones." "Shades of Memnon" has been optioned for movie production by Saligna and So On, the international production house owned by director Euzhan Palcy ("A Dry White Season," "Sugar Cane Alley"), the first black woman to direct a major Hollywood feature film.

SHADES OF MEMNON

Clyde Ahmed Winters, Brother G and Ra Un Nefer Amen

***Dedicated to Clyde Ahmed Winters and Ra Un Nefer Amen:
Two giants in the struggle to reveal the true history of ancient
civilizations.***

Acknowledgments:

I would like to first thank the creator for making this world in such a way that it challenges all of us to struggle and to strive, for without this there would be no progress. I must next thank the long chain of ancestors, those known and unknown, who sent me here and put it into my heart to carry on this work. To my mother, Geneva and father, Pat and the rest of the Walker clan, thank you for your support and love. Thanks also to the Ausar Auset Society for revealing the great wisdom to me. Thanks to Clyde Winters for revealing the facts to me. Thanks to Bill Duke, Joe Landsdale and Tim Truman for the kind words and assistance.

To my creative and spiritual homies Apuat En Heru, En En Sa Takhi(John Grey), Donnino Hill, Courtney Jolliff, Darryl Spicy, Auset N' Temu, Aung Mu Ra, Jah Bang Jah, Baba Oje, Frank Stevenson, Tony Akins, Reatha Hardy, SeneMaku En En, Hrupti Men Ab and Hra Ptah: Thank you for every line drawn, every image rendered, every verse kicked, every line spoken, every minute edited and all advise given- together we are the modern Medjay and I love you all. You are constant reminders to me that a fist can break through where a finger falters. ***Peace.***

SHADES OF MEMNON

AUTHOR'S NOTES:

"Shades Of Memnon" is the first series of the new African Legends genre being introduced by Seker Nefer Press. Based upon 10 years of research, the genre reflects the study of epic traditions that we call "Epicology," a word coined by Ayele Bekerie, a brilliant professor of Africana Studies at Cornell University.

In his ground breaking book "Ethiopic: An African Writing System," Bekerie defines Epicology as "the art and science of mythologizing, symbolizing, narrating, lamenting, prophesying, allegorizing and folklorizing. It could be looked upon as total history."

I realized total history was what I had embarked upon 10 years ago after reading Bekerie's book. In my quest I have studied traditions of history, legend and myth along with the sciences of archeology, linguistics and anthropology in an attempt to find out where the history and lore originated. I too discovered that "epic comes in and out of history" and that "some epic tales could literally and deliberately evolve out of history" as Bekerie mentions in his definition.

I will even go a step further, to say that, based upon my study of spiritual traditions and African religion, Epicology can sometimes be a stream of spiritual energy. It can be the process by which the ancestors give us guidance here on the earth, a way of keeping messages alive so that we will not totally forget, even in the darkest times.

The legends of Memnon are of this nature, having over the years taken on an almost magical quality, as if the legend had a life of it's own. They raise questions:

· *Who were these "blameless Ethiopians" praised frequently by the ancient Greeks from the earliest times?*

· *Why were they the central focus of "The Ethiopis," the third book in the Trojan War saga?*

· *Who was Memnon, the prince/king of these blameless Africans?*

· *Why was he chosen to receive a unique immortality, while his opponent Achilles was sent to Hades after death (see "The Oddessy").*

· Why were the statues of a local king named after Memnon in Egypt by the Greeks?

· Why did one statue emit a distinct sound as the sun rose, eerily backing the tradition that Memnon was literally the "son of the Sun?"

· Why have poets referred to Memnon when pondering the highest aspects of human nobility?

· Why did a group of German scientists in 1907 name a journal about the world's greatest artistic, cultural and archeological finds "Memnon?"

· Why is there a French journal today that presents studies of great archeological finds called "Memnonia?"

These are Epicological questions I have pondered and striven to answer in an Epicological fashion, through interpreting the legend. Not only about Memnon, but about many other legends I have come across in this process. So I ask you to read this epicological glossary, and this book series, and think of it as my attempt to honestly portray the accumulated legend and historiography about Africans in ancient times. Just remember, Bekerie says it is not the task of Epicology to be literally true, as in portraying a real man whose name was Memnon. What is necessary is that it be honest in portraying a legendary figure and what he has come to mean to the world—the highest aspirations of human kind.

SHADES OF MEMNON

SHADES OF MEMNON

BOOK I
CONTENTS

SHADES OF MEMNON

SHADES OF MEMNON

"Mythology Is Psychological Archeology"
George Lucas of "Star Wars"

AN EPICOLOGICAL GLOSSARY OF TERMS:

Aahmes Nefertari— The greatest hero of ancient Kamit. Queen
Aahmes Nefertari led the coalition from southern Kamit that defeated the dreaded Hyksos invaders. Though practically ignored
by historians today, this queen was made the most honored Sheps
of Kamit's entire history. Temples built in her honor rivaled those
of the Neteru, and parades were held in her name until the beginning of the Christian era.

Aat— Kamitic: A region of the Taut underworld.

Agaru— The sacred island home of the Anu, located off the
coast of modern-day southern India. Small blacks live on islands
in this area to this day.

Allat— A female deity, popular among South Arabian blacks
until the coming of Islam.

Amen — The most high, creator deity of both the Kamitians and
Kushites, and many other East African nations.

Amen-Ra—Kamitic: Another name of the most high, with em-
phasis on the deity's role as a creative power - see Ra.

Amorites—Ancient name for a nomadic, warlike Shashu people
in the Middle East during the Bronze Age. They blended with the
Hittites to become the Habiru, forefathers of the modern-day
Hebrews.

Anetch Hrak— Kamitic: Common greeting given to honored elders, priests and royalty in Kamit.

Ancestor communication— A spiritual science: Rituals and psychic abilities developed to ensure that the links between the living and the deceased are not severed after death.

Anu— The sacred ancestors of the Kushites. These small blacks, originating near the Mountains of the Moon, once lived all over the earth. They were related to the present day forest pygmies of central Africa, whose traditions claim they once lived in large cities. Anu remains have been found near ancient monuments worldwide, including Stonehenge, the Great Pyramid and in Olmec/ Xiu ruins. Highly skilled in the spiritual sciences, they were the source of legends of pixies, fairies and elves.

Apademak— Kushite deity of protection. Always depicted in lion form, this deity was popular in upper Kamit and lower Kush from very ancient times until the Christian era.

Araby—Ancient name for modern-day Arabia, especially South Arabia.

Atef— Kamitic: Brother/friend, potential father.

Aten— Kamitic: The sun.

Atl-anta—Ancient name for the fabled land across the Atlantic Ocean, known first to the Kushau, then to the ancient Greeks and others. Source of the story of fabled Atlantis, Atl-anta was north, south and especially, middle America.

SHADES OF MEMNON

Ausar—Kamitic: Deity representing the highest aspects of spirituality.

Auset— Kamitic: Deity representing mothering, nurturing and emotions.

Baa en pet— Kamitic: Metal from the sky, a meteor.

Bekhtan—A country located in the Middle East during the Bronze Age near the country now called Syria. A great trading nation of Shasu and Tamahu peoples. It was destroyed during the Great World War.

Blybos— A Canaanite city famous for its seaport and ship building.

Basileia— Ancient homeland of the northernmost contingent of "People of the Sea," located in northern Europe near the Baltic and North Seas.

Canaan— Ancient country once located in the Middle East.

Canaanites— The Kushite people who once ruled in ancient Canaan. They were migrants from Tamana.

Chi—Far eastern name for the life force. Called Rau by Kamitians and Kundalini by people from South India.

Children of Geb— Kamitic: Human beings alive on the Earth.

Children of Impotent Revolt— Kamitic: Unchecked emotions, assistants of Set.

Dark Deceased— Kamitic: Unruly human spirits that refuse to rest after death. Confused and in need of light, they stay on to plague the living.

Desher Sea—Kamitic: The Red Sea.

Djahy—A region of the Middle East just south of where Israel is today.

Eastern Kushites— Blacks related to modern-day Somalians, South Indians and South Arabians, with dark brown to jet-black skin, curly to straight hair and sharper features than Western Kushites. Originally from Tamana.

Five Great Kushite Nations— The five groups from Tamana, whose people most adhered to the great teachings embodied by the spiritual sciences and the Universal Principles. These are the Kamitians of North East Africa, the Haltamtians of ancient Iran, the Canaanites of the Middle East, the Meluhans of Southern India and the Xiu of Asia and the Americas.

Geb—Kamitic: The deity of the material plane, Earth. The world was recognized as conscious by the people of Kamit thousands of years before the Gaia theories of today.

Great Green— Kamitic: The Mediterranean Sea.

Great World War— Around 1200 B. C., the Mediterranean area became embroiled in devastating warfare. This was due to invasions by a mysterious coalition led by northern Tamahu dubbed

SHADES OF MEMNON

the "People of the Sea" by Kamitians. They destroyed great nations in Europe, Asia and on the islands in the Mediterranean before they were finally defeated by a coalition of Kushites in Kamit. At the same time, in West Asia and India, Eastern Kushites were fighting other Tamahu who swept down from the Eurasian steppes. This Great World War, some historians think, was the source material of the greatest epics in ancient world history, such as the Iliad; the Norse Ragnarok sagas; the Philistine tales in the Old Testament; the Indian epic "The Mahabharata;" the story of Atlantis; and "The Ethiopis," which featured the legendary Memnon.

Habiru—Ancient name for the semi-nomadic tribes of Tamahu (Hittites) and Shashu (Amorites) who settled in the Middle East just after 2000 BC. They came together in the land of Canaan, forming the Hebrews of the Old Testament. "And say, thus saith the Lord God unto Jerusalem; Thy birth and nativity is in the land of Canaan, thy father was an Amorite, and thy mother a Hittite." - 01d Testament, Ezekiel 16:3.

Haltamti—Ancient Elam, located in the country we now call Iran, was settled by various groups from Tamana. Linguistic studies indicate domination by the Xiu, who also dominated in regions of China and Meso-America.

Hapi— Kamitic: The river Nile.

Hatti— Ancient country once located in Turkey. Originally settled by Kushites, it came under the domination of Tamahu who adopted the local culture. Sometimes an enemy, sometimes an ally of the Kamitians, it was a mighty nation with a highly evolved society. They were destroyed by the People of The Sea during the Great

World War.

Hittites — The Tamahu people of Hatti. Some settled in areas of the Middle East, blending with the Amorites to become the Habiru, forefathers of the early Hebrews.

Heru— Kamitic: Deity governing heroism, stability and maturity.

Herukhuti— Kamitic: Deity governing justice, warfare and the upholding of natural law.

Hesperides— Greek mythology says that islands called Hespers or Hesperides were located in a fabled land across the Atlantic Ocean and that Memnon was raised there. In reality these were the settlements of the Xiu people in ancient Mexico. Archeologists today are puzzled by the engineering feats of the Olmecs (see Xiu), who moved thousands of tons of earth and stone to create artificial islands, platforms for temple complexes and giant stone statues. A careful examination will reveal that sophisticated earth moving and stone working was a common technology of Tamana migrants worldwide. Direct mention was made by the Greek writer Scylaxus of Coriandre, who recorded that Phoenicians traded with Ethiopians on an island across the Atlantic Ocean. Today major Xiu settlements are known to have been located on islands in ancient Mexico.

Het-Heru — Kamitic: Deity governing pleasure, sexuality and imagination.

House of Life— Kamitic: School, place of learning.

SHADES OF MEMNON

Hyksos—A coalition of Tamahu and Shashu who wrested control of Lower Kamit from approximately 1640 to 1532 BC They were overthrown by an army of Kamitians from Waset (Thebes) and Medjay warriors led by the great Queen Aahmes Nefertari.

Indu— Ancient name for Eastern Kushites who lived in Indus Kush.

Indus Kush— Ancient name for the area stretching from Pakistan up through all of northern India. It was once dominated by Kushites, who fled the area during the time of the Great World War. Anthropologists today call their culture the Indus Civilization. They were originally from Tamana in Africa.

Ifrits—Evil creatures from Arabic folklore, often representing the fearful and destructive forces of the desert.

Ish-Ra-EI—Ancient Israel of the Old Testament.

Ka— Kamitic: Individual spirit, the personal soul.

Kabba Stone— Ancient black rock considered sacred by Islam even today and also revered by worshippers of the "goddess" religions of ancient Arabia.

Kam—Kamitic: Meaning dark or black. Mistranslated in Biblical texts as "Ham." Africans are the children of Kam, not of a rump of pork.

Kam-Atef— Famous creature from Kamitic legend. His name means "friend of black people."

Kamit— Correct name of ancient Egypt, meaning the land of black people (Kushites). Part of the Tamana cultural/civilization complex, Kamit had both Western and Eastern Kushites within its population, which explains why many monuments do not look like the stereotypical "Negro." The Kamitians created the greatest achievements known to mankind, seeding the world with their knowledge and puzzling us with spiritual sciences that have yet to be fully understood.

Kamitians— The people of Kamit.

Kamitic— Things of and from Kamit (i.e., language, monuments, culture, etc.).

Kamitic Heresy— During the last years of the 18th dynasty a new king named Ankhenaten mounted the throne and tried to institute sweeping changes in the religion of the Kamit. Declaring his "Atenist" religion (the worship of the physical sun) the only legitimate faith in Kamit, Ankhenaten built a city and moved thousands of converts to it. In time the Kamitic people rose up in defense of the traditional Ausarian spirituality and dethroned Ankenaten. Then they defeated his chief priest Ausar-Mesh (known biblically as Moses) banishing he and his followers from Kamit. These exiled heretics joined with others from the Middle East to become the biblical Israel, concocting a false history based upon Kamitic history, spirituality and cosmology, including hateful stories about the nation that had banished them.

Keftui— The island nation of ancient Crete in the Mediterranean Sea.

SHADES OF MEMNON

Khepera—Kamitic: The sacred beetle representing the act of creation.

K'un Lun— Legendary regions of ancient China dominated by blacks (Xiu and Shang) who migrated there from Tamana. One of the greatest settlements was that of the Xiu in China's Shensi province. Today dozens of pyramids, one nearly as large as Kamit's Great Pyramid, can still be found there.

Kula Yoga— A spiritual science: The children of Tamana discovered a third great use for sex, which is known today as tantra or tantric sex. It is the use of yoga and meditation techniques during intercourse that combine male and female Rau for use in healing, psychic phenomena, spiritual cultivation or other marvels we sometimes call "magic." Today Kula Yoga is practiced primarily in Asian and African cultures.

Kush—Land to the south of Kamit, home to the Kamitians before they settled further north.

Kushau— The name that the ancient high culture blacks of Africa called themselves. When they migrated they usually created place names, such as Indus Kush, similar to what they called themselves.

Kushite— Things of and from the Kushau.

Kushite darts — An amazing weapon of the Kushites. These throwing blades were 3 to 5 inches long and made of finely honed bronze. Razor sharp, they were astonishingly accurate weapons in the hands of a trained warrior. Kamitic paintings depict them being used for warfare and hunting small game. A favorite weapon of the Medjay warriors.

Lower Kamit— The northern region of Kamit which borders the Mediterranean, is referred to as "lower" or "down there" because the Kushite people lived with a southern orientation. Middle to southern Africa was their homeland and was therefore "up," while areas farther north were considered "down."

Maat— Kamitic: The Kamitic deity who governs the natural balance of the universe. Depicted as a woman, Maat also represented the ideal of "right" behavior and social justice.

Makka— Ancient name for the city of Mecca.

Medjay— Kushite warriors who moved into Kamit after helping to expel the Hyksos. The Medjay were great trackers who also served as the police force of Kamit, and were legendary martial artists.

Meluha— Ancient name of middle to southern India where other Tamana people settled.

Meluhites— Ancient name for the Kushites who still live in Southern India and are also immigrants from Tamana.

Memnon— The most widely known heroic figure in world history. When the Greeks took over Kamit they named two statues near Thebes the "Colossi Of Memnon," who in Greek myths went to the battle of Troy with warriors from Susa (Iran) and his

SHADES OF MEMNON

own homeland.

"To Troy no hero came of nobler line, or, if of nobler, Memnon, it was Thine" Homer.

The name "Memnon" means immortal in Greek and Kamitic, backing traditions that say he was made immortal by the gods. Kamitic: Mem - cummin = a black seed; na = to go on; un = living. Greek: Resolute, always there.

There was a temple in ancient Haltamti (Biblical Elam, called Iran today) called "The Temple of Memnon" and recent scholarship on Greek myths point to ancient Meso-America (see Hesperides and Xiu) as his homeland.

In Asia, Africa and Europe there are many legends of Memnon; some indicating that there were more than one. Some people south of Kamit claimed relation to Memnon, while ancient Greeks claim he went to Kamit's Thebes. In reality, Memnon represents the worldwide influence of the children of Tamana, especially the Kamits and the Xiu.

Men Ab— Kamitic: Meaning "still heart." Meditation technique to gain control over emotions and assist spiritual development.

Mesh— Kamitic: Meaning "born of" or "son of" or "daughter of." Examples: Ausar-Mesh, Ra-Mesh and Tehuti-Mesh.

Middle Atl-anta— Ancient Meso-America, homeland of the Elder Memnon, who hailed from the mysterious Xiu people, who originated in Tamana.

Mountains of the Moon— Ancient mountain range near the traditional homeland of the Kamitians, other Kushites and the Anu. Situated near modern-day Uganda, it is the site of fantastic anthropological discoveries indicating that technical civilization began in this region nearly 100,000 years ago.

Mut— Kamitic: Mother or elder woman. The symbol for Mut was the vulture, often worn on the crown of royalty and deities to symbolize the nurturing aspects of government.

Mycenea—Ancient name of the region known today as southern Greece. In Greek myth it was the home of the legendary hero Persus and his Kushite wife, Andromeda. The Persus and Andromeda myth represents the peaceful coming together of Tamahu and Kushite peoples in pre-Greek history. Mycenea was nearly destroyed by the People of the Sea.

Myrmidon— Legendary warriors from Greek mythology, led by Achilles in the Trojan War.

Nabata— Ancient name for a South Arabian region settled by Kushites.

Nabataens— The people of Nabata, migrants from Tamana.

Nekhebet— Kamitic: The cool electromagnetic force of the Earth responsible for some psychic phenomena.

Neter— Kamitic: A deity. One of the conscious, governing natural forces put in place by the creator to run the universe.

Neterit— Kamitic: Natural forces manifested negatively; evil deities.

Neters— Kamitic: Plural -a group of governing spirits. They were never worshipped in the modern sense, but were revered as con-

SHADES OF MEMNON

scious forces of nature, assigned by the creator to run the universe. Statues and images were used as reminders of this, as well as focal points for meditation to control Neter forces inside human beings. Misunderstood to this day as "idol worship," this spiritual science is still a common practice of most African people.

Neteru—All of the governing spirits.

Nimrod—Legendary warrior from the Bible and other West Asian lore. He actually represents Kushau groups who migrated from north central Africa (Tamana) into West Asia to form the Elamites, Sumerians, Akkadians, Nabataens and others. "And Kush begot Nimrod...He was a mighty hunter before the Lord."—Genesis 10: 8, Old Testament.

Nome— Kamitic: A city; home district.

North Atl-anta— North America.

Oracle—A spiritual science developed to provide insight into the inner workings of a situation, decision or occurrence. True oracles are never fortune-telling devices. They provide a means of examining the underlying spiritual structure of a situation, similar to a computer program that analyzes stock market trends. Card games, dice and other games of chance of today are based upon oracles developed by the Kushite and Anu peoples thousands of years ago.

Oxhide—Various metals cast into the easily carried shape of an oxen's hide.

Pan-Kau-Rau-Shen— Kamitic: Means "defeating enemies with the force of Ra." A Kushite martial art. A form of it survives in Greece to this day and is called Pankration.

Petra— Ancient name of a city in northwest Arabia.

Petrans— The people of Petra who were its Kushite and Shashu settlers.

People of The Sea— An ancient group led by Germanic people who migrated from Basileia in northern Europe to the Mediterranean area. Renowned sailors, pirates and warriors, this coalition initiated the Great World War, circa 1200 BC

Ra—Kamitic: The deity representing the Great Power, the creative life force. Misinterpreted as the "Sun God" because the Kamitians often used the sun as Ra's symbol (see Aten). Through their spiritual sciences, the Kamites discovered that all life is sustained by interaction with the energy of the sun, currently acknowledged as a scientific fact.

Ra-Mesh III— Proper name for Rameses III, the great king who defeated the People of the Sea. (Ra, meaning "the great power behind all life," and Mesh, meaning "born of" or "son of" which then translates into "The Third Son of the Great Power.")

Rau— Kamitic: The life force or serpent fire (chi in Chinese).

Saba—Ancient land in South Arabia ruled over by a line of legendary Kushite queens, such as the Queen of Sheba (Saba) of the Old Testament.

Sabaeans—The people of Saba, who were Shashu and Kushau migrants from Tamana. Spiritual sciences — The Kushite technologies of spiritual upliftment, social ordering and natural resource manipulation. These included oracle systems, spirit possession/trance, natural healing, meditative techniques, Kula Yoga, the manipulation of earthly and human energies (pyramids, acupuncture) and the coercion of the laws of nature through heightened spirituality combined with hidden knowledge (magic). The Kushau and Anu shared in a civilization complex that recent anthropology indicates stretched back 100,000 years, originating near the Mountains of the Moon of Uganda. During this time they developed these spiritual sciences.

Set— Kamitic: Also called Setesh, the principle of evil and disorder, similar to the Christian Devil.

Shang— Ancient group of Kushites and Classical Mongoloids (brown skinned Orientals similar to Indonesians), who ruled parts of ancient China from 1500 to 1000 BC. These Kushites were Tamana immigrants, who settled in the area called K'un Lun.

Shashu— Kamitic: Arabic or Semitic peoples. Originally Tamahu migrants who came down from Eurasia around 2000 BC, the Shashu peoples developed by interbreeding with Kushites and adopting their cultures.

Shekem ur Shekem— Kamitic: Means "Power, Great Power." This was the common designation of Kamitic kings, not "pharaoh." The term pharaoh originally meant "Great House."

Shemsu— Kamitic: Follower, devotee.

Sheps— Kamitic: Honored ancestor. One of the Kushite spiritual sciences is ancestor communication, misnamed ancestor worship by western observers.

Shepsu— Kamitic: Plural- the honored ancestors.

Sky-boat—Kamitic: In ancient Kamit and other Kushite cultures there was a legendary tradition of flying vehicles. They were mentioned in magical tales like "The Stories of Setne Khamwas" and depicted and discussed upon the temple walls of Edfu. In Edfu the traditions say that the Neter Heru established a "foundry of divine iron" and maintained a flying vehicle used in the war with Set. Illustrations of this flying vehicle can still be seen on the Edfu temple today.

Sofik Aabut— Kamitic: The female deity of learning.

South Atl-anta— South America.

Spiritual sciences — The Kushite technologies of spiritual upliftment, social ordering and natural resource manipulation. These included oracle systems, spirit possession/trance, natural healing, meditative techniques, Kula Yoga, the manipulation of earthly and human energies (pyramids, acupuncture) and the coercion of the laws of nature through heightened spirituality combined with hidden knowledge (magic). The Kushau and Anu shared in a civilization complex that recent anthropology indicates stretched back 100,000 years, originating near the Mountains of the Moon of Uganda. During this time they developed these spiritual sciences.

SHADES OF MEMNON

SHADES OF MEMNON

Tamahu—People of European descent. (Kamitic: Tama means people and hu means white.) Various Tamahu peoples dwelled near the Mediterranean Sea, living in relative peace with their Kushite neighbors until the Great World War circa 1200 BC. At this time nearly all of these civilizations were destroyed by a coalition led by northern Tamahu called the People of the Sea.

Tamana—Ancient region of trading cities and countries located in what is now the Sahara Desert. (Kamitic: Tama means "people; na means "to go" or "to travel.") The children of Tamana the Kushau or Kushites, linked by similar languages, spirituality, technology and race. Tremendous engineering feats like stone tunnels hundreds of miles long beneath the north African sands, giant megaliths in Morocco and other north African countries, and well known Kamitic and Kushite monuments attest to the level of civilization attained by these people. When the Sahara (which is larger than the land mass of the continental United States) dried up, the people of Tamana migrated, giving birth to the major civilizations of the ancient world.

Ta Neter—Kamitic: Means "Land of God. Ancient birthplace of the Kushite people near the Mountains of the Moon.

Taut—The spiritual world. The place of residence of the dead and the source of all non-material life. In the lower regions of the Taut dwell the low spiritual forces, in the higher regions dwell the more pure.

Tehuti—Kamitic: Deity of wisdom.

Tem—Kamitic: Bad, negative.

Tenehu—Ancient Libyans. These people lived in the region just west of Kamit, and were the source of considerable trouble due to their attempts to invade Kamitic territory. They even formed a partnership with the People of the Sea against Kamit. The Tenehu were a mixed people, with Tamahu, Shashu and Kushites within the population.

Trojan War— The legendary war documented in Greek mythology by Homer in "The Iliad" and "The Odyssey" and by Arctinus of Miletus in "The Ethiopis," in which Memnon is the leading character.

Troy—An ancient trading city which was located in Turkey. In Greek mythology it was the home of Priam, whose half-brother Tithonos was the father of the Elder Memnon, who came to Troy's assistance. In real history, Troy was a trading center of the ancient world where Kushites, Tamahu and others lived in peace knowledge can work miracles.together. In the mythology, the city fell to forces led by Achilles and Agamemnon, whom many historians now believe represented the "People of the Sea" coalition.

Tu— Kamitic: Good, positive.

Uachet — Kamitic: The hot electromagnetic force of the Earth responsible for some psychic phenomenon.

Universal Principles: The Ancient Kushites' pattern of behavior inspired awe among the ancient Greeks, who called them "Blameless Ethiopians" and referred to them as "the most favored of the gods." This was due to a code of spirituality and ethics which the Kushites propagated to the world. Here is that

SHADES OF MEMNON

list, compiled from the traditions of the Kushites themselves and what witnesses such as the Greeks said about them:

1. Covet no land or riches that the supreme being does not naturally grant you.

2. Respect the opposite sex as your equal and your compliment.

3. Give unto the world what you would have the world give unto you.

4. Always seek balance in all things, for only in harmony can there be growth.

5. Honor your ancestors, especially those who sought justice and balance in their time upon the earth.

6. Seek not simply to do good, but encourage others to do good as well.

7. Always seek higher wisdom in all of life's endeavors.

8. Honor and safeguard the children, who have come to forge the future of the world.

9. Seek to be part of a brotherhood, sisterhood or group, for we accomplish more together than alone.

10. Have no tolerance for evil and injustice, so that you will forever be known as blameless.

Upper Kamit— Southern Kamit.

Uraeus—Whenever Uachet and Nekhebet were harnessed for a psychic attack or for protection, the uraeus, usually worn at the brow by royalty, was used to focus and discharge its power. For those who could not use the power, the uraeus is simply a representation of this ancient spiritual science. The Kamitic texts describe the power of the uraeus as laser-like and instantly fatal.

Urim and Thummin— Oracles used by the ancient Hebrews (Habiru) as mentioned in the Old Testament. (1 Samuel 28:6).

Western Kushites—Black people with broader noses, thicker lips and kinky hair.

Xiu— Tamana migrants who left the drying Sahara, settling in ancient China, Iran and Meso-America. The Xiu were Western Kushites, linguistically and culturally related to the Manding people who still live in West Africa today. In Iran they built "ziggurats" and left many artifacts, while in Mexico they built pyramids and carved huge stone portraits. The native American Maya called them "Tul Tul Xiu" and remember them as teachers. (Tul Tul in Manding means "supporters or teachers of the High Order") Today they are called the Olmecs, mother civilization of the Americas, and referred to as the "Shi Dynasty" by Chinese anthropologists. In China they left African physical remains and dozens of pyramids (many still standing) in that country's Shensi province, while artifacts and statues from settlements in Mexico indicate that the Xiu had Kushites and Asians among the population. This hints at an empire, or at least trade relations that may have stretched from China to the Americas.

SHADES OF MEMNON

THE MEMNON TRADITION AND THE XIU:

1. The Xiu were renowned for their architectural wonders and statues wherever they settled; the legendary character Memnon has been affiliated with architectural marvels and statuary worldwide.

2. The Xiu had major settlements in both the Far East and the Far West, which the Greeks confirmed by saying that Memnon led Kushites to Troy from both horizons.

3. The Xiu had settlements upon islands (like Laventa in Mexico), and the legends of Memnon say he came from islands called Hesperides, located on the far western shores of the Atlantic Ocean.

SHADES OF MEMNON

SHADES OF MEMNON

Come on tell a story,

Morning Glory,

all about the Serpentine Fire"

Earth, Wind & Fire—
"Serpentine Fire"

SHADES OF MEMNON

FOREWORD

What is history?

What is the context of reality within which we all live? All of the moments before
this moment. Why is it important to record it in a way that it reflects? Because
history is a way of saying that, "I was there too." I mattered. I contributed. I am
somebody. And the degree of that contribution gives validity to how I walk,
how I talk, my sense of aesthetics, how I wear my hair, my ornamentation, the
way I dress, the way I dance, my religion.

I have significance because so and so of long ago walked, talked, spoke,
danced, felt, realized in a similar manner. And if so and so walked, talked, spoke,
danced, felt, thought and heard music in a similar manner, and he was significant, and he accomplished many great things, and his aesthetics, his sensibility
is similar to mine, then perhaps even I, in this small shack, or this small ghetto
pad, or this island in the Caribbean, or this African hut, if he who is before me,
who looked like me, whose lips were thick like mine, whose nose was wide like
mine, and whose shoulders spanned the globe of his dreams, if he could
achieve greatness with his light, then perhaps, so can I.

But without my reflection in the mirror of history, if my reflection is nowhere to
be seen, if my reflection is insignificant or cast in the light of criminality, if my
light is not of importance, then of what importance could I be in this present
moment? Because if nothing of significance looks like me or has my voice or my
walk, wears his hair like my hair or thinks in the way that I think or wears his
clothes on his back that way I wear mine, then of what significance am I? What
significance do I hold dear to my heart if I am only a recent discovery, an
experiment. What is my significance?

The question of context and significance are not of intellectual import only. Young men passing through the passages of life, proving who they are, is something that we should pay attention to. Because if you and those that have gone before you, been like you, have proven themselves in a manner that is significant, that did not require them to defile themselves or their brother or any part of humanity, then perhaps you can copy that behavior.

But if that memory is not taught and if the only reflection I see is the present and around me is only the sociopathic that preys upon my ignorance of myself, and does not hold my mother and father, uncle and aunt, grandmother and great grandfather and relatives in high esteem, then my culture and my tribe is not worthy. Then I must prove myself to you. I must prove my manhood, my significance, my contribution to you in ways that sometimes are not only self destructive, but destructive to you as well. Because if I can not value my own life, I most certainly can not value yours.

So within this context of history, we perceive reality. *History is the moment reflected in the context of the past.* We are always struggling for something to hold onto, something that says, "I have a lineage of significance and importance like others."

This is why this book is not a book that is to be read by those who want to have a scholarly treatise on a great man of antiquity, but by all of us, black, yellow, white, and brown, who understand the importance of and impact of individual achievement and contribution. So that that contribution not only reflects the importance of the struggle of that particular culture, but of the human spirit and its importance. Because history is not only the chronicling of a single event or cumulative events or contributions of a particular individual only, but it is more importantly the chronicling of the process through which individuals and nations go, the process through which we all go to reach a certain goal. And history is also a teaching device in terms of chronicling what not to do, where not to go, what stoves not to put our hands on. It is the chronicling of the process of accomplishment itself.

What is the anatomy of accomplishment? It is the dissection of accomplishment. History is a dissection of tradition and rituals and rites of passage. And the dissection of ethics and sacrifice which is always involved in the process of accomplishment. The dissection of discipline, of commitment, of legacy and most importantly, the dissection of generational responsibility. These fundamental elements —the process of accomplishment, tradition, rituals, rites of passage, ethics, sacrifice, discipline, commitment and generational responsibility are some of the fundamental issues that are absent in the consciousness of the twenty-first century. I believe that if we do not begin to reexamine these fundamental principles of survival that had been utilized by cultures of the past, we will not be able to survive the twenty-first century.

SHADES OF MEMNON

SHADES OF MEMNON

So I celebrate this book and this author, and though it may be seen as the accomplishment of one man, Memnon, I would ask you to think of Memnon in a greater context. The context of his historical significance. Not as an individual, but as historical process itself, because he was truly the Homo Universalis, the universal man, who accomplished more than many. And if we examine the principles that he lived by, the rituals of his culture, the rites of his passage, the ethics by which he functioned and the legacy which he left that connects us to him through the chord of generational responsibility, then perhaps we will see that he is a symbol of all accomplishment and of all the processes thereof. As we celebrate Memnon, in essence we are in the light of the celebration of ourselves, because we all have the potential to be like him and more. We have the potential to move towards our light and our way. However, without the lantern of history, we are certain to flounder in the abyss of ignorance.

Bill Duke

"Go back again and find the divine dark,
Seal up your eyes and be as tombs,
See that yourselves shall be as Memnon was.
Then, if you have the strength to curse the darkness,
And praise a world of light, remember Memnon..."

Conrad Aiken, "Preludes for Memnon" - 1945

SHADES OF MEMNON

SHADES OF MEMNON

Preface

Absolutely astonishing.

Those words are about as close as I can come to describing the effort, research, and remarkable results of Brother G's monumental epic "Shades of Memnon."

Here is the story of one of the greatest and most legendary heroes of history, and unfortunately, few know anything about him. Few have any idea of the contributions of Africans to history, as most people's views of blacks are based on broad racist interpretations established by books, and even more, by films. A lot more went on in the black past besides "Yes Bwana."
It is unfortunate that modern readers will be astonished at the cultural and historical significance and contributions of Africans to history. It is even more disturbing that many of African ancestry will be surprised to discover the importance of their race to the developement of the world.

Art. Dance. Music. Literature. Politics. Government. Even Martial Arts. Africa and Africans were instrumental in the developement of all of these, and more. Besides this, "Shades of Memnon" is what the British love to call a "ripping yarn." It's the sort of tale that entertains while it enlightens, much the same way that "Little Big Man" entertained and enlightened us.
I don't really know how to express my respect for Gregory L. Walker's endeavors and the fine results. Everything I say seems lame. It's just not enough. I can only say that I have been entertained and I have been enlightened.
As Brother G states in the last line of the prelude of his tale, "This is the story of Memnon." Really, nothing else need be said. In fact, say no more. Read.

Joe R. Lansdale

SHADES OF MEMNON

PRELUDE: HE'S GOT TO FIGHT TO LIVE"

The doctor shifted uneasily as he stood at the foot of his patient's bed. Next to it the mother and father sat in two chairs pulled close, silently weeping. Clinging tightly cheek to cheek, their hot tears mingled as their bodies shook with grief. On the bed lay a dark-skinned young man beneath white linen sheets, his head and left eye bandaged, his visible eye closed. His breathing was shallow. Multicolored wires were attached to his face, head and chest.

Shaking his head sadly, the doctor made a mark on his notepad. The parents hadn't noticed him, so he decided to leave them alone. As he backed away towards the door, his shoe scraped the floor and both parents looked up.

"Mrs. Martin...Mr. Martin," the doctor said hesitantly.

"Is there any hope, doctor?" cried Mrs. Martin. "Will my baby come out of this?"

The doctor looked at the desperate, pleading looks on the faces of the Martins. He swallowed hard to keep his own voice from cracking. "I'm sorry. We've...done all we can. With this type of head injury...it's a miracle he's survived so far."

"He ain't gonna wake up," cried Mr. Martin painfully. "My boy is gone!"

"No," said the doctor. "No. There's a chance."

Mr. Martin stood up, his hands held out toward the doctor. "How much of a chance? How much of a chance does my boy have?"

The doctor clutched his notepad until his knuckles turned white. "Please Mr. Martin," he said. "Sit down, please."

"I'm asking you, doctor. How much of a chance does he have?"

Mrs. Martin rocked back and forth in her chair, hugging herself as the tears streamed down her face. "He's a good boy. Craig is a good boy. Please, God. Please, don't take him from us."

"How much of a chance, doctor?" Mr. Martin repeated, his eyes filling with tears.

The doctor sighed and wiped his hand over his mouth.

"Perhaps fifteen, possibly twenty percent," he replied solemnly. "If he comes out of the coma within 72 hours."

The doctor then gestured toward the medical equipment on the other side of the young man's bed. It emitted a low, steady beep as it monitored the young man's life signs.

"We've done everything we could do. It's up to Craig now. He's got to fight to live."

SHADES OF MEMNON

Mr. Martin sat down next to his wife as the doctor quickly left the room. They sat for long minutes, staring at the still form of their son. Both wished Craig had been home two nights ago, when a bullet meant for someone else struck him on his way to school. He was the first generation of their family to go to college, and he planned to be a writer. Now his hopes and dreams hung by a fifteen to twenty percent thread.

"C'mon, honey," said Mr. Martin. "You need to get some sleep...."

"I ain't goin' nowhere," Mrs. Martin said. "Nowhere. I'm staying here until my baby wakes up."

Mr. Martin sighed and held his wife close as the hospital grew quiet around them. Soon they were asleep with tears drying on their cheeks, while clinging to each other in fitful spasms of exhausted slumber.

All was quiet. All was still. In the mind of Craig Martin a deeper quiet of total silence and infinite darkness reigned. Then the voice spoke.

"Shula-ka-a! Awake! "

The dark void undulated as the voice spoke again. "Shula-ka a! Craig! Shula-ka-a! Awake! "

Craig opened his eyes. Before him stood a strange figure— a tall man with inky black skin, wearing a gray robe of strange shiny material. Mists swirled around the figure and Craig noticed that the man was sitting on something that looked like a cloud. There was a dim glow that seemed to come from everywhere and shadows flickered past the corners of his eyes. Suddenly, Craig felt fearful.

"What is this?" he asked. "Who are you?"

The figure took a step towards him and Craig noticed the man was incredibly handsome. His eyes flashing with streaks of light, the man smiled and introduced himself.

"I have been known by many names, over many lifetimes, as have you, Shula-ka-a. My immortal name is Shula-tet. I am your ancestor, your Sheps."

Craig took a deep breath as realization suddenly hit him. The last thing he remembered before this was an incredible pain in his head and falling to the ground.

"I'm...I'm dead!" Craig gasped fearfully.

Shula-tet's grin turned into a big smile. "I see you are still subject to the fear. No Shula-ka-a, you are still Craig."

Then Shula-tet waved his hands at their surroundings. "This...is you. I am the visitor here."

"But...why are you here?" Craig asked. "What's happening?"

"You surely are near death, Craig Shula-ka-a," replied Shula-tet. "But your time must not yet come. I am here to give you strength, so that through you, others can find strength as well."

Shula-tet waved his hand and Craig grabbed the side of his face, crying out in terrible pain. Shula-tet nodded grimly as he spoke. "You must know the challenges ahead of you if you choose to live."

Craig fell to his knees. The pain was searing.

"I...my eye! Where is my eye?"

"You must learn to live without it," said Shula-tet, matter-of factly.

"I can't," Craig screamed. "I can't live like this."

Shula-tet strode over to him. Effortlessly, he picked Craig up and stood him on his feet. The pain drained away as he touched him.

"You must live!"

"But I...."

"You must go back to your parents, back to the world, and you must live, Craig Shula-ka-a! Look! "

Shula-tet took a step back and lifted his palm upward. A flicker of light appeared above it, growing brighter and bigger as it swirled around.

"This is why you must go back! Look into this light which was my life. My most famous life!"

Craig stood as if hypnotized. The light increased to several feet across and images took form. Rapidly landscapes flew by, as if viewed down from the height of a flying bird. He saw forests, rivers, sand and gigantic structures that he had only seen as ancient ruins in books of times long past.

A shining pyramid flashed by and the voice of Shula-tet boomed out of the sky around him.

"Hear now, Craig Shula-ka-a! This was a time of change, a time when the path of mankind shifted. A time when the kingdoms of Elam, Kush, Atl-anta, Saba and Kamit stood out as glorious beacons of the black man's culture. When the lands of Hatti, Keftui, Mycenea and Bektan lived in peace and the cultures of man strived for harmony."

Craig's mind reeled as the images came closer. He could see an astonishingly beautiful building of pure white stone. Young people wearing white robes were walking up shining marble steps. Most were dark skinned, but some were lighter. They all walked into the building with an air of veneration and respect, carrying small boxes and wooden boards with brushes strapped to them.

"This is the end of the Age of Bronze, the twilight time of enlightenment, when the glory of civilization was at its peak, the spiritual sciences flourished upon the earth and the universal principles were respected. Black people were known as blameless, noble and wise. This was the age of my most glorious life. Memnon!" cried Shula-tet. "I was called Memnon, and this was the time of the Great World War!"

Craig saw a young man walking up the temple stairs whom he immedi-

SHADES OF MEMNON

ately recognized. It was Shula-tet.

"You are a scribe," Shula-tet continued. "The first scribe in our family line who can clearly hear me. Only you can let the world know! Through you the world can gain strength and faith that this age will return. Even those who hurt you. Especially those who hurt you!"

Craig nodded enthusiastically.

"Show me," he cried. "Show me, Shula-tet!"

"Craig Shula-ka-a, my soul-descendant! Gain strength! Choose life! This is the story of Memnon!"

"The Profound Philosophers Who Take Their History From Epic Poems Are Of Course Obliged To Make Two Memnons. This In Our Museum They Call The Younger."

GODFREY HIGGINS,
ANACALYPSIS, 1836

SHADES OF MEMNON

CHAPTER 1: "I WOULD BE A WARRIOR"

Year 3, Third Month of Inundation, Day 10 in the reign of Shekem Ra-Mesh The Third, King of Kamit, the strong Heru, endowed with life.

Master Shu-ha sat high upon the raised platform of teaching. His legs were crossed in the traditional manner and in his lap lay three scrolls of papyrus. The candles of teaching burned brightly in their tall golden holders behind him, the flames flickering over his shoulders, the light gleaming from the sides of his brown, bald head. He lifted one scroll, scanned it briefly and addressed his students.

"Who can tell me, words exactly, where are the Kamitians are from?"

I knew the answer. I had studied ancient traditions well. It was one of my few passions in learning. I was in a foul mood though, and so kept silent.

"Come, speak up," Master Shu-ha exhorted. "You who will be apprentice scribes on the morrow, speak up!"

Many students sat in the chamber of learning. Among the candles of enlightenment were those from as far north as Bekhten and as far south as Upper Kush. The right hands of all who would graduate on the morrow shot up, except mine. I was in a foul mood.

"Memna-un," Master Shu-ha said. "You know the answer. Speak it! Words exactly!"

I knew he would choose me. It was like this always. I, the reluctant student and he, the determined teacher. There had been many bouts with the rod between us over the years, but I had learned.

"Yes, Master Shu-ha," I replied. "From the writings of Hunefur: We are the Kamitians. We come from the Valley of Beginnings, near the Mountains of the Moon, where Neter Hapi dwells. We followed the waters of Hapi in the time of Ausar to partake of the gift of life and goodness, here, where Hapi touches the Great Green. We are the Kamitians, we come from Ta-Neter."

"Very good, Memna-un," Master Shu-ha said. "Next time, no hesitation."

He lifted another scroll and unrolled it. Each of the many students in the chamber waited silently, eyes forward, anxious for the next question. Except me. I dipped my brush into its ink and started a drawing of Khepera, the beetle, on my palette.

Master Shu-ha looked up, gazing into the faces of his students. "Now, who can say, words exactly. Who are the sacred ancestors of the Kamitians?"

I put down the brush quickly, smiling innocently as his eyes touched mine. He squinted and looked on to the next student.

"What is their nature?" he went on. "Where do they dwell?"

The hand of Amistan, son of Bekhtan ivory traders, rose high. The

SHADES OF MEMNON

Master nodded and Amistan spoke.

"From the writings of Shekem Pepi the Second, in the land west of Ta-Neter and south of the seat of Hapi, live the sacred ancestors of the Kamitians. Here in the shadow of the Mountains of the Moon dwell the Anu, the small ones, strong of magic."

Master Shu-ha seemed very pleased. Leaning forward with the papyrus in both hands, he congratulated the student from Bekhtan.

"You know well the traditions of the Kamitians for one so new among us. Speak on, son of the north. What else do these writings say?"

"As the first of all peoples," Amistan continued, "The Anu dwell daily with the Neters. It is their song that drowns the wailing of Setesh, it is their dance that brings smiles to the faces of the Neteru and makes fertility from womb to tomb. No man can keep the Anu bound. No man can stay the Anu's magic. Hail to the Anu! They dance the dance of life!"

The room suddenly exploded with clapping and enthusiastic cries. Not only did Amistan know the words exactly, but he had made good speech from his knowledge.

"Good speech, Amistan," said Master Shu-ha. "You will do well at your post in Bekhtan."

I did not join in the praise of Amistan. Giving him a sidelong glance, I went back to drawing my beetle. Master Shu-ha must have noticed, for an instant later his rod landed atop my palette, violently knocking it from my lap, spilling ink across the floor.

"Memna-un!" he cried. "You try my ka! Why do you not give praise to your fellow student for good speech? Why do you not pay attention in the House of Life?

The rod swished menacingly past my face as he drew it back. I no longer feared his stick, but I had gained a healthy respect for it. I knew speaking plainly would likely earn me a taste of it, but I spoke nonetheless. I was in a foul mood.

"Great Master," I cried angrily. "He is a northerner! He comes from a land where great speech means nothing, where the love of Maat is unknown! They curse the Universal Principles in his land! It matters not how well he speaks, for soon he shall be back among them. His space should be filled by one from a Kushite land..."

Indignant cries went up from many in the room, especially the other northerners. I heard some voices of agreement, though, especially the students from Upper Kamit and Lower Kush. The murmurs grew louder and louder.

"Silence!" cried Master Shu-ha. "Be silent all of you!"

The Master paced the floor as the room grew quiet. Holding his rod behind his back, he bowed his head as he searched for the right words. Then he whirled around towards me.

"It is true that most northerners cause trouble, as some Kushites have been known to do also. But what makes you think that they can not know Maat?"

I spoke hesitantly, knowing that a debate with Master Shu-ha could only end with my total defeat and likely humiliation.

"But...but look at their lands. They go about like wild game..."

As I talked, Master Shu-ha picked up the last papyrus. He looked at it and nodded. He wore a knowing smile as he looked up at me.

"You know as well as I Memna-un, that all northern lands are not like that. Noble Hattie and Alashia are two examples. Here is the last lesson, Memna-un: What was the first task of Ausar when he learned to perceive Maat?

I nearly choked. I knew the answer, and it made my argument worthless. Master Shu-ha knew this also.

"Speak, Memna-un! Words exactly! "

I looked around at the other students. They were all staring. Some of the northerners smirked, but Amistan looked sympathetic. I gathered my strength and obeyed my teacher.

"The first task of Ausar was to deliver the Kamitians from the wilderness and harsh living. To teach them the ways of cultivation and the prosperity of living in Maat, great Ausar led the Kamitians down the course of Hapi to the richness of the black valley. With freedom from earthly want there came time for the progress of the spirit. Next Ausar and Great Mut Auset created the fertility rituals...."

"That is enough," Master Shu-ha said. "You will never be a great scribe until you learn to apply the wisdom you recite. Get to your feet, student."

I stood before the Master. I was the tallest student in class; indeed, the tallest youth in the district, and I towered over him. He looked up into my face, flexing his rod. He was not intimidated.

"I know you have recently passed your rites, Memna-un. You are now a man. The time of the rod is over for you."

I breathed a sigh of relief as Master Shu-ha shook his head.

"I know not the reason for your anger, Memna-un, but you will now go to the Hall of the Chambers of the Neters. Let your head rest with Heru so your ka may know peace."

I gathered my palette, paints and brushes and strolled toward the entrance to the Hall of Enlightenment. The candles along the walls flickered as I walked past, playing dramatically with the shadows of all the students. Before I parted the curtain, I turned to look at the class. Sitting on their mats, they all seemed so content, so at peace with their destiny, but I was not. Though I would graduate on the morrow, I knew that the life of a scribe would not be mine.

SHADES OF MEMNON

I walked down the long corridors of the House of Life, past the dramatic paintings and huge statues of the governor and governess of wisdom and learning: Great Tehuti, with the face of the wise ibis bird, and Sofik Aabut, whose beautiful, piercing eyes bore the wisdom of womanly understanding. They seemed to stare down upon me, asking me, "Why? Why were their gifts not enough to calm my restless ka?"

I turned down the Hall of the Chambers of the Neters and walked past the images of Amen, Ra, Ausar and Auset. Finally, I stood before the Chamber of Heru and read the inscription above the curtains: Enter Blind Heru.

I entered the chamber, lifted the candle from the table at the entrance and closed the curtains behind me. The altar of Heru gleamed before me in sparkling gold, silver and inlaid lapis-lazuli. A golden statue of Heru, emerging from his lotus and wearing the crown of kingship, dominated the altar.

Beside Heru lay the golden crook and silver flail. A stalk of frankincense poked out from a holder before the statue and all sat atop strips of red and white weave-cloth. Bending the candle slightly, I lit the frankincense. As the smell of the fragrant stalk wafted throughout the chamber, I took up the crook and flail and seated myself on the floor before the altar.

"As the strong Heru subdued Set," I said, "my ka will subdue the followers of Set." I then breathed deeply and focused on the image of the governor of the will. "Begone, Children of Impotent Rage," I said. "Begone, foul followers of Set."

I grasped the crook and flail tightly, closing my eyes as the image of Heru took shape in my mind, growing in sharpness and intensity. There he stood before me, wearing the crown and holding the implements of sovereignty that were now in my hands. His eyes gleamed as he searched my mind for his prey. Then he thrust his beak menacingly, hungrily for the blood of the Children of Setesh. Each time his beak thrust forward, calm washed over me, freedom from the raging emotions, the wicked spawn of Set.

I was at rest with Heru for a long while, losing all sense of time or place, when on the edge of my consciousness I heard the tinkling of the bell of awakening. Slowly I struggled out of the place within myself as Heru faded. Opening my eyes, I saw that the candle on the altar had burned out, but light came in from behind me.

Master Shu-ha stood in the doorway, holding the curtain open. As he placed the bell back in its place, he said gently, "Memna-un, it is time to depart the House of Life."

I stood up slowly, replacing the crook and flail, then turned towards the entrance. Glancing up, I noted the words above the exit.

"Leave in Peace, Great Heru, your eye has now been restored."

Master Shu-ha was observing me closely as I slipped through the curtain.

"You have been in the chamber for a long time Memna-un," he said. "Come, we must talk."

As we strolled down the corridor towards the great doors of the House of Life, Master Shu-ha nodded in approval. "Memna-un, now that you are refreshed by the Neter, tell me...what troubles you so?"

We strolled out onto the landing before the entrance and stood between the House of Life's giant white pillars. Master Shu-ha looked inquisitively into my face, saying, "You have been a difficult, but brilliant student, Memna-un. Your scribal skills are unmatched by any in your class. Many posts await one such as you. Perhaps in the court of Shekem Ra-Mesh himself...."

I turned from the face of my teacher, gazing across the endless sand south of this place of learning. I imagined myself tallying boats and counting wheat. Jotting down names of those who had grievances in the courts of Maat and recording the building projects of the Shekem. None of these was what I wanted.

"Master Shu-ha," I cried, "I want to be like my pa. I would be a warrior!"

Master Shu-ha held up his forefinger as he always did when making a point. "There are many ways to win glory, Memna-un."

"But I want to fight for the protection of my people, just as my pa did," I said desperately. "I have tried to forget it. I have tried to follow my mut's wishes to come to the House of Life and learn the ways of a scribe. But my pa was a warrior! It burns within me! It haunts me night and day!"

"It is true that your pa won fame in his day. Emerging from the fabled land of the Atl-anta, he defended Maat with sword in hand and earned glory in many lands. But then he lost his life at Troy. Your mut would not see you go that way."

I gazed back towards the sand and held up my hands to Aten. Its rays dazzled my eyes as the orange orb sank toward the horizon.

"My mut, my mut, my mut, my mut" I cried. "I have followed the will of Meri-Ta all my days! Never has she asked me of my wishes! Never has she let me choose my own way!"

Master Shu-ha placed his hand on my shoulder.

"She has considered you at every step, Memna-un. She could see the fire of your pa burning strongly in you. This is why she wanted you far away from the fields of battle. She is your mut. You and Neftiji are the parts of Memna-un the Elder that she has left upon the earth."

His words penetrated and I understood. But my desire would not go away. "Your words are true Master," I replied. "I will think long on them."

I then started down the steps to make my way home.

"Hold, Memna-un," Master Shu-ha said. "One other thing."

I stopped at the foot of the stairs, gazing back up at my teacher.

"There have been reports of strange vessels along the merchant routes. Tell your mut to be wary. If you see anything amiss, go at once to the fort of the Medjay and report it."

SHADES OF MEMNON

"But master," I said, "there have been no pirates on the Desher Sea for many ages. Who would dare...?"

"It may be mere rumor, Memna-un. But your mut is Port-Mistress and so must be made aware. Go now and inform her."

As I strolled down the hill that supported the House of Life, I could see the entire nome, all the way to my mut's house in the far distance, on the banks of the Desher Sea. As the rays of Aten grew dimmer, activity in the streets became lighter. The market was closing down, as sailing men headed toward the saloon for a draught, and market women packed up their wares for the day.

I decided to go down the market street, in hopes of finding a flask of honey for Meri-Ta before they all closed down. Perhaps it would sweeten the sour taste that was sure to come when I told her of my plans.

The market woman took the barter note I gave her and handed me the flask of honey. She scrutinized the note closely as I walked away.

"It is a true note, mut," I said. "You can redeem it at my family's granaries anytime. Good evening to you."

She smiled, then slid the note into her pouch. "Just checking, my son, just checking."

I walked away, hefting the flask and wondering if she was as careful with her own product. As I considered opening the stopper to look inside, I spied a Tamahu youth near my age, walking with two large hunting cats on leashes. As I came closer, I saw he had a laborer's sack hanging at his side. Then I saw that it was my classmate, Amistan. Pretending not to see him, I went into a false examination of the flask of honey.

"Ho, Memna-un!" Amistan said.

"Greetings, Amistan," I replied.

"Going home?"

"Yes. I have honey for my mut"

"Must you hurry? I've something to show you...."

The two cats he had leashed were of the southern breed, from the lands above Upper Kush. Large-boned and strong, they were of the type normally used for catching birds in the marshes near Hapi. One cat was ebony black, the other ivory white.

"I go to make profit with my friends here," Amistan said, gesturing toward the cats. "Care to come along?"

"Amistan..." I said reluctantly, "about what I said in the Hall of Learning today...."

"Never mind that," he said cheerfully. "Come along."

We turned down a street and started towards the wealthier side of town, where the boat owners and traders lived. The cats seemed eager, as if anticipating some pleasant activity. Soon we stopped before a beautiful house with a noticeably huge garden.

Amistan held the leashes towards me. "Here! Hold these."

I seized the leashes as Amistan walked to the front door. Though I could not hear clearly, I could tell he was making some kind of deal with the woman who answered, probably a financial one. Finally, she made a gesture of resignation and Amistan walked back triumphantly.

"She has agreed to my price," he said.

"Price...for what?"

"Watch, Memna-un."

We walked towards the garden and the cats became frantic, straining against the leashes and hissing impatiently. Then Amistan opened the gates to the garden and let them loose. They bounded excitedly towards the thick plants and began their frantic hunt for prey.

I nodded at Amistan and smiled. "You Bekhtani," I said, laughing. "Always ready to make profit!"

"I can't help it," he replied with a grin. "My parents are traders."

The cats hissed and leaped for a few moments, and then the white one returned holding a large green snake. Springing over to me, the cat dropped it right at my feet. I was startled a little because it was still alive, but Amistan got to it first and stamped it to death.

The cats continued stalking and hunting until the black feline dropped another snake before us. I raised my foot, preparing to stamp it to death, when Amistan thrust his palm towards me.

"Hold, my friend," he said, "no need for that...."

I looked down and saw that my classmate was right. The snake was already dead.

The hunt continued as the orb of Aten settled beneath the horizon. I was wondering how we would see in the dark when Amistan pulled a pitch torch out of his bag. As I held it, he took two fire stones from his pouch and struck them together near the head of the torch, quickly sending enough sparks flying to set the torch ablaze.

The fall of night seemed not to bother the cats. As their pile of snakes grew larger and larger, Amistan beamed proudly as he spoke of them. "Ah, Memna-un," he said, "these cats are the best profit-making investment I have ever made. They kill the pests and I make the riches."

"I see they are well trained," I replied. "But why do they not kill all the snakes they bring out?"

"Ah, Memna-un," Amistan replied. "The dark one, he kills every one, while it is the white one that does not kill its prey."

"But why?" I asked.

"Only the Neters know. The white one delights in the hunt. The black one delights in the kill. They are of the same litter, and with their parents it is

SHADES OF MEMNON

just the opposite. Their mut, who is milk white, lives for the kill, while their pa, a black cat, loves the hunt only."

Amistan then looked into my eyes. "I suppose you cannot say how a creature will act based on where it comes from or how it looks. I suppose you have to judge a creature by its own actions. Don't you think so, Memna-un?"

I looked into the light-skinned face of my classmate, noticing how the torch-light was shining upon his straight black hair and only nodded in agreement.

"Indeed, Amistan," I replied. "Your wisdom is sound."

The pile of snakes grew larger and the hunt went on until Amistan called the cats back. As I held the leashes again, he counted the snakes and went back to the house. After another brief discussion with the mistress, he returned with a handful of shekels and a big grin. Nodding gratefully, he handed me three of them.

"For your help, Memna-un," he said.

I thanked him and we embraced. As we parted ways I silently thanked Amistan for the lesson he had taught me.   Passing the edge of town, I left the dim torchlights from the houses behind and picked my way over the well-worn trail in total darkness. I had no fear, having walked these trails all my life. My only worry was how my mut would react when I told her of my plans to be a warrior instead of a scribe in the service of the Shekem.

As I passed the Medjay outpost, a small fort to the north and west of my home, the moon was rising high. Moments later I strolled along the Desher Sea, casually noting the glowing orb's light bouncing off the waves. Little did I know that this would be the last carefree moment of my life.

In the distance the night torches that illuminated my home revealed a large ship docked nearby. As I came closer I heard loud voices, then shouts and the sound of metal striking metal. A battle!

I ran a few paces and stopped. "The Medjay!" I thought. "I must tell the Medjay something is wrong!" My Mut and sister had a dozen warriors to protect them, which should, I reasoned, give me the time to alert the warriors at the fort. I turned to run back, when a frightful scream pierced the air. It was my mut!

Dropping the honey and shekels, I ran frantically towards the house. Several small landing boats, obviously from the large ship, were pulled onto the shore. Dead men were laying everywhere. Rounding the corner to the entrance of the house, I saw a terrible battle taking place.

My mut's men were fighting a crowd of strange, pale-skinned warriors I had never seen before, speaking a language that was equally unfamiliar. I saw Teta, the leader of the Port House guard, fighting valiantly against four men, while several of his guards went down before the large mass of foreign warriors.

With strange round shields and long swords of a make I had never seen, the attackers were vicious and gave no quarter. No one had yet noticed me as I stood before the house, looking desperately for my mut and sister, trying to decide what to do. Then I spotted Meri-Ta, my mut, surrounded by four of her faithful warriors. They were hopelessly struggling to protect her against the imposing wave of attackers.

My mind was then made up. Springing forward, I seized the sword-arm of one of the attackers, striking him in the belly until he let go of his weapon. As several of the warriors turned towards me, Teta noticed and yelled out.

"Memna-un, flee! Go! Save yourself! "

As he said this he turned his head slightly, something he taught me never to do in battle. One of the attackers took advantage of this and viciously ran a sword through his belly.

I screamed as I watched my good friend die.

"Teta! Teta, nooo! "

Now my mut was also holding a sword. Only two of her men were left, determined to fight until the end, but several of the strange warriors were closing in on them, which sent me mad with rage.

"Leave my mut," I shouted. "Leave her!" I screamed, while grasping the sword the way Teta had taught me.

There had been many mornings Teta and I would sneak away and he would secretly teach me the arts of war. I used those skills now and waded in among the surprised warriors. As Teta had often instructed, I took advantage of my height, swinging down upon them at angles they found hard to block. Two went down at the advance of my blade before they realized that death walked among them. As fast as I could, I split two more heads and sliced the necks of three more.

Spattered with blood, my only thought was to kill everything hat lived between myself and my mut. By now she had noticed me and at first looked quite surprised. Then she began gesturing frantically toward the house.

"Mut!" I shouted. "I am coming!"

Finally the warriors recovered and had me on the defense. Blocking me from my mut, they pushed me back and away from her. I could see that her guards were fighting valiantly but would soon be overwhelmed. Now cut and bleeding, she assisted them as she called out to me.

"Neftiji," she shouted, pointing towards the door of the house. "Your sister!"

"But Mut!" I cried.

"Worry not for me!" she screamed, "Go! Save your sister...now! "

I hesitated briefly, then another scream came from the house. It was Neftiji! Whatever was going on, my mut seemed more concerned for my

SHADES OF MEMNON

sister's safety than her own, and though it pained me greatly, I obeyed her.

The battle was blocking the entrance to the door, so I rush to a window, but to turn and jump as they pressed me would mean certain death. After several wild swings toward the warriors to ward them off, I hefted a large flower pot from the window ledge and threw it. I then let fly other small pots from the ledge, then as they ducked, turned and leapt through the window.

Falling heavily, I ignored the pain and sprang up quickly. Outside I could hear the warriors cursing, but none were tall enough to jump as I did. I pushed furniture down before the door to slow them and ran further into the house.

"Neftiji!" I called as I ran through our many rooms. "Where are you?"

Then I heard her.

"Memna!" she screamed desperately, "Memna, help!"

I ran to her room to find it crowded with the savage warriors. They had her pinned down on her bed, groping and tearing at her clothes. Tears streamed down her face as she struggled against them.

I bared my teeth, saying nothing as I stepped before the doorway. One of the warriors spied me, and with sword in hand, rushed my way. As he emerged from the room, I sliced his neck and booted him to the side as others sprang to attack me. But they could only emerge one at a time, and I was ready. Sidestepping as they ran past, I cut them down one after the other.

After several had fallen, the others were more wary and stood back, poking at me with their swords. As their attention turned towards me, I glanced over their shoulders to see Neftiji gather herself up and slip silently through a window.

Breathing a sigh of relief, I ran back toward the front door to assist my mut, the remaining warriors close upon my heels. There I was met by the fiends I had escaped earlier, and now found myself trapped.

Gripping my weapon tightly, I decided to take as many of them with me as possible. Then the crowd of warriors before me parted and my eyes beheld a terrible sight. One of the vicious men dragged a limp body by the hair and tossed it down before me. It landed at my feet, blood spattering across the floor. It was my mut.

At first I was speechless, frozen in horror. Then I spotted the smiling, gleeful faces of the cruel warriors before me and flew into a terrible rage. Slashing right through the wicked smile of the nearest one, I began attacking those around me with all the hatred and force I could muster. The ferocity of my attack threw them back and I maneuvered into a corner, preparing to take them all with me into the next life.

I fought for long minutes, until fatigue and the overwhelming numbers finally overcame me. Cut, stabbed and bleeding from many wounds, I slipped on my own blood and went down.

The sword was wrenched from my hand and I was dragged over the body of my own mut and out the door. There before the entrance I was held upright, as rough hands tore my tattered robe from my chest. A warrior I had wounded stood before me. Holding a sharp knife in the flames of a torch, he eyed me hatefully. A few vicious kicks to my back and blood was spurted from my mouth. Then these villains began speaking to each other. Though I could not understand, I knew they were making plans for all the dreadful things they would do to me.

Suddenly the warrior with the heated knife threw away the torch and approached me, a cruel smile playing across his vicious face. I readied myself for death, but as he raised the knife a voice rang out behind him. It was in his own strange language but had an unmistakable Kamitic accent. He hesitated, then proceeded towards me again as the voice called once more.

The would-be murderer looked over his shoulder, speaking sharply to whoever had addressed him. Several of the others raised their voices in what seemed to be warnings, but he ignored them, raising the blade to stab me once again. Just as the weapon was about to fall, his body convulsed violently and he screamed in bitter anguish. Clutching at his chest, he dropped heavily to his knees, the knife tumbling from his grasp as he fell. Between his clutching fingers the flesh of his chest moved violently, bulging and palpitating unnaturally.

Then from out of the shadows emerged a Kushite man, his head clean shaven in the fashion of a Kamitic priest. His hands held high, he recited words of power, making gestures in the air as the man writhed and moaned. Finally, the magician stood over his victim, made a cutting motion in the air, and the man's chest burst open like a ripe fruit.

Muttering incoherently, the warrior watched as his own heart rose from his body, to be plucked from the air by the Kushite magician. Then the warrior's eyes rolled back and he fell, dead in his own flowing blood.

The strange Kushite put the heart into a sack at his side, casually shaking the blood from his hand. Then he spoke to me with a voice that chilled my heart.

"You fight like a panther, young one," he said.

I stared at him. He was indeed a western Kushite, like most Kamitians, and was even wearing the white robe of a Kamitic High Priest, but apparently he was also the leader of these strange pale warriors. I thought of the lesson I learned from Amistan.

"A shame about your mut, young one," he said, gesturing towards the warriors surrounding us. "These are...barbarians. At times they can be quite difficult."

Then he smiled. Cold fear such as I had never felt ran through me as I saw him smile. I wondered what he would do with the dead man's heart.

SHADES OF MEMNON

"What is your name, young panther?"

I could hardly open my mouth from the fear, and I knew that he had to see it in my eyes.

"I am Kho-An-Sa," he said. "Speak your name, young panther, and I may yet let you live."

"My...my name is Memna-un. Son of Meri-Ta and Memna-un..."

Kho-An-Sa put his hand to his chin.

"Memna-un...Memna-un? Son of Memna-un the warrior, the Great Memnon who fought at Troy?"

I looked at him, but my mouth would not open. Then he raised his hand as if to strike me. "Answer me!" he shouted.

"Yes!" I cried. "Yes, he was my pa."

Kho-An-Sa's eyes narrowed as he rubbed his chin thoughtfully. "I see now why you fight so well. Many of my allies would rejoice to see the seed of the great Memnon of Troy destroyed. But I...I have other plans."

Kho-An-Sa extended his hand, cruelly clutching my face. His fingers were bloody and hot.

"Young panther, do you wish to live?"

Struggling against the fear this priest made well up inside me, I spoke defiantly.

"I...I care not," I groaned. "I have defended my family."

"That you have done, young panther," Kho-An-Sa said. "And you have done it very well. But now you will be my defender! My warrior! "

"Never," I groaned. "You killed my Mut. Never would I serve you...you...."

He stepped back and clapped his hands and two warriors stepped forward. They were holding Neftiji.

"Memna-un," Neftiji cried. "Do not do it!"

Kho-An-Sa walked towards her. Raising his hands, he began speaking the words he used when he took the warrior's heart. Neftiji screamed.

"No!" I cried. "Leave her alone!"

Kho-An-Sa stopped the chant and turned back towards me.

"What is it you say, young panther?" Tears streamed down my face. I would have fallen if the warriors had not been holding me.

"Yes, Kho-An-Sa," I said.

"Yes...what...young panther?"

"Yes...I will serve you. Don't hurt my sister...."

Kho-An-Sa lifted my face again and smiled his cruel, wicked smile. "I knew you would see the wisdom in this decision. Do as I say and your sister will not be harmed."

He then barked orders at his men in their rough, crude language. Some hustled forward from the house with bags of shekels- dock fees earned by my mut. Kho-An-Sa counted the bags and sent the bearers towards the boats. Then he turned to Neftiji and I.

"Look well, young panther," he said, gesturing towards the house. "You will never see this place again. From this day forward, you are mine!"

As Neftiji and I were dragged towards the boats, I could not look at my sister. Overwhelmed by grief and weakened from my injuries, I felt that I had failed my family. Then my eyelids grew heavy and my mind slipped down into darkness.

SHADES OF MEMNON

CHAPTER 2: DESTINY IT IS INDEED

I awoke to feelings of pain and sickness, and the sound of great waters splashing all around me. I was lying down, my body swaying to the rhythm that accompanied the sound of the water. Opening my eyes, I beheld Neftiji kneeling over me, applying a cool wet cloth to my face. I tried to speak, but she quickly covered my lips.

"Quiet, Memna," she said in a low voice. "We must not let them know you are awake."

I nodded and looked around the room. I lay naked upon bedding rolled out on the floor. Neftiji knelt beside me upon sleeping sheets of her own, tears of happiness welling up in her eyes. Light came from a candle in a holder on the wall near us.

We were in a small cabin inside the ship, with one door as the only entry. Neftiji did not have to tell me that it was locked.

"I knew you would come back to me, Memna-un," she said. "The healer in service to Kho-An-Sa said you would not wake up. But I knew."

"Where are they taking us?" I whispered.

"I do not know. I have heard Kho-An-Sa talking to someone outside. They said we were near Ta Neter...."

I shook my head and tried to sit up, but my limbs failed me and I slipped back down to the bedding. Neftiji put her hand upon my chest. "Rest, Memna," she said. "You will be strong soon."

"Neftiji, we must get off this ship...."

"I know," she quickly replied, "but you must not let them know you are awake. Kho-An-Sa is planning something terrible for you. He keeps speaking of our pa, saying you will be a greater warrior than he was, but in service to him."

Just then we heard footsteps coming toward us. I closed my eyes and pretended to be asleep as I heard the door swing open.

There was the sound of two men entering the room, and then the voice of Kho-An-Sa.

"Girl, has your brother yet stirred?"

"No," Neftiji said. "His head is still hot."

The floorboards creaked loudly as they came closer and began rubbing their rough hands over my head and neck. There was a pause and another voice spoke in the strange language of the northerners. Kho-An-Sa made some reply to it and then he spoke again in Kamitic.

"Here, girl. Anoint his limbs with this. The son of such a mighty one should die in battle, not like this. I would see this panther roar once again."

SHADES OF MEMNON

Kho-An-Sa and the other man left the room and the door shut once again. I opened my eyes slightly and looked toward the entrance, then turned towards Neftiji. She clutched a small clay pot in her hands, staring at the door with burning hatred in her eyes.

"It is heat-ointment, Memna," she said as she turned toward me. "How can a man who knows so much of healing be so cruel, so evil?"

As she applied the heat-ointment, Neftiji told me what had gone on as I had lain near death. We had been at sea for a quartermoon. During this time she had been to the deck twice, both times to be shown how far away from home we had been taken. Kho-An-Sa thought this would make her give up hope and convince her to cooperate with his plans, but for her, it was a moment to memorize the lay of the ship and plot our escape.

We plotted patiently as time went by, my strength gradually returning as Neftiji shared her food with me. I spent hours stretching and exercising my limbs, interrupted by tense moments of feigned stupor when Kho-An-Sa and his healer came to check on me. After two more quarters of the moon had passed, I was at last strong enough for us to make our move.

Late one night, when all movement upon the ship had ceased, Neftiji stood at the door, holding her bedding. She kicked the door and waited for the guard to open it. When he did, she thrust the bedding into his hands and pointed at me. I lay with my eyes slightly open, to be ready at the right moment.

"Come, man, help me move him," Neftiji said as she pointed at me. "He has been on the same filthy bedding for weeks." The guard seemed not to understand her words and threw down the bedding in disgust.

He was about to slam the door shut when Neftiji cajoled him sharply.

"He is sick with fever," she said. "He must have new bedding. Kho-An-Sa will be angry if he dies because of your negligence."

At the mention of Kho-An-Sa's name a fearful look came over the guard's face. He frowned at Neftiji and slowly walked into the room. As they came toward me, Neftiji bent down and reached for my legs.

"You take his arms," she said.

As the guard bent down for my arms, I lunged up suddenly, seizing him firmly by the throat. He tried to reach his sword, but with a twist I threw him to the floor, all the while tightening my grip to cut off his wind. Neftiji darted through the door and came back quickly, holding a large water vessel. I was choked him vigorously so he could not cry out, but he was starting to pull his weapon.

"Memna, move! " Neftiji hissed.

As I removed my hands I could see the guard's lips forming a cry, but the vessel came crashing down upon his head and he fell limp. Then Neftiji and I looked at each other. Both of us were dripping with perspiration and breathing heavily from the excitement. I then took the guard's clothing and put them on my own naked frame, and after snatching up his sword, we cautiously made our way out the door.

We walked softly to the top of the stairs and Neftiji peeked apprehensively out onto the deck. She then gestured for me to follow and we slipped stealthily into the open air.

The ship was very large, as large as any I had ever seen, except for the grand vessels of the Shekem or the trading ships from Blybos. Behind us, towards the rear, was a large square structure. Neftiji had told me earlier that this was the sleeping quarters of Kho-An-Sa, and that behind it was the steering oar and oarsmen's quarters.

Directly before us lay another large structure, which was the sleeping quarters for the crew and warriors. On the far side of this sat the storeroom. Our goal was to get there for supplies, and then get to the small boats stored nearby.

The wind was high and the sails were full, which meant that no rowers would be about. As our eyes became adjusted to the light of the three-quarter moon, we moved silently past the sleeping area of the men. I heard snoring and movement as we crept and held my breath as we passed beneath their windows. I had no wish to fight these vicious men again and put my sister at risk.

As we passed the warriors' quarters, Neftiji stopped, pointing carefully around the corner. I looked to see a warrior leaning against the door that led to the ship's supplies, his arms crossed resolutely over his chest. My heart sank into despair. We had been fools to think that the storeroom on a ship full of barbarians would not be guarded.

Neftiji pulled me close and whispered into my ear. "I will distract him, Memna, and you...." She pulled her finger across her throat like a sword cut, and I understood what she meant.

Neftiji took her robe off and walked boldly out into the open. The warrior noticed and stepped forward, reaching for his sword. Then his eyes widened and he relaxed, a lustful smile playing across his face. He then said something to her in his strange language, which Neftiji answered with a giggle and a fertility dance. As her body swayed before him, he stepped forward and tried to seize her, but Neftiji danced a circle around him, keeping just out of his reach.

His breathing became heavy as he stumbled around and around to keep up with her. When his back was finally towards me, she stopped. As he poised to spring upon her, I rushed forward, plunging the sword as deep as I could into his back. Uttering one brief moan, the man dropped heavily to the deck, his eyes rolling up in a stare of death.

After Neftiji redressed herself, we opened the door to the storeroom and

SHADES OF MEMNON

stepped inside. Near the entrance we found a candle, lit it, and began gathering supplies. We chose sacks of dried meat and fruit and jugs of water, anything which would last a long time, because we knew not when we would see land again. Neftiji seized a large knife used to trim meats and tucked it into her robe. Then we put the supplies into two large sacks and dragged them around the storeroom toward the small boats.

There we found three vessels, each with a rope tied around its middle and length. One was larger than the others and was equipped for sailing. We chose this one and tossed our supplies into it. Nearby stood a large wooden pole with a rope and pulley attached. At the end of the rope there was a hook for latching onto the boats and lowering them into the water. Neftiji attached the hook and I began pulling it into the air, but the pulley squeaked loudly and sharply, piercing the salty night air.

We stopped suddenly. My heart beat quickly as Neftiji and I stared at each other for long seconds. Finally she looked around and shrugged her shoulders. We knew we had no choice but to go on. The pulley kept squeaking as I pulled the boat up. Though I knew it would arouse the sleeping warriors, I prayed that we would get into the water before we were caught.

Finally, the boat was high enough to push over the side, but by then we heard footsteps and cries from the other side of the storeroom. Neftiji stepped forward to help and we were rapidly lowering the boat toward the water as two warriors appeared. Their swords were drawn and I could hear more approaching.

"Get into the boat," I ordered my sister.

Neftiji hesitated at first, then climbed to the edge of the ship and leapt into the small craft. At that moment a warrior ran forward, swinging at me with his sword. When I stepped aside his blade cut the rope thread through the pulley, causing the vessel and my sister to plunge down into the dark waters.

I snatched up my own blade as the warriors rushed me. One slashed down at my head while the other thrust towards my legs. Blocking the downstroke, I leapt back to avoid the other blade, then came back at the warriors with vicious circular strokes that put them on the defense. But by now more warriors had appeared and I knew I had to make my escape.

Shouting and cursing, I beat back the two warriors before me until they became entangled with the advancing men. Taking advantage of the momentary confusion, I ran to the edge of the ship and leapt out into the sea.

Plunging deep, I let the sword slip from my hand and swam up to the surface. When my head burst above the waves, I saw the small boat close by and made my way toward it. There were shouts and curses from the ship as Neftiji pulled me aboard, then we smiled as the huge vessel glided past us, pushed on by the power of its sails. Seizing our oars, I began rowing immediately, wanting to put as much distance between us and Kho-An-Sa's ship as possible.

As the outline of the ship slipped further away into the darkness, I was determined to row until we could no longer see or hear the vessel that had held us captive. Losing all sense of place and time, my mind centered on the oars and the sea and escaping the evil of Kho-An-Sa. Several times I heard Neftiji speak, but I ignored her, focusing only on the task at hand.

Some time later Neftiji shook me. Lifting my eyes, I found Aten rising, the sea calm about us and no sign at all of the ship of Kho-An-Sa. After giving praise to Amen-Ra I collapsed into the bottom of the boat, falling into an exhausted, deep sleep.

Sometime later I awoke with a start as a stream of water crossed my lips. It was Neftiji trying to rid me of my parched, dry mouth. Gulping it down vigorously, I reach for more but she pulled back. "No, Memna," she said. "Slowly, take it slowly."

I gazed across the open sea and saw that it was still calm and peaceful. Aten was now midway to rest, so I had obviously slept for many hours.

"I rowed for a while," Neftiji said. "Then I went to sleep also, Memna. It is hard work."

I stood up and stepped over to the mast at the center of the boat. "Yes, it is," I replied. "Now we must hoist the sails so that we can travel faster. At night we will follow the stars."

Neither Neftiji nor I knew much of long range sailing, but as children of the Port Mistress of the Desher Sea, we knew how to set sails and had some knowledge of navigation by the heavens. As night descended we guided the boat toward the west. We knew we were on the upper Desher and hoped to reach Ta Neter before our supplies ran out. As we lay down in the boat, holding each other for warmth and watching the stars, our thoughts turned to our parents.

"Memna," Neftiji said. "Do you think mut and pa are together now?"

I hugged my sister closer, nestling my chin into her thick braided hair. "I think so," I said. "I would think that Ausar would unite them."

"Memna, why are the good killed by the evil?" Neftiji asked sadly. "Why do the Neteru not destroy all who would unbalance Maat and bring wrong into the world?"

"I don't know. Perhaps Master Shu-Ha would know. He taught that the good and the evil must fight, like the struggles of Set and Heru, until some balance comes about."

Neftiji sat up and looked at me seriously. "If...when we get back home, let us go to the temple. Let us pour libation for mut and pa."

"Yes," I said. "We will do that for our parents."

We sailed for many days without seeing land or any other vessels. Our supplies were running low, especially water, and our spirits were beginning

SHADES OF MEMNON

to fade. Then one morning after a full moon had passed I awoke to the heat of Aten upon my face and sat up to find a cloud of mist in the distance. I leapt to my feet when I saw the outline of what appeared to be hills or mountains. I could see a great many sea birds flying overhead, crying out as if to greet us, while the breeze brought us the comforting smell of fresh vegetation and earth.

I shook Neftiji joyfully. "Look," I cried happily. "Land! We have reached Ta Neter!"

Neftiji stood up beside me, wiping the sleep from her eyes. A broad smile played across her face as she joined me in viewing the still distant sight. But as we came closer, her smile faded. She looked up at me, pulling on my arm and saying grimly, "Memna...that is an island. This is not Ta Neter."

As we came closer I could see that she was right. The mist was clearing and I saw that it was indeed an island, but even from a distance I could see how green and beautiful it was. Yet, there was something strange about the way it shimmered, and the fragrance of the vegetation was like none I had ever experienced. I considered this a trick of my mind due to our long weeks away from land.

"Well, let us at least stop there for food," I said. "We must at least have fresh water."

Neftiji nodded and started gathering the empty water jugs. I squinted at the island and a strange feeling came over me. I felt as if we were being watched.

As we sailed closer, the sea birds seemed to gather thickly before us. Crying out loudly, they hovered over the boat like a cloud. Moment by moment, more birds joined the flock in a flying jumble between our vessel and the land.

"What is wrong with those sea birds?" asked Neftiji. "Is there a group of fish nearby?"

We both looked into the water. We had seen birds gather on the edge of the sea in this manner to hunt large schools of prey fish after a hatch. From their movements I knew they were preparing to dive into the water and attack. Almost too late I realized what they were doing.

"Neftiji!" I shouted. "Get down!" The sea-birds screamed in unison as they dived toward the boat. I had no doubt that we were the prey. I grabbed a thick sail lying nearby, pushed Neftiji down and lay on top of her, covering us both as best I could. With deafening screams, the birds pummeled into my back and violently battered the boat.

"Memna," Neftiji asked fearfully, "why are they attacking us?"

"I don't know, Neftiji," I huffed. "I don't know!"

As the attack continued, I heard tearing and rending. Risking a peek from beneath the cloth, I saw the cloud of birds tearing our sails to pieces and slashing the cloth we lay under. I knew they would soon get to us. I also knew that there was no way to fight so many. I started to despair.

"Neftiji, they are tearing through the cloth!"

"Get off me, Memna. Let me try something," she cried.

I rolled off her as she started moving around in the dimness under the shredding sail. Suddenly she pressed a large stone vase into my hands. "Will this fit over your head?" she asked.

"What?" I asked, half listening as I heard the birds pecking frantically at the cloth. I could see small holes tearing near my head, and had to hold on tight as they tried to pull the sail off of us.

"Will it fit over your head?" Neftiji repeated. "Hurry, Memna, we have no time!"

The holes in the cloth were getting larger and the birds were striking my back more viciously, but I slipped the vase over my head. "Yes, it fits," I cried from inside it, "but what...?"

She then pulled me toward the edge of the boat.

"Hold onto my arm," she said, the ringing sound of her voice indicating her own head covered. "Keep the vase on and get into the water. On three, we will jump in. Keep the vessel on your head and hold onto this rope, here!"

Seizing my hand, she and ran it across a rope attached to the side of the boat. "One...two...three!"

As we rapidly slid over the side and into the water, the birds screeched horribly and descended down upon us. Holding onto the rope, we floated in the water up to our heads. As we waded, blow after vicious blow pounded against the vases. At first it had me reeling, until I thought of Neftiji's safety and steadied myself. Leaning my encased head against the side of the boat, I wrapped my free hand around my sister's waist.

"Are you all right, Neftiji?" I asked, trying to shout over the noise of the birds.

My sister said nothing as her body went limp and fell towards me, causing the stone vases to strike together loudly. I hugged her close, bracing both our heads against the side, determined to hold out against the mad attack.

The birds kept striking for long minutes, until they realized they could not get at us through the stone vases. When they stopped striking us, I could hear them tearing things apart in our boat.

The vases were getting heavier, while Neftiji was dead weight in my already exhausted arms. I knew I could not hold on much longer, and the choice between death under the waves and death at the claws of the birds crept into my mind.

Then suddenly, the tearing and screeching stopped. Listening carefully for the sounds of the birds, I slowly lifted the stone vase. Aten blazed brightly

SHADES OF MEMNON

and I half expected an attack upon my eyes, but I looked around to find that the sky was clear. Our sails were totally ravaged and there were marks all over the boat, but, thanks to my sister, we had come through alive.

I pushed my vase into the boat, then pried the vase off Neftiji's head. She had totally lost her senses and had an ugly bump on her forehead, but her breathing was even and steady. Gathering her into my arms, I pushed her into the boat and pulled myself up after her. I intended to gather the oars and row as far away from this island as I could until I glanced at our supplies.

The water vessels were toppled and fouled and the bags of fruit and meat were empty. I sat down next to my sister, stroking her still face. We had no choice now but to get to the island.

Neftiji awoke as Aten was low on the horizon. Though we both wished it otherwise, she agreed that we must get to the island. Thankfully, the birds never returned and after a rest I started rowing toward land. As we both looked nervously to the skies, Neftiji sang a temple hymn to cheer us:

"As the love Amen is eternal
As the law of Amen is just
The Two Lands will endure forever
Through the work of all, it must.
As Ausar came back to save us
As Hapi saves the land from dust
The Two Lands will endure forever
Through the work of all, it must...."

Neftiji was about to begin a new verse, when suddenly something struck the boat with such force that we were nearly tilted over. My sister screamed and held on to the side as I lifted the oars and peered into the water. Several dark, sail-shaped fins emerged from beneath the waves, which I immediately recognized.

"Sea beasts!" I shouted. "Neftiji, stay away from the sides!"

The fins of the sea beasts were circling the boat slowly. These were the terrible creatures that I had heard about from sailors, who say that when a man falls into the sea near them, he is torn to pieces and eaten. Tales of these beasts, with their frightfully large jaws and multiple rows of teeth, are used to frighten children and those who never leave land. I could not understand why they would attack a boat, but after the sea birds, nothing could surprise me near this strange island.

As the fins of the sea beasts circled faster and faster, I turned to Neftiji. "Tie yourself down," I said. "You must not fall into the water!"

My sister took rope and frantically tied herself to the mast that once bore the large sail. I started rowing towards the island, but one of the sea beasts charged, crashing into the side violently. I held onto the oars with all my strength and tried to row again, but another sea beast rammed us. The creatures were huge and I could hear the wood splintering with each blow. I knew if this continued our small vessel would be torn apart.

Lifting an oar, I bashed it against the next one that charged. But it ignored my blow, smashing itself against the boat, nearly throwing me over the side.

Neftiji screamed. "Memna, be careful! Just row! Please row, you can-

not fight them!"

I looked at my sister and shook my head. "They will not let me row! Where is your knife?"

As Neftiji pulled the knife from her robe, another sea beast battered us. The knife slipped from her hand and tumbled towards the waves. I dove for it frantically, snatching it up just before it fell into the sea.

The sea beasts continued circling. Taking turns, they dashed themselves against the sides, nearly succeeding in tilting us over several times. I sat down in the middle of the boat, hacking away at the oar with the knife as water had begun leaking from the sides. Suddenly I stood up, holding the sharpened oar and gazing at my sister grimly.

"Neftiji, if I don't...if you find yourself alone, swim to the island. It is your only chance...."

SHADES OF MEMNON

"Memna, what are you going to do?"

I said nothing and turned toward the water. Bracing myself, I spotted one of the beasts rushing towards us. Lifting the oar high, I brought it down, stabbing into the side of the beast with all my might. A loud, shrill noise emerged from the water and I leaned upon my makeshift spear, pushing it deeper into the body of the beast. The creature thrashed violently and began turning, and I found myself being hoisted from the vessel as I held on my makeshift weapon.

Looking back, I screamed to Neftiji. "Swim, my sister, while I distract them. You must live! Live for me, please!"

"Memnaaaaa!" she shrieked.

Then the sea beast dove into the water, taking me with it into its airless depths. Holding my breath as we plunged, I twisted the oar as it thrashed, determined to slay the beast. As long moments went by, the creature's struggles became weaker and my chest throbbed painfully for air. Finally the beast gave up and we bobbed to the surface.

Poking my head above the water, I gulped desperately for precious mouthfuls of air. After catching my breath, I pulled the oar from the body of the dying creature and blood poured into the sea. I turned to swim away, only to find the fins of the others fast approaching, forcing me back against the creature I had just killed. Bracing myself against the dead beast, I prepared to strike at its approaching comrades with the oar.

As the first of the others came near, my heart nearly stopped. It was twice the size of the one I had just killed, and I knew I could not stop it. But I was determined to go on fighting, and dove beneath the waves, hoping to strike at the beast's soft underbelly. The huge creature hurtled toward me and I poised myself to strike. But, suddenly, it veered away from me and surged up towards the surface.

As I looked on in utter surprise, the beast bit into its own dead companion. Swimming further back, I watched as the others rushed forward, joining in a the cannibalistic feast. As the sea filled with blood and the sounds of tearing flesh, I cautiously swam back to the boat.

Tossing in the oar, I dragged myself up over the side, gasping for breath as I fell in. I called to Neftiji, but there was only silence. Lifting my head, I gazed into every corner of the ravaged vessel, but my sister was gone.

Looking toward the island, I saw nothing but waves. I looked behind and there was nothing but the sea beasts, continuing their feast. Then I looked back to the island, hoping against all odds that she would be there.

I rowed as fast as I could, my arms aching from the day's ordeals. As I drew closer, I noticed that the sand of the island had a strange glow, but paid little attention to it as I scanned the shore for Neftiji. Finally, I beached the boat and dragged myself ashore.

Immediately I spotted a set of fresh footprints, small footprints emerging from the waves that I knew must be Neftiji's. Following the prints, I called to my sister several times, but heard nothing in return. Undeterred, I followed the footprints for a long while, until, to my dismay, they abruptly disappeared.

For more than an hour, I searched frantically in all directions. But I could find no further sign of my sister. There was only a deep impression in the sand that looked as if a heavy rock or giant log had been dragged away.

When the rays of Aten began to grow dim, despair overcame me and I shouted to the sky. "Amen!" I cried. "Oh, Amen! Do not take from me the only one I have left!"

I sank to my knees, staring down at the strange sparkling sand. I was weak and tired. Tears streamed from my eyes down onto my wet and tattered robes. As the waves crashed against the shore, I reached into the sand, clutching it in despair. It was then that nature of the sand distracted me. It was heavier than any sand I had ever known, and looking closer, it dawned on me that it was not sand at all. Suddenly I realized that the entire beach was made of gold. Gold ground to the fineness of sand.

Just then a loud noise exploded across the beach, and the ground shook with the force of an earthquake. I struggled to remain upright as the beach rolled beneath me, and then without any warning, Aten disappeared.

Slowly turning, I looked up and was paralyzed with awe. A creature of huge proportions blocked out the light. It was a giant serpent, fully 40 cubits long and no less than 10 cubits across. Dazzling scales covered its body, gleaming like silver as it eclipsed Aten's fading light. A curious glow surrounded it also; and when it moved, its sinuous form produced a tinkling sound like softly shaken sistrums.

But the strangest thing about this impossible creature was its head. Though its skull was shaped like a serpent's, its face had remarkably human features. Intelligent eyes beamed from beneath brows of pure blue lapis and a golden beard jutted from its chin that was identical to the false appendages worn by the kings of Kamit.

Made speechless by its size and awesome beauty, I stared at the creature in utter disbelief. Then it bent its huge head and spoke to me, in a voice so loud that it took my breath away.

"Who has brought you here, little one?" the creature boomed.

I covered my ears and lowered my head. My mind could not believe what my ears had just relayed. The creature spoke perfect Kamitian.

"Who has brought you here, little one? Who has brought you here?" it thundered. "Speak!"

SHADES OF MEMNON

I tried to, but no words would come. With an impatient nod the serpent rose up menacingly, recoiling itself to bring its golden beard right near my chest. "Say what has brought you to my island!" it shouted again. "If you do not tell me at once, I will show you what it is to be burned utterly into nothing and become a thing of ashes. Speak quickly, I am waiting to hear!"

I looked up into the face of the serpent. Its eyes glowing bright gold, penetrating to my very ka. Pondering his question, I found the strength to say one word.

"Destiny."

"What?" the serpent replied, tilting its head to hear. "What is it you say, little one?"

"Destiny...brought me here," I repeated.

Then the serpent rose and let out a tremendous peal of laughter, shaking the entire beach.

"Ha ha, ha ha, ha ha, ha ha! Yesss! Yes little one, you are right! It is destiny that has brought you here! Destiny it is, indeed!"

And with that, the creature leaned over me, opened its huge silver mouth and snapped me up into its gaping jaws.

SHADES OF MEMNON

CHAPTER 3: "GUARDIAN OF AUSAR"

Terrified, I found myself tumbling from side to side inside the dark mouth of the huge serpent. Sure that my end had come, I waited for the huge ivory teeth to crush me and for the massive, rough tongue to press me down into the tunnel-like gullet. Long minutes passed as I felt the serpent moving and heard strange sounds, like waves of the ocean, coming from somewhere inside its body. Finally, the giant head lowered, the mouth opened and I slid out, landing gently on a glowing, golden floor.

Dazed and surprised, I looked around at a tremendous cave with walls that glowed like heated bronze. Behind the serpent was a huge pool of blue water with speckles of light playing beneath the surface. Next to the water stood Neftiji.

"Oh, Memna," she cried as she ran toward me. "He said you would come! The serpent said you would come and he was right!"

The serpent slithered its huge bulk into the blue water and turned around towards us. A smile appeared on its strange face as it nodded its huge head knowingly.

I hugged Neftiji close, thanking Amen for bringing her back to me. Then I turned back toward the huge creature, stepping protectively before my sister.

"What...who are you?" I asked. "What place is this?"

The serpent dipped its head into the pool, brought it back up and vigorously shook off the water. Moisture and light sprayed in all directions as soft musical notes chimed from the scraping of its silver scales.

"I am the king of this island. Who are you, little ones?"

"I am Memna-un, and this is my sister Neftiji. We are Kamitians. You said you are a king. Where are your subjects?"

"I am my own subject. I am my own king."

"Are there no others like you, then?"

"So many questions, little one! Do you not wish to refresh yourself? Allow your sister to show you the way."

Neftiji took me by the hand and led me from the cave. Nearby was a grove of beautiful silver trees, filled with delicious looking fruit. As we neared one large trunk, a limb lowered, putting a juicy red fruit in reach of our hands. I marveled at this and turned towards Neftiji as it hovered near my head.

"Take it," Neftiji said with a smile. "You will like it."

I plucked the fruit and the branch rose back into place. Neftiji took it from my hand, twisted it, and it split perfectly down the middle. Biting into her half, she smiled, juice dripping from the corners of her mouth. Then I bit into mine.

SHADES OF MEMNON

An explosion of sensations engulfed me. Waves of pleasure washed over me and I found myself greedily devouring the fruit. Neftiji plucked more and we consumed several before she led me back into the cave.

As we walked, I felt as if I were floating. Every sense seemed to be heightened, my mind was clear and my weakness had gone away. We stopped before the pool again, standing beneath the gaze of the serpent.

Looking deeply into our eyes, he spoke gently.

"You have passed the tests of worthiness to come unto this land," he proclaimed. "The test of intelligence from the creatures who fly. The test of strength from the beasts who swim. And the test of courage from the beast who is not a beast. You have earned the high fruit of the Tree of Life and great knowledge can now be yours."

My mind tingled. The fruit seemed to draw out long forgotten memories, and I recalled where I had heard of this serpent before. As he spoke, Neftiji and I looked at each other. I knew she recognized him also, from stories we had heard as young children.

"I am Kam-Atef," the serpent said at last. "Guardian of Ausar. It was I who safeguarded the body of the sacred one after the treachery of Set, for the salvation of all Children of Geb."

We fell to our knees and bowed our heads in reverence.

"Know this also chosen ones: You have not come to this Island of the Ka by chance, but by destiny ordained by the Neteru and by your ancestors. Prepare yourselves! Tomorrow your lessons begin!"

The great serpent shook his glowing coils again, then disappeared beneath the surface of the pool. Neftiji and I went to a corner of the cave. There we lay down in each other's arms and fell into a peaceful sleep.

Our lessons indeed began the next day, at the rising of Aten, with Kam-Atef leading us to see the wonders of his island. There were hills made of gold and precious gems. There were groves of the sweetest myrrh and fields of fragrant khol and cypress trees. Delicious fruits were everywhere and there were gardens where vegetables rose from the soil into your hands at the beckoning.

Small, beautiful animals with brilliant colors and many strange forms roamed at will. Some resembled squirrels or hares, while others were puffs of fluffy blue hair with large eyes and small human-like claws. These proved to be the friendliest, running up and down the trees and tossing down fruit when we could not reach it. All around we saw nothing but peace and joy. It was truly an enchanted island.

We stopped near a stream that had the fragrance of fruit incense, with brilliant red bushes burdened with fat purple berries lining its shore. As Neftiji and I dined upon the berries and drank from the stream, Kam-Atef settled his huge body into a spiral and spoke of the nature of his land.

"You stand upon an island that was one of the first in creation. This Island of the Ka has all that men desire. It is a paradise, like Ausar's Fields of Peace, but it exists in this world and not the next."

"Great serpent, why is it so difficult to get here?" I asked, drawing a cool handful of water from the stream. "Why so many challenges and hardships?"

"This place is only for the worthy, only for those whom the Neters deem it necessary to send," Kam-Atef replied. "When there is great strife in the world, a few Children of Geb are called to this place to gain knowledge for the world's salvation."

"Are we in such a time now, great serpent?" asked Neftiji.

Kam-Atef nodded. "Yes, little one. It is revealed to me that the Children of Geb will be plunged into a great war. Dire times, unknown since the slaying of Ausar, are coming to all your lands."

I rose and stepped towards Kam-Atef, who looked down at me as I raised my hands excitedly.

"This is why I long to be a warrior, like my pa. He fought to preserve Maat, and I would do the same. This my mut could never understand..."

Kam-Atef's long forked tongue flicked out, nearly striking me. I jumped back, startled into silence.

"Your mut has much wisdom, young one," said the great serpent. "I myself can see the state of your ka. You are not yet ready to fight as a true warrior."

I sat down next to the stream and pondered Kam-Atef's words for a moment. "What do you mean?" I asked, finally.

"You have fire without discipline. Strength without humility. Knowledge without wisdom. Tell me, little one, would you fight in the service of Ausar or in the service of Set?"

"Ausar!" I replied quickly. "Yes, Ausar of course!"

"Then you must first develop Heru, the son of Ausar, inside yourself. You must conquer the evil forces within your own spirit, if you would fight against it in others. Right now you are strong with the influence of Set. This is why you have been sent here."

"Why have I been called here?" asked Neftiji.

"You have come to learn to heal, my child. With the help of the fruit of the Tree of Life, you both will achieve your destinies upon this island. As I said, great evil is rising among the Children of Geb, and you must help fight against it."

"What is this evil, great serpent?" I asked.

Kam-Atef rose, his scales chiming and gleaming in the light of the new day. "Follow me."

We went back into the cave and stood before the pool of sparkling blue water. The flickering lights flashed beneath the surface, looking almost alive as Kam-Atef waved his head above them. The lights came together and

SHADES OF MEMNON

formed glowing orbs, then the orbs blended to form a surface which shone like a polished mirror. Images started to form upon it as Kam-Atef began to speak.

"There are other beings like myself in the world of Geb. Most play no part in the affairs of men, as they await their time to go back home to where we all come from: the Taut. Our home is in the higher regions of the inner planes and we are explorers of the worlds without. We are spirits who travel to different regions to experience and gain wisdom. Do not ask me why. This is our nature; it is what we do."

The pool showed groups of serpents gathering and moving together. Landscapes changed from cold mountains, to hot green forests, to long flat plains. Gradually, the serpents changed also, some becoming larger, some shrinking in size and some changing in different ways: growing legs, or wings or fins. Some remained more snakelike, while others took on more human features like Kam-Atef. The images gave the impression of the passing of immense time.

"We have lived here since your world was young, little ones. All was well until the Great Neter caused your numbers to grow and your abodes to expand. For we are beings that adapt to the ways of the dominant creatures of the worlds we live upon, and sadly, some of us have fallen under the influence of the immature Children of Geb."

Images of human beings worshipping serpents, running in terror from them, making war against them and other activities flashed upon the surface.

"We are beings of great power and intelligence who prefer to remain neutral to the affairs of your world. This is why we live far away from you in remote places. But sometimes you move near us, influencing us according to the nature of your spirits. Luckily, I dwelled near Kamit and fell under the sway of a righteous people, the Kamau...."

"As your priests say, I protected the body of Ausar, while Heru battled Set for the throne. But after the time of Heru, I was forced to leave, for the turmoil in the spirits of the Kamitians after Ausar's time became too much to bear. Now I live here, protected by my ancient magics and the Neteru of your world, who send me pupils to teach when the Children of Geb become endangered. You see, there are others like me who are not in league with good forces. Look here! These are my brethren who have fallen under the sway of unjust peoples."

More images of serpents appeared in the pool. Some were being worshipped like deities. To my horror, they appeared to be receiving human sacrifices. Knives in the hands of black-robed priests fell upon victims lying on bloody altars before them. Other more terrifying images appeared, showing thousands of people gathered before the serpents and their bloody priests. Their backs bent low in reverence, most of the worshippers looked like the northerners who ran with Kho-An-Sa, but some were Kushites, and some were Shashu.

There were also yellow- and red-skinned people that I had never seen before. All carried swords or spears and seemed to be preparing for war. I shuddered at the evil these serpents emitted, and at the eagerness with which their worshippers seemed to revel in it. Individual images of serpents appeared one by one, as Kam-Atef spoke their names:

Narti-ankem-sen, allied with the wicked of the Fenku. Herfekem-qeb, allied with the wicked of the Indu.

Ankh-em-fentu, allied with the with wicked of North Atl-anta.

Sam-em-qesu, allied with the wicked Az-tec-a.

Ha-hu-tiamsau, allied with the wicked of South Atl-anta. Shept-temesu, allied with the wicked of the Basilia.

Un-em-sahu, allied with the wicked of far eastern K'un Lun. Sam-em-snef, allied with the wicked of the southern homelands.

Akh-embetu, allied with the People of the Sea.

Kam-Atef shook his head sadly as he continued.

"These are the 9 fallen ones of my kind, who have absorbed evil and developed a taste for blood. They give support to those who would bring them power and influence through sacrifice, and they in turn, empower evil men and negative forces from the Taut. Prepare yourselves well here, little ones! For the evil in men's minds is becoming flesh. Monsters now walk your world, and you, Memna-un, must use your skills as a scribe to prepare for the war against these evils."

"How, great serpent?" I asked. "What must I do?"

"You must sit before me and write what I relate to you. Only this knowledge will save the Children of Geb from the Reckoning."

"What is this Reckoning?" asked Neftiji.

"Those with the hearts of beasts shall become them," replied Kam-Atef. "And other creatures so terrible that men will come to call them myths and legends. But they are real, and you must know them to defeat them."

Thus began our time of learning on the Island of the Ka. Day after day, we sat before Kam-Atef, fulfilling our destinies as his students. Due to the enchanted fruit of the Tree of Life, our minds opened tremendously, allowing us to learn in months the equivalent of years of study in the House of Life. The great serpent gave me stylus and papyrus and assigned me to prepare a sacred volume for the salvation of the Children of Geb.

In the shadows of sparkling hills of gold, I learned the nature of the Taut underworld and the creatures that dwell within and those that can come forth from it. Among glorious groves of rainbow trees, I learned that all dreams and all nightmares exist in the Taut and that at certain times and places, they

SHADES OF MEMNON

emerge into the realm of the living. I named this sacred volume "The Book of Knowing the Creatures of the Taut."

This book, I was told by Kam-Atef, would ensure that all the great Kushite nations, those who most adhered to the spiritual sciences and held fast to the Universal Principles, would be equipped to combat the forces of the Reckoning. In preparation for my task as the keeper of the book, I was required to learn the languages of these other Kushite peoples, three of whom I had only heard of in legends and tales told by my pa. But, according to Kam-Atef, they were real, and one day I would be required to deliver a copy of the book to each of them.

I also prepared for being a great warrior by learning to calm my restless spirit. The great serpent taught me to rest my mind and to breathe properly, in order to go within and keep my heart stable. This technique, called the great ritual of Men Ab, was once taught to Heru by Tehuti in the war against the usurper Set.

Neftiji also fulfilled her charge by studying the great Spiritual Sciences used for healing. In this enchanted place where every herb needed for healing grew, my sister mastered their use by learning the speech of the plant world and the nature of the minerals in the body of Geb. Kam-Atef also taught her to detect the Patterns of Life in the body, and how to manipulate them by hand or by small sticks inserted into their flow.

I found that Neftiji's ministrations brought ease to aching muscles and that her herbs gave vitality to the heart and mind. She kept us both vital and strong as we filled our charge as students. I knew that my sister would be a truly great healer in the world.

Time seemed to stand still upon the island, and for a long while we forgot about our lives in the outside world, until one fateful evening. That day's lessons were ending for me, while Neftiji sat mixing herbs in a pot over a small fire. The sweet fragrance filled the cave and put me as ease, but when I turned to ask her what she brewed, I found her sobbing. Excusing myself from my discourse with Kam-Atef, I rushed to her side.

"My sister," I cried. "What is it? Why do you weep?"

She tossed a mushroom into the pot and a puff of yellow smoke wafted toward the ceiling. "Memna," she answered tearfully. "We have not spoken of Meri-Ta for a long time. I miss her so..."

I lowered my head and my mut's sweet face automatically came to mind. "You are right, my sister," I replied. "We have not given her or pa their honor, nor have we sent them our love. We will libate for them both tonight."

Grasping the hot pot with two pieces of cloth, Neftiji removed it from the flames. Then she looked past me to Kam-Atef, who sat on his coils nearby. "Great serpent," Neftiji said. "Is this Taut you are teaching my brother about the same underworld in which the dead dwell after life on Geb?"

"Yes," said Kam-Atef. "It is all a part of the endless otherworld created by Amen for spirits who live without flesh."

"Can you show us our parents, then?"

Kam-Atef uncoiled himself and rose high, his head poised above the sparkling pool. Then he looked at Neftiji and asked in a serious tone, "Are you sure this is what you want, little one? Often the condition of a newly passed spirit is not pleasing to see." Then he nodded at me and added, "And you, Memna-un, do you wish this also?"

I thought about the last time I had seen my mut. I had lost her during a time of violence and we never spoke parting words. As for pa, he simply left one day when I was small and Neftiji newly born. He said he was going to aid allies in a battle at Troy, and never returned. I longed to speak to them both and to hear their voices again.

"Yes, great serpent," I replied. "I would like to speak to my parents."

"As you wish," Kam-Atef said, waving his silver head above the pool. Light mists washed across the surface and colorful images flashed by. Bright corridors appeared with strange walls that pulsated as if alive, leading to a door that opened to a shining chamber. There, sitting high upon his throne of pure white, sat Ausar. He was wrapped in white cloth from the neck down, his face black as charcoal, with the crook and flail held tightly across his chest. His head slowly turned and he seemed to be looking at us. Then he slowly nodded, as if giving us permission to go on.

The view then flashed past Ausar, down long corridors where tendrils of darkness and light flitted to and fro. Finally, I saw my mut. She was lying upon a silver bed, her hands entwined peacefully across her breast.

"She sleeps the slumber of the newly passed," said Kam-Atef. "If you would take council with her, you must libate."

Neftiji and I looked around the cave, then back at Kam-Atef. "There are no libation bowls nearby," Neftiji said.

"Use your hands," said Kam-Atef.

Neftiji and I reached into the pool, withdrawing two handfuls of water each. We poured it onto the ground and spoke the libation words.

"En en Neter, Keper-ankh. Ea Ti En Meri-Ta!"

Small flashes of light appeared to sink into my mut's head. Her brows moved and she stirred, but only slightly.

"Again," said Kam-Atef. "Say it louder."

We dipped our hands into the water and poured it onto the ground again, shouting the libation words in unison.

"En en Neter, Keper-ankh! Ea Ti En Meri-Ta!"

This time much more light engulfed my mut. She shook and moaned, then opened her eyes and sat up. Meri-Ta blinked and looked directly at us.

"I am awake, my children."

SHADES OF MEMNON

"Mut!" Neftiji cried, her eyes filling with tears. "We miss you so!" I said nothing at first due to the knot welling up in my throat. Holding back tears of my own, I bowed my head in shame.

"Mut, I am so sorry...." I finally exclaimed.

"Shush, Memna," spoke Meri-Ta. "Look at me."

Gazing into my mut's face through the mist of the pool, I found her smiling sweetly. I could still feel the affection she had always given me as she gazed into my face.

"You did the best you could, Memna, and I am proud of you. Mourn no more for me, my children, for I have only crossed over. It is you who have work to do in the world of Geb."

"Mut, we are here on the island of the Ka," Neftiji Said. "We are with Kam-Atef, the great serpent from the stories you told us of Ausar."

Meri-Ta sat up higher on the silver bed and turned her face toward the great serpent. "Hail, Kam-Atef! My children are blessed by your presence."

"Hail, Spirit in the bosom of Ausar! " Kam-Atef said in reply. "Your children are to be prepared for a great struggle that threatens their entire world. Does this have your blessing?"

My mut gazed first into my eyes, then into Neftiji's. "Is this what they will to do?" she asked.

I grabbed Neftiji's hand and we nodded our heads in unison.

"Yes, mut," Neftiji declared. "It is."

"Then teach them well, great Kam-Atef. This endeavor has my blessing."

"Mut," I said. "Where is pa? Can we speak to him?"

My Mut shook her head. "When I first arrived, he did not come to greet me. I do not believe your pa is here."

"What?" I cried. "But why is this so? Surely, he is not consigned to the outer darkness. Our pa was a righteous man, he would not be in the place of sinful spirits...."

My Mut held up her hand to silence me. "Memna, your pa is not here in the Taut at all. He still dwells in the bosom of Geb. He is still alive."

Neftiji and I looked at each other in utter amazement.

"But, mut," Neftiji said. "They said he died at Troy."

"Your pa does not dwell with Ausar, dear one. Somewhere, he still lives."

Feelings of joy, fear and confusion overwhelmed me. Ever since I was a young boy, I had grieved over the death of my pa. To find he had survived brought only one question to my mind. "Mut, where is my pa?" I asked.

"Alas," Meri-Ta said sadly, "this I do not know."

"But you of the Taut can observe the doings of Geb. How can you not know where he is?"

My Mut placed her hand upon her brow. Lowering her head she spoke solemnly. "This is true. But when I seek to observe my husband, I see only darkness. Darkness. Your pa yet lives, but he is held down in darkness and he cannot move. I can tell you only this...it is in a place in the north, for I can feel the cold that he feels. His place of captivity bears a harsh and bitter chill that never ends."

The thought of my pa being held in cold darkness disturbed me greatly. All my life I had been told that he died an honorable death defending Maat in a far-off land. I turned towards Kam-Atef.

"Great serpent! You have heard this yourself. You must let us leave to find our pa. We must leave here now!"

"You are no prisoner here, little one," Kam-Atef said. "But your lessons are not yet finished. Would you give them up now, so close to completion?"

I opened my mouth to speak, but my mut's voice was there before mine. "My son," she said. "I too would see my husband freed from the cold prison in which he dwells, but you have a task there that needs completing."

My mut's tone was as it had always been when scolding me for impetuous behavior. I bowed my head. Even after her death, I was humbled by her wisdom. Neftiji held my hand as we both listened respectfully to the shade of Meri-Ta.

"My children, you have been given a sacred task. You must learn all from great Kam-Atef and go back to give the wisdom to the world. Then go and find your pa, with my blessings. You must fulfill this destiny. Promise me you will!"

"I promise, mut," I said.

"I too, promise," said Neftiji.

"My children, you make me proud. Libate for me and I will send you help when I can. Be strong and listen to the great serpent. I am tired now, my children, farewell."

Meri-Ta lay back down upon the silver bed and the images faded from the pool. Kam-Atef then disappeared beneath the surface of the sparkling water, and Neftiji and I retired to our corner of the cave. Though I stilled my emotions with the breath of Men Ab, I went to sleep thinking of my pa and dreamed of him being held down in cold darkness.

Twelve moons went by during our stay on the Island of the Ka and my sister and I learned diligently from the great serpent. All was peaceful until one sunny morning when Neftiji and I were out picking fruit. A strange object appeared suddenly in the sky. High above the trees it hovered, looking like a stiff sort of bird. As it came closer, I saw that its wings did not move and that it gave off a low musical hum. As it flew back and forth over the island, like a bird of prey seeking victims, Neftiji and I ran back to the cave to inform Kam-Atef.

When we burst into the cave, he was lying atop the pool, floating serenely as the sparkling lights reflected off his glowing scales.

SHADES OF MEMNON

"Great serpent," I puffed excitedly, "there is a strange flying thing above the island."

"Yes," added Neftiji, "its wings do not move and it makes a strange noise."

Kam-Atef glided from the water and rose up before us. "Where is this object?"

"It is near the grove of the Tree of Life," I said.

The great serpent listened to our fearful voices and a huge grin appeared across his face. He then let out a loud peal of laughter that shook the entire cave.

"Ah ha ha ha ha! Look at you, little ones, shaking in fear. Have I not taught you to be more observant than this? Follow me!"

We trailed Kam-Atef back to the grove, strolling through the trees until we came to a well-worn clearing. Kam-Atef looked to the sky, pressed his lips together and let loose a piercing whistle. Soon the object appeared directly above the clearing, emitting an identical sound. Then it began lowering to the ground. As it came closer Neftiji and I looked on in amazement, finally realizing what this strange object was.

"A sky-boat!" I cried.

As it came closer to the ground I could see it clearly. Its wings were stiff and attached to each side of the vessel to cut through the wind. It had a tail that stuck upright for steering and was perhaps 50 cubits long. Painted white on the top and black on the bottom half, it bore a mix of Kamitic symbols along with other odd and unfamiliar signs. Neftiji and I had heard of these magical vessels in tales told to us as children. Now, like Kam-Atef and his island, we knew they were actually real.

The great vessel floated gently to the ground, landing a few cubits away. Then a door opened on the side and two very small Kushite men stepped out. Both wore loincloths in the style of early Kamit and bore wreaths of white flowers around the tops of their heads.

They stepped forward holding spears, bowed to Kam-Atef, then took their places at both sides of the door. Then a very small woman with radiant, reddish-brown skin stepped from the ship. She was dressed regally in a long blue robe held at one shoulder by a pin with a huge clear diamond. Around her neck was a wreath of flowers of brilliant colors and vibrant hues. Her hair was closely cropped in the style of southern Kushite women and her eyes were large, liquid and expressive.

She stepped aside and a small man emerged. He too had striking reddish-brown skin and was dressed as she was, with blue robes and a sparkling wreath, but his pin held his robe on the opposite shoulder. Looking closer, I noticed a soft golden light radiating from their skin. They bowed to Kam-Atef and spoke in unison.

"Hail, great Kam-Atef. We bring you greetings from the land of the Anu."

"Hail, princess Nu-At. Hail, prince Aunk-At. Welcome once again to the Island of the Ka."

Neftiji and I were shaking with delight. Here again was another legend come true. The great Anu, the sacred little people, stood before us. Kam-Atef noticed how we were shaking and nodded at us with a chuckle.

"These are my charges, Memna-un and Neftiji," he said. "Kamitians who have come to the sacred island to learn."

The prince and princess bowed their heads towards us.

"Hail, Memna-un. Hail, Neftiji," they said in perfect unison again.

We both bowed nervously, too overwhelmed to speak.

The royal Anu turned towards the sky-boat and clapped their hands. Out came lines of Anu men and women carrying baskets. There were dozens of them. Most were black-skinned and looked like the small peoples far to the south of Kamit. But some had the reddish-brown complexions of the prince and princess. They all ran joyfully into the trees and started picking fruit, singing songs of transcendent beauty as they worked.

As their exquisite songs filled the air, the atmosphere became charged with a vibrancy unlike anything I had ever known. Neftiji and I swayed to and fro as we experienced the legendary music of the Anu, the songs of healing that only a privileged few had ever heard.

The prince and princess excused themselves and went among their people, directing them and overseeing their harvest. Neftiji and I were speechless for long minutes as we watched them work. Finally I pulled my mind away from their songs to pursue the questions raging in my mind.

"Great serpent," I asked, "what is your relation to the Anu?"

Kam-Atef watched the little people dashing amongst the trees, nodding his own head to their music. He answered me without taking his eyes off them. "They come to harvest during this season yearly. They are the only race of Geb's Children, who as a whole, are worthy to eat of the Tree of Life. They are the oldest of your kind, those who for the longest have given thanks to Amen-Ra."

One small Anu ran by, a basket balanced precariously upon his head. Hesitating, he winked at Neftiji before scurrying on his way. My sister giggled. "They must be very wise to eat so much of the Tree of Life," she said.

"Indeed," Kam-Atef replied, "they are the most wise of all the races. Very soon they will leave the world of Geb behind. They will be the first race to cross over all together, and go on to be one with the Neters."

I was astonished at the implications of Kam-Atef's words.

"You mean their people will die all at once?"

Kam-Atef shook his head. "No, little one. No. Soon they will gather on their sacred island of Agaru for the great ritual of Coming Forth. As a people, they will give up this world and go to live in the Taut forever."

SHADES OF MEMNON

We watched their flurry of activity for hours and listened to Kam-Atef's many stories about these little magical people. Finally, they hauled the fruit aboard and prepared to leave. As we stood watching the small folk file into the sky-boat, the royal couple walked up to us, giving us an open-handed salute I had never seen. As we bowed in return, they stepped closer.

The princess took the colorful wreath from her own neck and placed it around Neftiji's, whispering something in her ear. Then the prince took a ring from his forefinger, and, seizing my hand, pushed it upon my finger.

I did not believe it would fit me since his hand was like that of small child. But as it moved up my finger, the band grew, slipping onto my forefinger easily. The band was solid gold and bore a pitch-black stone of a sort unknown to me. It was carved in the likeness of the head of a great cat, with a face that seemed to change expressions. Upon the cat's brow was a symbol I had only observed in the most ancient of Kamitic documents. It was the symbol for a chief or great leader. Then the prince whispered into my ear.

"By this ring you will be known."

I had no idea what he meant, but Neftiji and I thanked them reverently for the gifts. They saluted Kam-Atef and then disappeared into their sky-boat. As we watched it rise among the clouds, Kam-Atef made a fateful announcement.

"Little ones, you have received everything you came to this island to get. Your world awaits you. It is time for you to leave.

SHADES OF MEMNON

SHADES OF MEMNON

CHAPTER 4: "WELCOME BACK, CHILDREN OF MEMNON"

It was a clear early morning on the golden beach of the Island of the Ka. The sea was calm and the water bright blue-green as we stood between our small boat and the great serpent. It was with great sadness that Neftiji and I restocked our vessel in preparation for leaving. Tears filled my eyes as I carefully wrapped my greatest possession, The Book of Knowing The Creatures of the Taut, in cloth and papyrus for the trip.

Kam-Atef lifted his head high to scan the waters and flicked his huge tongue out to test the wind. The rays of Aten bounced off his glowing scales, reflecting light onto the golden sand and waters of the sea. He had never looked quite so beautiful to me.

"It is a good day to sail," Kam-Atef said with a nod.

Neftiji and I looked at each other, but said nothing as we placed jugs of water and bags of food into the boat. Knowing one day we would have to leave, we had repaired the small vessel during our stay on the island. But as we stood there on the glowing golden sand, neither of us realized how difficult we would find leaving the presence of the great serpent.

Noting the sad looks upon our faces, he tried his best to cheer us up. "Come now," bellowed Kam-Atef heartily. "Still your hearts! Be at peace with your destiny, for you have achieved great things during your stay here!" We put down our jugs of water and ran to him, rubbing our hands all over his scales in an futile attempt at hugging his huge bulk. Lowering his head, he gently shook his immense frame, causing the musical chimes of his scales to fill our ears.

"Ahhh, little ones," Kam-Atef said affectionately. "I am very fond of you also. But we all have our duty. Go back to the world with what you have learned. Be strong, for the Children of Geb need you.

"Great serpent," Neftiji said sadly, "we will miss you so."

I stepped back and looked up into the face of Kam-Atef.

"Could destiny bring us back to this island, great serpent? Will we ever see you again?"

"It is possible, it is possible," Kam-Atef said with a smile. "It is more likely, though, that you will never come back. But there is a way for us to always speak to one another, if you choose to accept it."

"What is it, great one?" Neftiji asked. "How is it that you can always speak to us?"

"You can accept my venom," Kam-Atef replied. "It will allow me to be with you in spirit and speak to you in times of need."

"How do we take the venom, great serpent?" I asked, the answer to the

SHADES OF MEMNON

question dawning upon me as soon as I spoke the words.

"Step back," Kam-Atef said.

Neftiji and I did as he bid as the great serpent's lowered his head to our height and opened his mouth. Four long fangs I had never noticed before jutted from his jaws. As they came close I couldn't hold back a gasp of instinctive fear.

Kam-Atef pulled back asking, "Do you not trust me, little one?"

"Yes..." I said, having to think for a moment, "yes, I trust you."

Lowering his head again, he bit lightly into my shoulder with two sharp fangs. There was a sharp pain that was quickly gone, and a peculiar sensation of cold liquid entering my body. Withdrawing the fangs left not a trace of blood, only two small marks shaped like a crescent moon.

After he bit Neftiji he coiled himself before us and spoke. "Memna-un and Neftiji, there is now a sacred bond between us that can never be broken. Not even by death."

Neftiji and I looked at each other in astonishment. The words Kam-Atef spoke now came into our minds before they reached our ears.

"We are now connected across all spaces. Still your heart and call my name, and I will answer to give you guidance...if it is safe to do so."

"How might it not be safe to answer?" I asked.

"If the forces of the evil ones are near, they may hear me," Kam-Atef said gravely. "They would be able to use our communications to track you down. You would be in great danger."

"We thank you for this gift, great serpent," Neftiji said.

"We will cherish it above all worldly possessions," I added, "and will take care not to abuse it."

We boarded the boat and Kam-Atef nosed us gently into the waters of the sea. As soon as we unfurled the sails, a gust of wind flew into them, carrying us swiftly away from the island. Kam-Atef stood there as we sailed further away, getting smaller and smaller in the distance. Finally, we saw him turn around and head back into the hills and forests of his enchanted island, but we heard his voice in our minds as his form disappeared into the trees. "Farewell, little ones. Farewell!"

We sailed north for many days, with greater ease this time since Kam-Atef had taught us more about using the stars to guide us on our journey. We had been on the Island of the Ka for a full year, and wondered what was going on back home. We longed to see a trade vessel or diplomacy ship going to or from a port of Kamit, to get news and finally speak to familiar people. One day, three quarters of a moon into our journey home, I spied a ship in the distance.

"Neftiji! "I cried. "Look, a ship! "

Neftiji stood up with me and we watched it come closer. It was a large vessel, as large as any trading ship from Canaan or Saba, and it seemed to be going the same way we had come. This meant it was probably traveling to the incense-rich lands of the southern queens of Saba or Ta Neter.

As the ship grew closer, Neftiji waved a white cloth, signaling to them that we wished to come aboard. They spotted our signal and veered towards us, when a strange feeling suddenly seized me, and I snatched down Neftiji's waving arm. While she looked at me in confusion, a wave of horror and recognition washed over me. I had recognized the ship too late.

Suddenly the deck was lined with archers. All were Tamahu, pale northerners with red and yellow hair, aiming their bows carefully to cut us to pieces with their arrows. Cold chills swept over me when I saw a dark Kushite emerge among them. It was Kho-An-Sa.

"At last, young panther!" he shouted down with a wicked smile. "We have been looking for you!"

They threw down a ladder and two men scampered down. I thought of fighting, but there was nothing I could do. Neftiji stood motionless, her mouth open and eyes filled with fear. I had to shake her as the warriors stepped into the boat.

"Be brave, my sister," I whispered. "We will find a way out of this. For now, do as they say."

I hugged her as the two warriors stepped towards us, swords drawn. Then they shoved us up the ladder, climbing after us with the points of their weapons at our backs. As soon as our feet touched the deck, other men scampered down to retrieve our belongings. We were then shoved toward the middle of the boat. There Kho-An-Sa sat in a throne-like chair, his hands folded in his lap, and evil glint of diabolic joy in is eyes.

"Welcome back, children of Memnon," he said coldly.

"How did you find us?" I cried. "Why don't you leave us alone?"

"My...devices told me that you had never left the south Desher Sea," he replied, "and that somewhere you still lived."

"You have been out here," I asked, "for a whole year, looking for us?"

Kho-An-Sa leaned forward in his chair, pointing at me menacingly. "I told you, young panther, you are destined to serve me."

"No!" I cried. "I will never serve you. I would die first."

He stood up and clapped his hands and several warriors seized me, while others snatched Neftiji away from my side.   They dragged her towards Kho-An-Sa who asked cruelly, "It is clear that you have no fear of death, young panther, but what of the life of your sister?"

Neftiji struggled against her captors. "Memna-un, don't do it! "

"Don't hurt my sister!" I cried.

Kho-An-Sa turned to the warriors near his chair and gestured. From among them stepped the largest man I had ever seen. He was a veritable

SHADES OF MEMNON

giant, harshly pale, with a thick red beard and a strange horned helmet topping his bright red hair. A thick leather corselet encased his massive frame, and the skin of a large beast served as a cloak. He walked towards Kho-An-Sa and bowed, then turned toward Neftiji and drew the largest sword I had ever seen. The double-bladed weapon was a hand and a half wide, big enough to cut down a small tree, and he held it against the throat of my sister.

"No, young panther," Kho-An-Sa said. "I have not just been prowling the Desher Sea looking for you. Your departure forced me to seek a new warrior from the north to serve me, and he will cut your sister in half at my bidding. What say you?"

Neftiji was petrified with fear as she looked up into the bestial face of the Tamahu warrior. I had no choice but to bow my head to Kho-An-Sa.

"Leave her be," I muttered. "I will do as you say."

"Very good, young panther," Kho-An-Sa said. He waved his hand at the men holding my sister and they dragged her away. The huge man sheathed his sword and stood motionless.

"Where are they taking her?" I cried. "Leave her with me! Why do you take her away?"

"Not this time, young panther," Kho-An-Sa replied. "You will not see your sister again until I am sure you will obey me."

The warriors let me go as Kho-An-Sa whispered into the ear of the huge Tamahu. He then walked towards me and began pushing me roughly towards the hold of the ship, the same hold I had escaped from a year ago. He pushed me once too roughly and I whirled around to confront him. My anger overcoming me, I slapped his hand away and raised my fist threateningly.

Growling like a beast, the Tamahu seized my neck like a stick and lifted me from the deck with one hand, choking me and waving me about like a small child. As I kicked him and pawed at his arm, the light began to dim before my eyes, until a word from Kho-An-Sa released me from his deadly grip. I fell to the deck, dizzy from the lack of air. Suddenly Kho-An-Sa's face appeared over me, and the ring given to me by the Anu was roughly jerked from my finger.

"You are mine now, young panther," he said, turning the ring over in his fingers, "as are all your possessions. You will join this northerner in service to Kho-An-Sa, and you will never escape me again."

I sat in the hold for many days, pondering the destiny that brought us back into the clutches of this evil magician. I thought of many plans for escape, but none seemed workable because I knew not where they kept Neftiji, and because of the presence of the huge warrior outside my locked door. As constant as the waves bouncing against the ship, he stood there day and night, never seeming to rest or sleep.

When he opened the door to pass in my morning and evening meals, his

SHADES OF MEMNON

strange blue eyes were ever alert and penetrating. His heavy breathing and the odor of the putrid skins he always wore were a constant reminder of his presence. I could see why Kho-An-Sa had chosen him to guard me, for he had the qualities of a hunting animal. A dangerous, deadly beast.

Three quarters of the moon passed as I languished in the hold of the ship. Then one morning I heard a commotion on deck, and felt the ship come to a stop and lower anchor. Later the door swung open and my huge guard beckoned me to follow him.

On deck the whole crew was preparing to depart, furling sails and lowering barrels to the shore for restocking. I looked out at the small town where we had docked. It was an ordinary trading center, with long streets filled with creaking wagons and colorful markets. Several taverns and gambling houses were nearby, indicating the sort of loose administration under which this port must operate.

I was escorted off the ship and loaded into a wagon along with my huge guard and several other warriors. In a nearby wagon I caught a glimpse of Neftiji. She saw me also and turned to speak, but was jerked roughly by two men sitting near her. At the head of her wagon I spied Kho-An-Sa.

We left the town and traveled across sandy plains towards the east. As we traveled along, I looked for any opportunity to escape, but my ever-vigilant guard seemed never to sleep.

Each time I woke up, his piercing blue eyes would be there, boring into mine.

After several days, we could see the outlines of a large city. To the south I saw fertile fields and huge monuments of stone rivaling those of Kamit. To the north, the fields gave way to trackless desert and endless brushy wastelands. It looked much like parts of Kamit, but the huge monuments had been built differently. The name of the place came to me as I recognized the tremendous temple towards the middle of the city.

Hundreds of Kushites and Shashu were marching around a tremendous stone building, chanting, their heads lowered in reverence. Even from this long distance I could hear the worshippers' litanies as they praised the name of Allat, Mut Goddess of the Sabaens, and her gift inside the temple, the holy black Kaaba Stone. We had reached the sacred city of Makka, in the fabled land of Araby.

We stopped near the northern side of the city, got out of the wagons and went inside a large building that bustled with activity. Kho-An-Sa went ahead with Neftiji and a few warriors, leaving the rest of us near the large entrance with the piles of trade items stacked against the walls and the men who guarded them.

There were many sorts of people milling about the area— Kushites, Shashu and even some Tamahu. Most ran to and fro with tablets of clay and pieces of papyrus in hand, no doubt keeping track of trade agreements and sale items. Finally a guide came and escorted us down a long corridor and into a small room. Inside Kho-An-Sa was seated at a table with a Shashu man with wily eyes and a crafty demeanor.

"Ah," said Kho-An-Sa. "This is the one I spoke of...."

"Where is my sister, Kho-An-Sa?" I demanded.

"She is safe, young panther," he answered. "Look, Khalibar, see my latest warrior, the son of the great Memnon of Troy."

The Shashu looked at me. Nodding his head, his narrow eyes appraised me from head to toe. "The son of Memnon," he said. "He is worth much on the open market..."

Kho-An-Sa looked at Khalibar suspiciously. "Do not think of it, Khalibar," he said. "He is to be my warrior. Soon he will fight for me."

Khalibar's eyes shifted nervously. "No, my dear friend," he replied. "I would never betray you. It is simply my mercantile instinct...."

"I want to see my sister, Kho-An-Sa," I interrupted.

"Young panther," Kho-An-Sa answered, "you will see your sister when I say. For now, I must attend to business in the Sabaen lands south of here. You will stay here under the watch of Khalibar, and your guard, Cronn."

"But where is my sister?"

A vicious expression appeared on the face of the evil magician. "You will see your sister later, son of Memnon! Alive if you obey Khalibar, dead, if you disobey him or attempt any foolishness. Is that clear?"

I lowered my eyes.

"Is that clear, young panther?"

"Yes," I answered.

"Good," he said. "When I return, we journey to the city of Petra. There your training shall begin."

They locked me in a room inside Khalibar's storehouse and stationed Cronn as my guard once again. One small window allowed me to see the wastelands to the north, where I watched the sands blow for hour after hour. Many lonely days went by as I wondered about the fate of my sister and contemplated ways to escape. Despair was my daily companion, and as I sat on the floor of my cell, worrying about Neftiji, the days on Kam-Atef's Island of the Ka seemed a distant dream. One day I saw the great serpent's face in my mind, imagined his voice and longed to hear him, and then suddenly his voice came into my head.

"Yes, little one, I am here."

I jumped to my feet. "Kam-Atef! Is it really you?"

"Yes, little one. Are you troubled?"

"Oh Kam-Atef, things have gone terribly wrong...."

"Tell me, little one."

SHADES OF MEMNON

I told Kam-Atef of our second capture by Kho-An-Sa and about our present situation. I asked him if Neftiji had contacted him.

"No, I have not heard from Neftiji," he said. "And there is no one nearby who I can send to assist you, little one. I am sorry."

I sank back down to the floor, holding my head in my hands. "I cannot send you direct assistance," Kam-Atef said, "but listen Memna-un...trust no one you meet in that land of the Shashu, and if you can escape, flee to the court of the Queen of Saba. She is a just ruler and even the power of Kho-An-Sa cannot stand against her. Flee south to the Queen of Saba if you can, little one."

As the voice of Kam-Atef faded, I found renewed hope, a rise in my spirit to keep fighting. Peering from the window again, I watched the rays of Aten grow dimmer, and felt assured that our chance to escape would come.

When Aten's rays disappeared beneath the horizon, I heard a loud thump near the door. Turning around, I expected to see Cronn handing me my evening meal. But the Shashu merchant, Khalibar stepped through the door instead. "Come, young one. I will take you to your sister."

At first I hurried to the door, but then remembered Kam-Atef's words and hesitated. "Where is Cronn?" I asked suspiciously.

Khalibar smiled and pointed to the floor near the door.   "Ha, ha!" the Shashu laughed. "The filthy barbarian lies here, the victim of drugged wine."

I walked toward the door and peered out onto the floor. There the huge Tamahu lay face down in a pool of spilled wine. A tumbled flask lay nearby.

"He will bother you no more," said Khalibar. "Death will take him within moments. Come! Why do you hesitate?"

I followed Khalibar through the doorway. We stepped over the still body of Cronn and hurried down the corridor.

"Careful, young man," Khalibar said. "There are men in Kho-An-Sa's employ still about."

We came to a large room filled with clothing of many forms and fashions. "Choose a robe for concealment," said Khalibar.

I picked a long brown robe with a hood, pulling it tightly about me. With the hood pulled over my head, no one could distinguish me from the many pilgrimagers to the great stone of Makka.

Khalibar thrust another robe into my hands. "For your sister," he said.

Seizing the robe from him, I stuffed it inside my own. We walked rapidly out into the moonlight, heading towards the north end of the city. I watched Kahlibar's manner as he greeted those he knew along the way. Even if Kam-Atef had not warned me, I would have had deep suspicions about him. He was Sebek-Tem, crafty and dangerous.

"Why do you do this for us?" I asked. "I thought you were a friend of Kho-An-Sa?"

"Young one," he replied, "profit is my only friend. And rest assured, this will require payment..."

I stopped immediately and demanded, "What form of payment?"

Khalibar stopped ahead and turned around.

"Kho-An-Sa told me that a book he found in your possession indicates you have been to the Island of the Ka. The land of golden shores! Ruby hills and streams lined with diamonds!"

I nodded. "Yes, we have been there..."

"Then you must lead me there. I must have the riches of this island! "

"But Khalibar..." I began.

Raising his arms, he clenched his fists greedily and hissed, "The island, young one! The island for your freedom and for the life of your sister! You will lead me there. You will do it! Or I will leave you in the clutches of Kho-An-Sa!"

I said nothing as we resumed walking. Presently we came to a huge stone building with torches burning at each corner. The guards outside the front doors knew Khalibar and let us through. Inside were trade items from the ships, no doubt stored to be taken overland to market. As we approached a small room toward the rear, I saw two more Tamahu warriors lying on the floor. Both were soaked with wine and neither was breathing. A Shashu man wearing desert clothing stood over them. He saluted Khalibar with a bow, said something in the Shashu language, then turned toward the door the men had been guarding.

I strode forward and thrust it open and there stood Neftiji, holding a vase over her head and about to strike me. I pulled down the hood, then the vase tumbled from her hands and she rushed into my arms.

"Memna-un, Memna-un," she sobbed.

"Are you well, sister?" I asked, handing her the extra robe. "Did they harm you?"

"I am well," she replied, looking at Khalibar. "Who is this with you?"

"This is Khalibar," I replied. "He will lead us away from here."

"Hurry!" said Khalibar, while he and his friend looked around nervously. "We must go. Now!"

As Khalibar and his man walked ahead toward the door, I reached down and stealthily snatched a sword from one of the dead guards, quickly concealing it in the folds of my robe. We then caught up with the Shashu at the entrance. But when we walked out we found the guards barring our way with their spears lowered.

Khalibar spoke to them in a different language, similar to Kamitian, but I could not make it out. He turned to me and translated. "They were told that the girl was the property of Kho-An-Sa. They want to know why we are taking her."

SHADES OF MEMNON

SHADES OF MEMNON

I prepared myself to fight, reaching inside the robe to pull out the concealed sword. But before I could draw it forth, Khalibar spoke to them again and they smiled. Reaching into his pocket, he produced two small bags and tossed one to each guard. Then they stepped out of our way, falling back into place near the door. One guard stared at his feet, while the other averted his eyes towards the moon.

"We must go to the northern edge of Makka," said Khalibar, as we walked rapidly away. "We will find a caravan waiting there to take us to a northern port. From there we will gather a ship and supplies for the voyage to the Island of the Ka."

Neftiji looked at me incredulously and I gestured for her to keep silent. She and I both knew that the sacred island could not be reached by normal means, but we had to deal with the more immediate concerns first. I had spent many days watching the sands blow towards the northern wastelands and I knew they were barren and dangerous. I had no wish to journey into them.

"Why can we not acquire a vessel at the port nearby?" I asked. "Let us save the trip through the northern deserts."

Khalibar shook his head. "By now they must know of all the dead warriors," he answered, "as well as the missing gold I stole to finance this venture. I can never again go back to Makka or to the nearby docks. But about these things I no longer care, for the riches of the enchanted island are soon to be mine."

Once again Neftiji looked at me in disbelief, but said nothing. We reached the edge of Makka, and, as Khalibar had said, there was a small caravan waiting to transport us. Two wagons pulled by asses were filled with supplies and several men. A third wagon was empty, except for a few sleeping mats, a small amount of provisions and a driver. Several men astride camels and armed with spears rode ahead and behind them.

The moon was high and bright as we boarded the empty wagon and headed north. Khalibar sat across from Neftiji and I, and as we jostled along into the night, he began to doze. The torchlight from the front of the wagon was playing along the side of his sweaty face when I decided to whisper to Neftiji.

"My sister," I explained, "I would never promise the sacred island to anyone, least of all to a man like him."

Neftiji looked across at Khalibar, shaking her head in disapproval.

"Then why does he think we will take him there?', she asked.

"I had to go along with his madness to get him to free us..."

"I understand," she said, "but what must we do now?"

"We must escape from him also, and make our way to the Queen of Saba in the South. Kam-Atef says she is a just ruler..."

"Kam-Atef?" she replied. "You have been talking to Kam-Atef?"

As I opened my mouth to answer, a loud, horrified scream echoed through the night air. The caravan came to a halt and Khalibar bolted upright. A mounted warrior came racing up to the wagon, speaking the Shashu language and sounding terrified. Khalibar gave orders to the man and then translated for us.

"A huge beast has appeared. It snatched Ali off his camel and broke the animal's neck. Ali has been dragged off into the darkness...."

While he was talking, another scream pierced the night air. Khalibar shouted orders to his men and the wagons closed into a defensive triangle. We got out and made camp in the middle, while riders came in close and the men in the wagons got out their weapons. Sitting close around the camp's fire, we peered up into the moonlit sky.

"Some beast stalks us," said Khalibar. "Another man was just taken."

Neftiji huddled closer to me. "What is it?" she asked. "What kind of beast?"

"The men don't know," Khalibar answered. "It behaves like a lion, but they were all hunted down generations ago. Besides, I have never heard of a lion breaking a camel's neck with one blow. My men are very afraid."

Another man screamed horribly and a camel bleated. Both cries ended abruptly.

"The fool!" Khalibar said as he stood up from the fire. "I told them all to close ranks near the wagons."

A mounted warrior rode up to us, shouting desperately. Khalibar shouted orders back and his riders gathered closer to the caravan. Suddenly the crafty Shashu was holding a spear and handing me one also. "This beast is tearing my men apart!" he shouted. "Prepare to fight, son of Memnon!"

In each wagon five men stood holding spears and peering into the darkness. Suddenly, a cloud covered the moon and a huge dark beast charged a wagon, toppling it sideways and sending men flying in all directions. The warriors in the other wagons screamed curses as their spears sliced through the night air. Just then, a tremendous roar of bestial rage rolled across the sand, causing the camels to rear up uncontrollably and throw their riders. One unlucky man who landed out in the darkness screamed suddenly, his voice accompanied by the sound of breaking bones.

Standing back to back in the middle of the three wagons, we waited for the creature's next charge. Gradually the clouds moved away from the moon, flooding the desert with dim, but welcome light. Long minutes went by, and there was only silence from the wasteland. Khalibar shouted and his men answered back from all sides.

"It seems that the beast is gone," he said with relief.

We sat down near the fire again as Khalibar's men put right the wagon and took a count of heads. They shouted the number back to him and he shook his head bitterly.

SHADES OF MEMNON

"Five dead," he said. "And we still don't know what sort of beast it was. Praise to Allat that it is gone."

The camp was tense for the rest of the night with all of us peeking into the darkness, afraid and still wondering about the strange beast. No one slept as we all waited for the light of day, and when the rays of Aten broke over the desert horizon, the men gladly prepared to leave.

I cradled Neftiji in my arms as she dozed, while I watched the activities of the breaking camp. In the distance I saw two men piling sand over the dead bodies. As I watched, a large figure approached them from out of the desert. The two men leapt at the figure, who pulled a huge sword and killed them immediately. They fell atop the bodies they had been burying.

As two camel riders rushed towards the killer with their spears raised, I realized who it was and gave Neftiji a nudge. "It is Cronn," I whispered. "Be prepared to flee."

Khalibar now stood watching as his warriors fought the giant Tamahu. "It is that big barbarian," Khalibar said in astonishment. "I gave him enough poison to kill five men! Why is he still alive?"

We watched in amazement as Cronn battled his way toward the caravan, swinging his huge blade as he dodged the thrusts from the camel rider's spears. One flashing sweep cut down a rider, sending him sprawling to the sand, clutching his gushing wound. More men ran out to oppose him, but the huge warrior was unstoppable, ripping through them all with his flashing sword.

As Khalibar's men fell like stalks of wheat, fear flashed into his eyes. "That man is possessed by evil things," he said. "Come, young ones, we must go."

We jumped into a wagon and left the caravan with only two of Khalibar's men accompanying us, the driver and the man who had helped get Neftiji from the storage house. The rest he abandoned to fight the huge northerner.

I looked upon Khalibar with utter contempt for leaving his warriors to die while he escaped. He noticed this and shrugged his shoulders, smiling maliciously. "They do not matter, young one," he huffed. "The only thing that matters is the treasure of the Island of the Ka. I will be richer than all the Queens of Saba!"

I waved my hand in disgust. I was tired of this man's pettiness and greed. "Khalibar, there is no treasure," I said, finally.

"What!" he shouted. "What are you saying?"

"No one can get to the Island of the Ka for treasure," I answered.

"You lie!" Khalibar screamed. "You lie! You want to go back for it yourselves! Driver! Stop!"

The wagon halted and Khalibar stood, drawing a long curved sword.

His face was twisted with anger. "If this is true then why did you not tell me before?"

I stood up between Neftiji and the mad merchant, sliding my hand into my robe. "You were our only way to escape...and I never promised you! I never promised you anything!"

Khalibar raised his blade. "Then I will take profit out of your hide! A queen's ransom can be had for the son of Memnon of Troy! "

I pulled my sword out just in time to block his downward stroke. Khalibar's man leapt down to assist him, but I booted him away before his feet could hit the ground. When his lackey tumbled to the sand, Khalibar howled with rage. "Take my treasure?" he screamed. "Take my treasure, will you!? Die, young fool! Die!"

He sliced wildly at me and I managed to block each stroke, but the momentum tumbled me from the wagon. When I rose he had his sword raised over Neftiji, who held her hands before her, helplessly looking up at her doom.

Leaping up quickly, I stabbed Khalibar's leg. His painful scream filled the desert air. "Aaaaaiiie!!!!"

He fell from the wagon, his sword dropping from his hand. I leapt forward to finish him, but his man was suddenly there, thrusting at me with a spear. As he jabbed at me, he turned his back toward the wagon, giving Neftiji the chance to seize his face and scratch his eyes. As he cursed at her, I pushed the spear aside and thrust my blade through his chest. He crumpled to the ground before us.

When I turned back to Khalibar, he had gotten back to his feet and had retrieved his weapon. At first he stood his ground with his sword raised, spitting upon us horrible curses and jeers. Then a fearful look came over him and he turned to flee, dropping his sword in his blind panic. Stumbling pitifully due to the wound I had inflicted, Khalibar looked back with an expression of total terror.

Realizing he was not looking at me, I turned around to see his wagon driver falling to the sand, clutching a heavily bleeding wound. Standing over the dying man was Cronn, holding his huge blood soaked sword.

The giant walked past me and I stepped aside, watching carefully as he stalked toward Khalibar. The merchant was now crawling along pitifully, muttering in fear. Reaching desperately into his robe, he withdrew pouch after pouch of golden shekels, tossing them before the approaching giant.

"No!" Khalibar screamed in terror. "No!! Here take it! Take it all! Just spare me. Spare meeee!"

Cronn ignored the pleas and the pouches, treading them into the sand as he approached his trembling victim. Finally he stood over Khalibar and roared terribly, sounding strangely like the beast that had attacked the caravan.

SHADES OF MEMNON

Khalibar held his hands before him, quaking in helpless fear. "The beast!" he screamed. "The beast! Aaaaahhh!"

Cronn's sword came down in a gleaming arc, cutting Khalibar precisely in half and spattering blood in all directions. The giant roared again, kicking Khalibar's remains viciously while flicking the blood from his blade across the dead man's face. Then he turned back to me.

SHADES OF MEMNON

CHAPTER 5: "SEE NOW, SERVANTS OF THE SERPENTS"

As the giant Tamahu approached, I raised my sword in defiance. I knew I could not stand long against him, but I planned to hold him off just long enough for Neftiji to escape. Casting a quick glance over my shoulder, I saw her leaning over the side of the wagon, gravely concerned about the battle. My only hope in the fight was the knowledge that Kho-An-Sa wanted me alive.

Cronn approached me warily, tossing his sword from his right to his left hand. He made several small leaps and feints in an effort to unnerve me, but I held my ground, circling around him like a panther. He swung his sword again and I jumped back. Then he swung again, incredibly fast for a man of his immense bulk, and I sidestepped. Then suddenly he rushed me.

Blow after blow rained down upon my sword and I had no choice but to block them. Cronn knew that my arms, as small as a child's compared to his, would tire and then he would have me. As the tremendous blows came down, I heard Neftiji call my name, but I could not let her sway my attention.

Sweat poured from my body beneath the hot robe and I began to falter. The giant, however, never seemed to tire as he jabbed and sliced his blade towards my head. As I heard my sister calling again, I hit upon a desperate plan to trick my opponent.

Standing still with my sword upraised, I let him rain blow after blow as I blocked them. I knew he could see the perspiration flowing down my face and I pretended to wheeze and gasp. When he hesitated slightly, I fell to the burning sand as if stricken by the heat. Watching with my eyes half closed, I saw Cronn lower his weapon and nudge me with his foot. After nudging me again, he shoved the huge blade into the sand and bent to pick me up.

Quickly I seized my sword again and reared back to plunge it into him. But he was a seasoned warrior and twisted his body the second he saw me move, causing my sword to stab into his side, instead of his heart, as I intended.

He howled in pain as I jumped to my feet, wrenching the blade from his body as I rose. Though he kneeled before me, his large head was at my chest and I aimed my blade for it, determined to put an end to the bestial giant forever. Then a familiar voice cried out.

"Stop!"

I looked over my shoulder at the wagon to find it surrounded by Tamahu warriors. In the midst of them stood Kho-An-Sa, holding my struggling sister.

"Great Sekmet, young panther!" Kho-An-Sa shouted across the sand. "You are indeed your pa's son! But the time for this battle is over. Put down that blade if you value your sister's life!"

SHADES OF MEMNON

I looked down at Cronn, then stepped back and let the sword drop to the ground. Though he bled heavily from the wound I had inflicted, he immediately seized his sword and sprang to his feet. He raised his weapon over me while Kho-An-Sa shouted at him in the language of the northerners. He then looked towards Kho-An-Sa, then back toward me, letting loose an angry roar of bitter frustration. Then, very slowly, as if it pained him to do it, he lowered his blood-encrusted sword.

"Now," Kho-An-Sa said smugly. "Let us leave this place and journey on to Petra."

Kho-An-Sa had with him a six-wagon caravan. They put me in with the injured Cronn, a healer who was working on his wound and several other warriors. Neftiji was forced to ride with the magician. Then we turned towards the north, following the trail that Khalibar had been traveling. The trip lasted many days and since Neftiji and I were not allowed near each other, I took the opportunity to observe the strange habits of the Tamahu warriors more closely.

They were careful to cover themselves with white cloth and seemed especially concerned with avoiding the rays of Aten, which, unchecked, caused painful red inflammations upon them. As I watched them quarrel over the cloth at the hottest times of the day, I realized that they were just as curious about my skin. At first some of them touched me, then looked at their hands as if expecting something to rub off. Obviously most of them had never seen a Kushite, just as many Kushites had never seen a Tamahu of the light haired sort that these men were. As for me, I hoped that Aten would burn them all to ashes or chase them back to their cold barbarian lands forever. It was indeed a puzzle to me how a Kushite, even an evil one like Kho-An-Sa, could have become connected with these strange men.

Finally, after many days of riding, the great red mountains around Petra loomed before us. Soon we negotiated a narrow winding highway flanked by otherwise impassable cliffs. Great falcons circled above as we made our way up a long undulating road.

About midway through the trail, a stone structure appeared. Built from wall to cliff wall and strongly garrisoned, the gate effectively barred our path. As we approached, its large wooden doors opened and a group of Shashu emerged, brandishing swords and spears. Confronting us aggressively, they seemed to demand information. Kho-An-Sa spoke to them briefly and they opened the gate to let us pass.

Soon we came to a second gate and went through a similar routine before we continued. Then we approached a tall main gate, more strongly fortified than the others. Once again a few words from the magician was all that was needed to allowed us to pass through.

Passing the final check point, we entered the city, where I was immediately struck by its beauty and wonderful sense of order. The streets were lined with colorful, well-constructed dwellings of clay, mud and wood, laid out in carefully planned squares and triangular patterns. But what really set the city apart from others I'd seen, were the huge temples and tombs carved directly into the red stone of the surrounding cliffs.

Great columns of intricate detail lined the entrances and the walls were covered with delicate carvings and vibrant paintings. Never had I seen workings in stone to match these except for the greatest temples of Kamit. The people who had carved them must surely have been favored by Tehuti.

The caravan stopped before a temple, where Kho-An-Sa's men began unloading items. The magician himself went inside, followed by several warriors and Neftiji. I was hustled in behind them, still amazed at the effort it must have taken to carve all this from the living stone. After walking down many long and winding corridors lit by torches, we finally stopped before a huge doorway. Kho-An-Sa hesitated, straightened his back and puffed out his chest, then we entered.

The room we stepped into was huge, dominated by several large thrones situated upon a high dais. Several dozen men and a few women stood before the thrones, milling about two large candlelit tables covered with maps and writing instruments. When we entered, a tall Tamahu with yellow hair and a long white robe stepped forward. After greeting Kho-An-Sa in the language of the northerners, he shot a glance at Neftiji and I.

Kho-An-Sa pointed to me, smiling as he talked, but the yellow haired man seemed to be angry. A chill ran up my spine when he looked at me again with a bitter scowl, pulling his finger across his throat in a cutting gesture.

Others approached them and offered greetings before joining in the argument between Kho-An-Sa and the Tamahu. After several minutes, Kho-An-Sa raised his hand for silence and spoke again, briefly. They all seemed to accept this and turned back to their tables, all except the yellow haired Tamahu in white. Giving my sister and I an evil sidelong glance, he sulked angrily from the room.

I looked at Neftiji to see if she had noticed this. But she seemed to stare blankly ahead. I was beginning to sense that something was wrong with her when a loud gong sounded and everyone directed their attention toward the thrones.

Several men and two women walked up to the dais and seated themselves. Kho-An-Sa was one of them. The gong sounded again and the rest made two single file lines facing each other, creating an aisle leading to the thrones. Neftiji and I were shoved down it and pushed roughly to the floor. I seized my sister's hand to comfort her and found it limp. Then I looked into her eyes and to my horror, found them quite expressionless.

SHADES OF MEMNON

"Neftiji," I cried desperately. "My sister, what has he done to you?" I pleaded while seizing her and holding her close, but she was lifeless and did not return my embrace.

I looked upon the dais to find Kho-An-Sa sitting upon his throne, smiling knowingly. Squinting up at the magician, I raised my fist in anger.

"What have you done to her?" I screamed." What have you done to my sister?"

Kho-An-Sa looked at the others sitting near him. All nodded and smiled, except the yellow-haired one, who sat upon the far right throne with a hateful and disappointed expression.

"It became clear to me, young panther," said Kho-An-Sa, "that you would continue to try foolish escapes unless drastic action was taken."

"What drastic action? I screamed. "What did you do to her?"

"Your sister is now bound to me," he replied. "I have left her with a small sliver of life, which only my knowledge can maintain."

A rage, so terrible I never wished to feel it again, came over me. "You...monster!" I cried. "Some day..." I tried to continue but was snatched closer to the throne by two warriors.

Kho-An-Sa leaned forward. "Your threats are meaningless to me. I have your sister and all those seated here are to witness your pledge to serve me."

The room was totally silent. All eyes were upon me as I stood there trembling with rage.

"There are some among the Servants of the Serpents who have a blood grudge against the seed of the Great Memnon of Troy," said Kho-An-Sa, gesturing toward the yellow-haired Tamahu. "They would have sought you out eventually and taken your life. I give you a chance to live. Serve me and live. Refuse and I give you to them. You...and your sister."

I looked into Neftiji's face again, only to find her blank stare too much for me to bear. I then scanned the faces upon the thrones, locking eyes with the yellow haired Tamahu. He stared back, scowling with such intense hatred that it was almost palpable. Though I knew nothing about him then, I sensed that this man would forever be my mortal enemy, and that one day we would fight to the death over it.

Kho-An-Sa's voice broke our link of hatred. "What say you, Memna-un, son of the Great Memnon of Troy?"

I pulled my sister close to me. I knew not if she understood me, but I whispered into her ear regardless.

"Forgive me, my sister. One day I will find a way to free you. Forgive me for what I must do."

"Your answer, young panther," Kho-An-Sa said. "I will not ask it again."

All of those seated on the thrones leaned forward in keen anticipation. A hush fell over the entire room. Looking up into the evil eyes of Kho-An-Sa, I got down on one knee.

"Yes," I said. "I will serve you."

The yellow-haired Tamahu stamped his feet, then rose and stormed from the room, while the rest of those present exploded in cheers. I realized what my pledge meant to them, as they began chanting my name in the northern style they had used years ago for my pa.

MEM-NON! MEMNON! MEM-NON! MEMNON!

They rejoiced because the son of the most famous fighter for justice had just pledged his arm to the forces of evil. I looked down at my feet and thought of my parents. I could only beg their forgiveness until I could find a way to free my sister. The chanting grew louder as I prayed.

"MEM-NON! MEM-NON! MEMNON! MEM-NON!"

"May Amen the great...."

"MEM-NON! MEM-NON! MEM-NON! MEM-NON!"

"...have mercy...."

"MEM-NON! MEM-NON! MEM-NON! MEM-NON!"

"...upon my ka."

Days later I sat in a large chair in the room assigned to me by Kho-An-Sa, brooding over the fate of my sister. My mind was jumbled and confused, and I could not still my heart due to the turmoil. That and the shame I felt for pledging my loyalty to that evil magician would not let me contact Kam-Atef.

I glanced at the door to my room, expecting Kho-An-Sa's messenger to arrive at any second. This was the day I had been told I would begin my "training," and what that meant I did not know. Kho-An-Sa said it would involve "strengthening my bones," but my only concern was that it strengthened me enough to one day plunge a blade through his evil heart.

At last the man appeared. Bowing low, he beckoned for me to follow. As we left my chambers, I observed him closely. By the look of his long, straight black hair, dark brown skin and sharp features, he was an Eastern Kushite. A brand upon his shoulder marked him as a slave. Then it dawned upon me that I had only seen Kushites in servile positions in Petra. As we walked down the long corridors, I tapped him on his shoulder.

"What is your name?" I asked.

He stopped and turned towards me.

SHADES OF MEMNON

"Can you understand me?" I asked. "Can you speak Kamitic?"

The man looked around suspiciously.

"Yes," he replied in a low voice.

"Why do you whisper?" I asked.

Two Shashu warriors turned down the corridor and walked towards us. My guide immediately lowered his eyes and turned away from me to bow to them. They seemed to barely notice him as they walked by, but looked at me with great curiosity. After they turned down another corridor we were once again alone. I drew close to him and lowered my voice also.

"Do not be afraid," I said. "Please, tell me, what goes on in Petra?"

"My people are the Nabata," he replied. "We came here from the land of Nimrod and built Petra long ago. For centuries we prospered as a trade center and peaceful meeting place for all nations. Then they came, and through deception and cruelty, conquered us. Now we are slaves in our own land."

I noticed the pain in the man's voice. His loss was great and terrible.

"Who?" I asked. "Who came?"

"All of them. The Shashu we already knew, for we had traded with them for ages. We knew little of the Tamahu, who along with the Shashu, laid siege to our defenses as if we had had none at all. But we held our ground successfully until others came. These others we could not stop. They came from the sky. Strange Kushites came from the sky! Then their monsters attacked. . .and all was lost."

"What is your name?" I asked. "How is it you know the Kamitian language?"

"I am Hazz. I was once a trader. I have traveled to Kamit many times."

I listened intently as he told me more about Petra. His great land had been subjected to inhuman suffering under the domination of this strange coalition. He looked at me inquisitively and shook his head.

"Even here we have heard about your pa's exploits against these people. Why do you serve them? How can you betray your very blood?"

I turned from him in shame, gazing down the corridor to keep from looking him in the eye.

"I do not do it willingly, my friend," I answered. "Of that I can assure you. Now, take me to Kho-An-Sa."

We walked down several corridors until we came to stairs that were cut into the wall of the temple. Here Hazz stopped, pointing up the long torch-lit tunnel.

"I am allowed to go no further, Memnon," he said. "I hope we can talk again soon."

"Surely," I replied. "And I thank you, Hazz."

I mounted the stairs and found them dark, narrow and endlessly winding. They seemed to go on and on, and I once again marveled at the craftsmanship needed to cut such a pathway through solid rock. For long minutes I climbed from stair to stair, sometimes winding to the right, sometimes to the left. I felt I must be ascending to the very top of the mountain, and when I at last emerged I was struck by the intense rays of Aten.

As my eyes adjusted to the light, I saw that I was indeed at the summit, standing in an open air temple at the very top of the mountain. Several large wooden shrines were situated atop tables of solid white rock, which gleamed brightly from the intense light falling from the sky. Directly before me a long outcropping thrust out from the face of the mountain, jutting towards the southern wastelands in the distance. Upon the outcropping sat an altar carved from the white stone, polished to a dazzling sheen. Next to the altar stood Kho-An-Sa and another man, a Kushite I had seen upon one of the thrones.

"At last, young panther," Kho-An-Sa said, gesturing at the man next to him. "This is Sung Li, your trainer and instructor."

I looked closely at this man called Sung Li. Never had I heard a name like his, nor had I ever seen a Kushite quite like him. He was very short, with straight hair and dark shiny skin like an eastern Kushite. But his eyes were greatly slanted in a way I had never seen. He wore a dazzling blue robe of gleaming material I had noticed only on the very rich, or on members of the Shekem's court. As Sung Li bowed gracefully, Kho-An-Sa noticed my curiosity.

"Sung Li is of the Shang peoples. They rule a large kingdom far to the east, on the other side of the world. You must obey him as you would me."

I approached Sung Li, bowing humbly in return. Then he motioned for me to sit down upon the altar. To my surprise, the white rock felt cool under the direct rays of Aten, and I wondered what sort of stone it was carved from.

"I learn Kamitic words just to teach you," Sung Li said with a strange accent. "You must listen. Listen and I make you strong. Understand?"

I nodded and Kho-An-Sa looked on approvingly.

"First thing, take off clothes. Lie down and I be back," Sung Li said.

I took off my robe, waist wrap and sandals and lay down upon the altar.

Kho-An-Sa approached and stood over me. "Long ago, young panther, men had the fire of Aten, the force of Ra in their marrow," said Kho-An-Sa. "The bones of men then were unbreakable, but we lost that and much more many ages ago."

Sung Li appeared with a pot and put it down next to me on the alter. He then reached inside, withdrawing a handful of a strange smelling oil. He rubbed it on my skin and I flinched, for wherever the substance touched me, the rays of Aten intensified and burned. I tried to get up, but they both held me down by my shoulders.

"Be still," Sung Li said. "This make you strong. Strong like long ago."

SHADES OF MEMNON

"Do you know why a stone is hard, young panther?" Kho-An-Sa asked. "It is because the force of Ra is tight within that stone and hardly leaks out. This is what will happen to your bones. No one will ever be able to break them."

Sung Li continued rubbing the oil all over me. Soon I became accustomed to the heat and now felt my bones tingling inside my body.

"The chi will be solid in your limbs, young man," said Sung Li. "You will be great warrior."

"Chi?" I asked. "What is this 'chi'?"

"Chi! Rau! It is Life!" Kho-An-Sa said. "Whatever the name, it is the force of life, the serpent fire that dwells within us all."

I had never felt such intense heat, but it was not like normal fire. It was as if my body was absorbing the very rays of Aten and storing it inside. The altar became cooler as my own heat intensified. I started to become sleepy.

"What...have you...done to me?" I asked weakly.

The voice of Kho-An-Sa seemed to come from far away. "I give you strength, young panther," Kho-An-Sa answered. "Strength beyond your dreams."

My eyes closed and weariness overcame me. As I drifted into slumber, Sung Li poked at my limbs and rubbed more of the oil into my skin.

I know not how long I slept, but when I awoke I found my body totally paralyzed. Only my eyes were still under my control, which revealed the hundreds of small silver needles poking into my skin. Sung Li stood over me, poking me with more of the strange silver rods and methodically tapping them into my flesh with a tiny hammer.

"Ah, young man," said Sung Li. "I see you wake."

He pressed his face down close to mine, smiling.

"You, no worry. You be strong. You, be best I ever work on. You see," he said and continued tapping in his needles. Suddenly, I felt a rush of energy course though my body. My limbs jerked uncontrollably as it raced though me. After a while, I recognized that the force seemed to be following specific pathways throughout my body, especially up my back.

Sung Li seemed greatly pleased with what was happening to me. "Yes!" he cried gleefully, clapping his hands. "The dragon moves within you! The serpent fire awakes! Young man, move your fingers!"

I concentrated on my hands. But my muscles would not
respond. Then I felt a special heat whisking through my body, racing down my arms. I was then able to wiggle my fingers and twist my hand around slightly.

"Oh, you doing good," Sung Li said excitedly. "Now move toes."

I then focused on my toes. Once again, the muscles would not respond at first, but then the energy raced down my legs to my feet and I wiggled my toes vigorously. Sung Li clapped his hands gleefully again. "You the best I ever work on! You control the chi so quickly! Move leg now."

I moved my leg in the same manner, then Sung Li made me move other parts of my body with the force of this Rau-chi. I was amazed at how it animated my limbs without using any particular muscle. The implications of this control dawned upon me when Sung-Li extracted the needles from my arm. When I once again felt my muscles, he instructed me to reach toward him. When I did, my arm shot out with such force that I almost fell from the altar. He then removed the needles from my face but I could not speak. My jaws jerked and my tongue clicked vigorously in my mouth when I tried.

Sung Li laughed like a child, placing his hand upon my head. "Focus chi, young man," he said. "You now aware and it will stay with you. Now you learn to control it."

I lay upon the altar for many days beneath the needles as Sung Li taught me to control the force and direct it. Soon I was able to hold the force down and move normally. But even at rest I felt it bursting and rushing throughout my body. I asked Sung Li about the nature of this energy.

"This force you call Rau and I call chi is in all creation," he replied. "All men born with it. More come from food and sun. Kushite men get more from rays of Aten, absorb more Rau than others, but lose it because few can direct it."

"Why then can I feel it?" I asked.

"You been upon altar for full moon, young man. Your muscles shut down by needles and your chi increased by herbs. I open your awareness of these channels, the rest come from you."

I remained in the open air temple for five more moons, alternating between long periods of sleep under the needles and herbs and study with Sung Li when I would be awakened.

My Shang instructor introduced me to many strange practices, including the consumption of only vegetables, which he said I would have to continue for the rest of my days. He also kept me under the baking rays of Aten, but because of his ministrations, I rarely needed water. Other things happened as I learned to manipulate the Rau force through my body.

My sense of touch extended beyond my flesh, allowing me to feel the presence and shape of objects before seeing them. And when I opened my mouth for food, I could taste it without placing it on my tongue. Even my eyesight and sense of smell were greatly enhanced when I channeled this powerful Rau force into these senses.

After accidentally breaking plates during meals and crushing drinking vessels, I found I had to relearn every movement of my body to compensate for this rise of power inside me. Sung Li taught me techniques to rest my head and still my heart, similar to those Kam-Atef had shown me. But these

SHADES OF MEMNON

exercises were for the manipulation and redirecting of the Rau force, not simply to calm the spirit.

Kho-An-Sa came to visit us many times, and seemed greatly pleased with my progress. On these occasions he would appraise me like a prize bull, always assuring me that my sister would be safe as long as I did as I was told. I never liked the sinister tone he used nor the strange looks he gave me on these visits.

"Soon," Kho-An-Sa would say, "soon you will be ready young panther."

One day Sung Li used an unpleasant demonstration to show me what he had done to my bones. I was sitting upon the white altar, naked and bathed in the rays of Aten at midday. My feet were touching the ground and my knees were pointed toward Sung Li.

"Tell me, young man," he asked, "how do your limbs feel?"

I focused on my arms and legs. "They feel...heavy," I said. "Somehow thicker, but I have not grown."

"Oh, you have grown, young man," Sung Li replied knowingly. "You have grown on the inside, in your bones."

Suddenly he produced a knife from the folds of his robe, and before I could move, he plunged it into my right knee. I howled in pain and seized him by the throat, but he flicked my hands away effortlessly and withdrew the blade.

I pushed him away, and leapt from the altar, limping towards the entrance to escape this man who I thought had gone totally mad. But before I could reach the doorway, Sung Li dashed before me with incredible speed, barring my way to the exit.

He then brought the knife up for me to see and I gasped in astonishment. The bronze blade was bent and cracked. Dripping with my blood, it was destroyed as if it had been dashed against a stone. Looking down at my knee, I found it cut to the bone, but instead of ivory white, the bone gleamed ebony black. Sung Li addressed me with a satisfied smile.

"Rau is in your bones and nothing will break them," he said. "Like the days of the last age, when men were nourished only by Aten, your bones have been burned by chi."

I awoke on the morning of my last day in the temple to find Sung Li and Kho-An-Sa standing over the altar. They held a bull's hide between them, looking at me expectantly.

"It is time for the last phase of your training, young man," said Sung Li.

"You have been given strength that few besides the Shekems of Kamit know in this age, young panther," said Kho-An-Sa. "It is time for the Ceremony of Rebirth."

I stood up as they laid the bull skin onto the white altar. They then directed me to lie on it as they performed a special ceremony. Kho-An-Sa made signs in the air and chanted, while Sung Li wrapped the skin around me and stitched it closed. As Kho-An-Sa's strange words echoed out into the desert air, I was overcome by an urge to close my eyes and sleep. As I drifted into slumber, I felt water being poured upon the skin and smelled the fragrance of myrrh, the incense of Seker, governess of power and death. I then fell into a deep and dreamless sleep.

I was drawn back to consciousness by the sound of drums and the incense of Auset, the Neter of birth. When I opened my eyes, I found myself still inside the skin, but felt tugging and pulling from the outside. Suddenly the stitches tore loose and light from several torches flooded in. Voices were all around me as I stood up confused. When my eyes finally adjusted to the light, I found myself in the great hall, before the thrones once again.

The room was filled with the people of the coalition that had conquered Petra. On one side stood dozens of Tamahu, on the other side Shashu, and behind me stood a group of the mysterious Kushite Shangs. This time though, a group of red-skinned people were present, wearing long robes and feathered headdresses. Before me sat the leaders on their thrones, with Kho-An-Sa once again in the middle.

"See now, Servants of the Serpents, I have before you the son of your greatest enemy, empowered and ready to serve me," Kho-An-Sa shouted to the crowd. "There are some here who would do all they can to destroy the seed of Memnon of Troy, but I say to you, what better revenge than to make him work for our cause? What sweeter vengeance could there ever be?"

Interpreters translated for the various peoples of the crowd, and loud cries of approval rose from the Shashu and the Shang. The yellow-haired man and many of the Tamahu remained silent. Kho-An-Sa gazed at me intently as I stood there, naked and reborn in this place of evil.

"Young Memnon, are you ready to serve me?"

"Where is Neftiji?" I asked.

He clapped his hands and a warrior led my sister out into the open. She still had the same blank look upon her face, and I vowed silently that Kho-An-Sa would pay for her suffering.

"Yes," I said hesitantly. "I am ready to serve you."

Loud cheers erupted again throughout in the chamber, until Kho-An-Sa held up his hand for silence. "Those of you who doubt my wisdom will think differently as you watch our enemies fall before my power, under the sword of my warrior that stands before you. Cronn! Step forward!"

The giant Tamahu stepped out of the crowd.

"Give the young Memnon a weapon," Kho-An-Sa ordered.

SHADES OF MEMNON

Cronn walked over to the crowd of Tamahu and snatched a sword from one of them. He then walked over to me and put it in my hands, while Kho-An-Sa and the others leaned forward on their thrones.

"Now Cronn," Kho-An-Sa ordered. "Kill him...if you can." The crowd moved back as Cronn drew his huge sword with a savage howl. I stepped back and prepared to defend myself.

The giant rushed me immediately, charging forward with a scowl of rage. His sword came down with enough force to split me in two, but I side-stepped, and, quicker than I had ever moved before, flicked my sword past his defenses and slashed him on his side. The crowd gasped in surprise as the unbeatable Cronn turned towards me, blood gushing from the wound I had inflicted. He then raised his sword to beat it down upon me as he had done in our last fight, but this time, as blow after blow rained down upon my upraised sword, I hardly felt the shock.

For long minutes I held my hand aloft, blocking blow after blow with ease, as Cronn continued pounding away. My blade began to dent and bend from the blows while the sound of metal striking metal rang out. Finally, the giant tired and stepped back, a puzzled look upon his face. Kho-An-Sa leapt to his feet.

"You see!" he cried. "You see! Witness my work! Cronn, try again!"

This time Cronn took a different tactic. He came at me charging like a bull, swinging his sword at my midsection. I knew he expected to knock me down, so rather than trying to dodge him, I ran toward him instead. Our swords clashed, shooting sparks high in the air, as our bodies slammed together like two heavy stones. Locked together tightly, we snarled and pushed each other, trying to make the other give ground.

I stood my ground, but though the Rau in my bones made me resistant to his bulk, he was still far heavier. Slowly he pushed me back toward the raised platform underneath the thrones. As we came closer to the wall, he increased his efforts, no doubt thinking of smashing me against it, then striking me dead as I reeled.

Almost as if by instinct, I focused my Rau through my arms and up the blade, until I could feel Cronn's body pressing against it. As I focused the force against him, his eyes widened in surprise as he felt it. Tense moments passed. Perspiration poured from his face while grunts of hateful determination poured from his throat. Finally, I threw the Rau force forward in a might surge, causing him to push back in stubborn defiance. I then stepped lightly aside.

Launched forward by his own strength, Cronn crashed violently into the dais and fell upon his face. The entire chamber exploded with laughter, with even most of the Tamahu joining in his humiliation. Growling angrily, the giant leapt to his feet, but when he turned around the tip of my sword was at his throat. The chamber fell silent as the giant gazed down upon me, his eyes filled with fear and surprise. I looked to Kho-An-Sa for the signal.

"He lives," Kho-An-Sa proclaimed. "Let him go, Memnon."

I snatched the point away from his throat, slicing into his red beard as I drew it back. Cronn lowered his head and dropped his sword, then turned and walked slowly from the chamber. Once again cheers rocked the room, and Kho-An-Sa stood up proudly, shouting above the crowd and pointing at me.

"Yes!" he cried. "Yes! And he is mine! Mine!"

Once again the yellow-haired Tamahu left his throne and stormed from the chamber. A few Tamahu from the crowd went with him. Kho-An-Sa watched them leave with a smug grin, then continued to rant before his throne.

"Such a warrior needs a fitting weapon," the evil magician cried. "So within the week we leave for the north. There the great blacksmith shall forge my warrior a fitting blade. Let our enemies tremble! Tremble! Our own dark panther will stalk the plains of this world! And he is the son of their greatest protector!"

SHADES OF MEMNON

"Six Days The Silent Memnon Waits,
Behind His Temple's Folded Gates"

Oliver Wendell Holmes, "The Organ Blower" - 1872

CHAPTER 6: "UNDERSTAND THESE ISH RA ELITES"

As I strolled down the long dark corridors of the temple on the morning of our departure for the north, I wondered why Kho-An-Sa had summoned me to meet him alone before we mounted the caravan. Hazz was a few steps ahead, leading the way to a section of the temple I had never seen. As we rounded corner after corner, I noticed a slight decline in the floor and realized that we were going down, deep into the bowels of the this amazing structure. Finally, we approached a huge door. Hazz pointed to it and bowed.

"Enter, Memna-un," he said. "I shall await you here."

"Thank you, good Hazz," I said, returning his bow with one of my own.

"Please, my friend," Hazz whispered, nervously looking around. "Be careful not to show me respect before others. As a slave...I would be beaten for it."

I looked into his fearful expression and felt pained. Here was a noble man, afraid to receive common courtesy from another. I placed my hand upon his shoulder and drew him close.

"One day, Hazz," I whispered, "I shall return here. Together we will overthrow these evil ones who have taken Petra. This I swear to you, my friend—your people shall one day be free."

Hazz smiled and looked deeply into my eyes. "I believe you my friend," he whispered. "I truly believe we can."

I pushed open the door and found myself in a small torch-lit corridor. At the far end, thin curtains hung before an entrance to a well-lit chamber. Pushing through the curtains, I entered a large room containing several large tables covered with smoking containers and strange devices. Small covered vases along the wall shook slightly, as if they contained something alive. Upon one of the tables sat several transparent flasks containing swirling colors and odd images.

Standing over one of the tables was Kho-An-Sa, staring intently at the pages of a book. I took a step forward and recognized it as my own Book of the Taut.

"Young Memnon," he cried as he looked up from it. "Come! Enter! "

I approached the table upon which he studied my writings.

"Careful!" he cried. "Do not touch anything."

I walked around the table, immediately hearing strange sounds coming from the flasks and other containers. Peering curiously into a small jar, I spied tiny glowing eyes staring back at me and I jumped back, startled. "What is this?" I asked.

Kho-An-Sa thumped the book with his fingers.

"This is the work of magic, young one. My work and the wisdom contained in this Book of the Taut.

SHADES OF MEMNON

"You have no right to use that book!" I said angrily.

Kho-An-Sa slammed the book shut haughtily and walked around the table towards me. "I claim the right!" he said, pointing his finger close to my face. "I take the right! I am the master here! "

"But that book is sacred," I began.

"I am the master here," Kho-An-Sa repeated. "Do not question me, younger Memnon."

"Yes, Kho-An-Sa," I said, my sister's blank face appearing in my mind.

"Much better," Kho-An-Sa said. "I called you here to speak to you privately for three reasons. First—this is a brilliant book you have written. Your scribal skills are quite excellent. If I did not need you as my warrior, you would surely be my scribe. The wisdom of the legendary Kam-Atef is extraordinary. What was he like?"

"He was good to us," I replied. "He is very wise. He is sacred..."

Kho-An-Sa nodded. "He is very knowledgeable about the Reckoning. I have used this book to summon certain...spirits." Kho-An-Sa pointed to the vases along the wall and the transparent flasks upon the table.

"These we will take with us on our trip to the north. It will be quite dangerous. We will have to go through territory that is saturated with the forces of the Reckoning ."

"Why?" I asked.

"Only there can we find the great blacksmith. Only He can forge the blade needed for your tasks."

I pointed to the flasks and vases. "And you will use these...spirits for defense along the journey?"

"Yes," Kho-An-Sa replied. "I have summoned and bound them to these containers. I have only to release them when needed and assign them their tasks. But there is another reason I called you here."

He turned to the table and picked up a small silver box. Lifting the lid, he displayed its contents. "Of course you remember. . .these?"

Inside the box was the ring given me by the Anu prince and the flower necklace given to Neftiji by the tiny princess. I lunged for the box, but the magician snatched it back.

"Give them to me!" I demanded. "They belong to us."

"No!" shot back Kho-An-Sa. "Now they belong to me."

I stood with my hands close to my sides, fists balled, rage seething in my breast. I longed to tear the sacred objects from the hands of the evil magician, but I dared not do it. Kho-An-Sa smiled wickedly and placed the box back on the table.

"I have examined these objects with all my devices," said Kho-An-Sa. "Yet, I cannot discern their nature..."

Lowering my eyes, I prepared to lie. I thought it best not to reveal the true nature of the ring or the necklace. Kho-An-Sa folded his arms and looked inquisitively into my face. "Where did you get these items, young Memnon?" he asked.

"They were given to us," I replied.

"By whom?"

"By the great serpent," I lied.

"Hmm," said Kho-An-Sa, placing his hand upon his chin. "So far as I can discern, the ring is a mere bauble. But the necklace is made of flowers that never decay. I believe it has some medicinal use."

"They were presents to us, Kho-An-Sa," I said. "They were given to us."

"If you serve me well I will return your beloved ring," replied Kho-An-Sa. "As for the necklace, your sister has no need for it now."

"But...Kho-An-Sa," I started.

"Enough, young panther," Kho-An-Sa said, throwing his hand up to silence me. "We will speak of this no more. There is one more reason you have been summoned before me."

He clapped his hands loudly and a woman emerged from a corridor across the room. I was immediately struck by her beauty. She was of the eastern Kushites, with fine features and softly flowing black hair that caressed her shoulders and ran down her arms. Her eyes were light brown with flecks of gold and her skin glowed like burnished bronze. She wore a long, tight blue garment of the same material worn by the Shang and walked on sandals imbedded with sparkling gems.

She was quite graceful, and an enchanting fragrance swirled about her, making my nostrils flare and my skin tingle. I had never seen a womanly frame as perfectly curved or as delicately formed. She was truly the most beautiful woman I had ever laid eyes upon.

Tearing my eyes from her, I looked at Kho-An-Sa, who smiled at me knowingly and gestured for her to come closer.

"This is Nala," he said. "She will be your teacher for the next phase of your training."

I gazed at her with my mouth wide open. She smiled and bowed gently. "Greetings, Memnon," she said. "I am of the Indu from the east."

I looked at her again from head to toe. Her beauty was intoxicating.

"Kho-An-Sa," I asked, "what am I to learn from her?"

"Nala, show him," ordered Kho-An-Sa.

She came close to me and threw her hands around my shoulders. I felt the heat of desire rising as she pressed her body against mine. Then I felt her touch me at the base of my neck. My legs immediately gave way and I fell to the floor. I could neither feel nor move as Nala and Kho-An-Sa leaned over me, laughing at my futile attempts to rise.

SHADES OF MEMNON

"Ah ha, young Memnon," said Kho-An-Sa mirthfully. "You see things are not always what they seem. She is beautiful, yes, but she is deadly!"

"What have you done to me?" I asked angrily.

"I have merely touched a power point," Nala said. "Your legs will return to you momentarily."

The control of my legs came back as she spoke and I leaped to my feet. Nala jumped back in surprise.

"Oh," she cried. "You are a strong one!"

Kho-An-Sa gestured for Nala to come near as he explained. "The people of Indus-Kush have perfected the knowledge of the power points of Rau within the body. Nala will teach this knowledge to you. She will also teach you how to build your Rau without the rays of Aten or the eating of vegetables."

"How is this done?" I asked.

Nala reached up to touch my face. I flinched, then let her caress my cheek.

"It is called Kula Yoga, The Way of Uniting One's Rau with That of Another," she said with a sensuous smile.

"Uniting...with another?" I asked. "What do you mean?"

Nala smiled. "I will show you what it is."

Moving her hand down from my cheek, she brushed past my neck and chest, finally resting her fingers against my belly. Once again I felt fires of desire for this strange woman.

"Do you feel that?" she asked. "Is it hot? Is there desire there?"

I swallowed hard. Her long fingernails slightly scraped the muscles above my waist wrap. Kho-An-Sa chuckled slightly as he looked on.

"Yes," I said weakly. "Yes, I feel it."

"That is Rau," Nala said. "The life force. We will unite and I will teach you to strengthen yourself with the life force of your desire."

I looked at her in total disbelief.

"Unite?" I asked. "You mean..."

"Yes, that's exactly what I mean," said Nala with a playful smile. "Do you not find me desirable?"

I looked at Kho-An-Sa. He smiled and threw his hands into the air.

"Trust me, young Memnon," he said. "It is the best way."

I did not trust Kho-An-Sa, but I was a young man. Only twenty years from the womb, and I had never been intimate with a woman. The beauty of this one overwhelmed me.

"It is truly the best way of replenishing Rau," Nala said with a sensuous gleam in her eyes. "Some say it is the only way worthwhile."

"I'm sure," I replied eagerly. "When do we begin?"

Kho-An-Sa stepped forward. Placing his hands upon both our shoulders, he looked into our faces.

"You can begin when we sail from the port of Gaza in Canaan, but first I have a task for you both."

We left the temple hours later with Kho-An-Sa's six-wagon caravan. As we rolled away from the stone-carved walls and columns, I noticed Neftiji standing at a window, motionless. I waved to her, though I knew she would not respond. Whatever Kho-An-Sa had done kept her in a state more death-like than alive. Once again I had to stifle my rage and sadness as I watched her blank face and unblinking eyes as we left. The only comfort I had was Hazz, who was standing next to her as we left. He had promised to look after her when I learned she was to be left behind.

I shot a quick glance across the wagon at Kho-An-Sa as we wound down the path away from Petra. He seemed not to care that my hatred for him grew by the minute. As he sat next to Nala discussing the task we were to complete before sailing to the lands in the north, I wondered if the day would come when I would have to consider my sister lost and take my revenge upon him. But before that day came, I vowed to do all in my power to free her. And for that I had to learn more about Kho-An-Sa.

"Young Memnon," Kho-An-Sa said as the wagon jostled along. "Once more, let us review the task I have given you."

I nodded wearily. This was at least the tenth time we had gone over these plans.

"Yes, Kho-An-Sa," I replied.

"We are five days away from the port of Gaza. To get there we must pass through the land of the Ish-Ra-Elites. As I have told you, they are a small confederation of Habiru tribes, Amorite bandits and Canaanite castoffs bound together by descendants of the great Kamitic Heresy. They have raided the area for generations, stealing from caravans, wayward travelers and the like. As a people they are really of no consequence, just a few thousand fleas biting at the rump of Canaan and nearby lands. But they have something I want—they possess the Baa en pet."

"Metal from the sky," I said.

"Correct," said Kho-An-Sa. "It fell from the stars a few generations ago, landing near a Canaanite outpost. This was when the various tribes making up the Ish-Ra-Elites stopped warring and came together. Taking the fall of the sky-metal as a sign, they laid siege to the outpost and took it."

Nala leaned forward and joined in the telling.

"Now they keep the Baa en pet and use it for consultations."

"Yes," added Kho-An-Sa. "They use it as an oracle. They call it the "Urim and Thummin," but they have no idea what its true powers are. Those who use the metal in raw form become exceedingly strong due to its effects, but also subject to fits of madness."

SHADES OF MEMNON

"The fools think they are being overcome by the spirit of their deities," added Nala contemptuously. "But it is the power of the metal from the sky."

"They will come out to meet us when we cross over to the lands they control, demanding tribute," said Kho-An-Sa. "When they do, young Memnon, you are to take Nala to their leader and offer her to him. His name is Samson, a very simple man, who, I am told, has a weakness for beautiful women. Trick him and bring me that sky-metal."

"I understand," I said. "We will be thieves robbing from thieves."

Kho-An-Sa shrugged his shoulders. "I care not how you reason it," he retorted. "Just bring the Baa en pet back. It will be used to forge your weapons in the north."

On the evening of the third day, as Aten settled below the horizon, the hills of Canaan appeared in the distance. As we drew closer, a large group of men appeared upon the road and started towards us. As they closed in, I recognized them as the nomadic raiders called Habiru. With their short spears, slings and dusty goatskin waistwraps, they were well known to Kamit as troublemakers and thieves.

They stopped several cubits before us and two men stepped forward. Kho-An-Sa stepped down from the wagon to greet them. They began talking in the Habiru language and Kho-An-Sa repeatedly pointed back towards Nala and I. After a few minutes, the Habiru leader stepped over to the wagon and looked at Nala. His eyes widened and he went back over to Kho-An-Sa, nodding his head vigorously. Finally, their conversation broke off and Kho-An-Sa came back to the wagon.

"You must go now," he said.

Nala and I stepped down from the wagon. After I seized a bag of supplies and slung it over my shoulder, Kho-An-Sa pulled me close.

"We will await you at the third hill north from this spot. Do not fail me."

Nala and I joined the group of Habiru as they turned back towards their home. It was now completely dark and one of them lit a torch as we left the road and started across the fields of their land. After several hours, we arrived at their town. A great wooden wall encircled it, complete with a large gate and sentry post. When we neared, the torch bearer waved his torch and shouted a password. Then the huge gate creaked open and we walked inside.

Torches were burning everywhere, revealing a modest town of mud-thatched dwellings and small, round grain bins. There were very few people in the street, but sheep milled about in large numbers, their eyes glowing in the torchlight as we waded through them. Near the center of the town we were led toward a large building. Two wooden statues of winged men stood outside it, surrounded by several armed guards. I assumed it was the home of their leader.

We were led into the building's corridor, where the torch bearer knocked on an inner door. It soon opened and three young women appeared. The torch bearer spoke to them briefly and one disappeared, returning a moment later nodding affirmatively. She beckoned us to follow her and we did, trailed by the two other women.

We were led into a large room filled with the sweet smell of frankincense. In the center of it there was a large table covered with scrolls and tablets. There sat a large Habiru man, peering intently at a scroll by the light of a candle. The young girl nudged him and he grunted unpleasantly. She nudged him again and he pushed her hand back with his elbow. She nudged him yet another time and he finally looked up.

"Greetings," I said.

"Greetings," he answered. I was surprised that he spoke clear Kamitic.

Nala bowed low. She had been told not to speak unless spoken to, as is the custom among the Ish-Ra-Elite women. The large Habiru rose to his feet and came toward us. He looked much different from the rest of them. Though his curly hair and beard were long, they were very well washed and neatly combed. Sparkling rings adorned his thick fingers and a silver necklace accented his throat. His robe was of finely woven white material.

"I see you have brought me tribute," said the Habiru, eyeing Nala. "But where is the tribute for my people?"

"She is all we have," I said.

"Oh, but I hear you have six wagons in your caravan," he replied. "Six wagons must be carrying something of value."

"Yes," I replied. "It is her. Take a close look, great king."

"I am no king," said the Habiru. "I am a judge, the law of my people, and my name is Samson. I will take a closer look at your tribute."

He walked toward us and seized the torch from our guide. Holding the flame before Nala, he examined the contours of her body and let out a loud, long whistle.

"She is indeed rich tribute," said Samson with a lustful smile. "Perhaps I will let you go without further payment."

"I am glad she pleases you," I said.

"She does indeed," he replied, placing the torch into a holder on the wall. "What is your name, young man?"

"Memnon," I said.

Samson stroked his beard. "Memnon...it seems I have heard that name before..."

"Perhaps you have," I replied.

"Well, Memnon, it would please me if you would break bread with me. What say you?"

"I would be honored, great Samson," I replied.

SHADES OF MEMNON

He spoke to the young woman next to him and she scurried from the room. Another young woman brought out a chair for me.

"Come, sit," Samson said, beckoning me towards the table. I sat down as Samson pushed the scrolls to the side and waved his hand to dismiss our guide. He started from the room, seizing Nala's arm on his way.

"Leave her!" ordered Samson. "She goes to the women's quarters later. It...pleases me to look at her."

The man let go of Nala's arm and left. The two other young women stood nearby, shooting angry glances at Nala. One was a Tamahu with delicate pale skin and red hair. The other was a western Kushite, perhaps Nubian, with brown skin and short, tight hair like my own. Both were very beautiful and obviously jealous of Nala. Samson flicked his hands at them and they hurried from the room. He shook his head as he watched them leave.

"Women!" he said. "Were they not useful for making sons, I would have nothing to do with them." Then he looked at Nala again. "Except for women like this one. Where did you find such a treasure?"

"We...bought her from southern Shashu," I lied. "They told us she comes from far to the east."

"Indeed, she must be from the east. I have never seen a woman like her," Samson replied. "And believe me, I know my women."

The first woman came back with a flask of wine and two bronze goblets. She was a southern Shashu, with long brown hair and light brown skin. She too was beautiful and smiled prettily as she poured the wine. Samson saw me appraising her and chuckled lightly.

"Can I offer her to you for the night?" he asked.

"Thank you, great Samson," I replied. "But no. I must leave soon."

He lifted a goblet and gulped down the contents. "As you will," he said, slamming the goblet down upon the table. The young woman immediately filled it again.

"Tell me, great Samson," I asked. "How is it that you speak the Kamitian tongue?"

He gulped down more wine, wiping his beard with the back of his hand.

"It is required of all judges since the time of Ausar-Mesh. It was he who led our people from bondage in Kamit and was given the Commandments and the Urim and Thummin by Yaweh."

I nodded and took a sip of wine. As he continued to talk I began to understand these Ish-Ra-Elites. It seems that they had taken a part of Kamitic history, twisted it, and were using it as doctrine to unify their people. For the Kamitian records say that this Ausar-Mesh was an exiled priest of Kamit who led followers of the Kamitic Heresy decreed by the mad king Aunken-Aten. It was they who nearly led to the ruin of our people before we finally drove them from our land. But I was not there to argue with Samson. I wanted to learn where they kept the Urim and Thummin.

The Shashu woman brought in plates of food and more wine. I only ate the vegetables, leaving the lamb's leg and fowl lying where they were. Samson noticed this and questioned me.

"Why do you not consume the meat?"

"I am forbidden to eat it," I replied. "I have undergone...changes recently that will not allow it."

"Ah!" cried Samson, raising his goblet high, "You've found a new faith! A toast to your new way of life!"

We dashed our goblets together and drank heartily. Then I glanced over my shoulder at Nala. She was still standing near the entrance, giving me an impatient look. I turned back towards Samson as he guzzled more wine.

"Great Samson," I began carefully, "I am interested in your faith also. What is the Urim and Thummin?"

"It is the sacred way that Yaweh speaks to us," he replied, biting into a large hunk of meat. "It advises us in war, in peace and in life."

"Could it answer a question for me?" I asked.

Samson tore into a lamb leg with great enthusiasm. Rarely had I seen anyone eat with such relish. As he spoke, food trickled from his mouth.

"Surely, but I would have to ask the question myself. Only a judge of Ish-Ra-El can consult the sacred stone."

We finished the meal and the Shashu woman cleared the table. On her way out Samson said something to her in the Habiru tongue, and she drew a curtain behind her. Then he pointed to Nala.

"Woman, turn around," he ordered. "No females are allowed to view the Urim and Thummin."

After Nala turned around, Samson walked over to a table in a corner of the room and returned with a bronze candleholder containing seven candles. He lit them with a torch, then touched the fire to a stalk of frankincense. He returned to the corner, lifted a wooden box with great reverence and brought it back to the table. Slowly he opened the lid, revealing a large, dark lump of rock nearly a half cubit around. Speckles of glowing metal glistened from it.

"The Urim and Thummin," said Samson reverently, clasping his palms together. He stood over the stone and said a prayer in the Habiru language, then he removed two small rods from the box. One was of bronze and the other silver.

"What is your question, Memnon?" he asked.

Though I doubted the accuracy of this oracle, I decided to ask something of real importance.

"Will I ever see my pa again?"

Samson lifted the silver rod and said, "If this rod sings longest, it means yes." Then he lifted the bronze rod and added, "If this rod sings longest, it means no."

SHADES OF MEMNON

He closed his eyes and slowed his breathing. Then he tapped the rock with both rods and it began to vibrate. He struck it again as the box and the whole table began to shake. Suddenly a loud piercing note came from the silver rod, then the bronze rod started to sing also. Samson's hands quivered and his mouth opened and closed as if he wanted to speak.

The piercing pitch of the rods grew louder and louder and I covered my ears to block it out. Moments later the bronze rod went silent, while the note from the silver rod went on, but lower and lower. A few moments later the rock and table ceased shaking and the piercing sound stopped completely.

Samson opened his eyes. "You will see your pa again, Memnon," he said. "Yaweh has declared it."

"Thank you, great Samson," I said. "You have given me much comfort."

Sweat was pouring from Samson's face and his robe was soaked from the strain of his oracular task. He placed the rods back into the box and was reaching for the candles when he suddenly fell to the floor. Then Nala appeared from the shadows behind him.

"Take the rock, Memnon," she said. "Let us leave this place."

I looked up at Nala, very surprised. I had not noticed she had moved. Then I looked down at Samson. Though his religious doctrine had truly appalled me, I was starting to like him. Now we could never be friends. I seized the heavy rock and slipped it into my pouch.

Nala took a flask of wine and poured it on Samson as he lay there. Then she dashed some on me, placing the empty flask in Samson's still hand. "Let us go," she said. "You must pretend to be drunk until we leave this city."

We walked from the room and strolled down the corridor towards the entrance. Nala seized a blazing torch at the door and held me up as I stumbled and feigned drunkenness. Samson's three women laughed as we went past them, waving their hands and holding their noses. Even his guards outside the door looked amused as I shuffled past in a fake stupor.

As we walked further from Samson's house, I increased my speed and began walking normally. Nala seemed disturbed and was urging me to go even faster. "There was something. . .strange about Samson," she said. "His body felt different. I don't know what it was, but we must get away from here quickly."

As we went through the town we saw many wagons sitting near houses and draft animals all about. Nala stopped at one of the dwellings and pointed to two asses tied nearby.

"Memnon, get those animals. We must leave quickly. Samson will not remain asleep very long. I know he won't." she said very nervously.

We hitched the asses to the wagon and quietly rode toward the gate. I waved the torch to signal the tower, and the huge wooden doors swung open for us to ride to freedom, but as the doors were closing behind us, I heard a loud commotion from the city. I then slapped the reins on the asses to hurry them along.

"Hurry these beasts, Memnon," said Nala fearfully. "He will soon be after us."

A shout rang out from the tower and several arrows flew past us. Though the three-quarter moon was bright and Nala carried a torch, the road was very dark and unfamiliar. We sped along as fast as I dared to drive the beasts, when Nala suddenly seized my arm.

"Oh, no!"

"Are they after us?" I asked.

"Yes! And they have horses!"

As she spoke I heard the hoof beats, then glanced around to see another wagon gaining close behind. The men carried spears and stood ready to throw them as their wagon closed the distance between us. I knew they would soon be upon us, and we had no protection from their weapons.

"Nala," I shouted above the clatter of the pounding hooves, "what is in the back of this wagon? Look quickly!"

Nala turned around and held the torch aloft to see. "There are some bags of grain and small vases..."

"Take the reins!" I ordered.

When Nala had the reins, I seized the torch and leapt to the rear of the wagon. A spear flashed past, barely missing me. Our pursuers were now perhaps 30 cubits away and closing in fast. I could not make out the approaching figures, but I could hear the voice of Samson, shouting over the thunder of their horses hooves.

"I gave you the hospitality of my people and you stole our sacred Urim and Thummin!" he cried. "Thief! You shall not leave the land of Ish-Ra-El alive!"

Another spear whistled past, landing on the seat right next to Nala. I knew I had to work fast or we would surely be struck down.

"Your trick did not work!" Samson shouted hysterically. "Yaweh is my shepherd! Yaweh is my strength!"

Crawling along the bed of the wagon, I seized two large bags of grain and dragged them to me. Then I leapt to my feet, clutching one of the bags close to my chest.

"Here!" I cried, waving the torch overhead. "Here I am! Kill me if you can!"

SHADES OF MEMNON

Three spears whistled through the air, plunging into the thick bag of grain I held before me. Tossing it aside, I lifted the other sack as the pursuing wagon came alongside us. As I prepared to hurl it I could now see Samson under the torch light. Sword in hand, he crouched low, preparing to spring over into our wagon. But I did not give him the chance. Lifting the bag high, I hurled it to the ground before the rapid hooves of their horses.

The lead beast tripped and fell as I had planned, the two others ran over him, and then the wagon exploded as the wood hit the horses. The men went flying high into the air, their screams and curses joining the painful cries of their horses.

Leaning over the side of the wagon, I dripped with perspiration. The wrecked wagon disappeared into the darkness behind us as Nala cried out gleefully.

"Well done Memnon!"

I looked up and grunted, then lay down on the floor of the wagon. Watching the stars, I let Nala drive us on into the night.

Hours later I placed the Baa en pet in the hands of Kho-An-Sa. He grasped it enthusiastically, hefting it high into the air. The flecks of metal in the rock gleamed and glittered under the light of the three-quarter moon.

"Ahhh!" he exclaimed. "The sky-metal!"

He took some time to admire it, then handed the rock to a warrior, who walked to a nearby wagon and placed it carefully inside a heavy sack. Satisfied that is was secure, Kho-An-Sa turned back to Nala and I.

"Did you encounter much trouble getting it?" he asked.

"Not as much as we could have," I began, "but we..."

"Memnon was magnificent!" interrupted Nala.

"We would surely have been killed if not for his quick thinking."

Kho-An-Sa smiled slightly. "We will discuss this along the way. Let us leave for Gaza before they come searching for us."

We mounted Kho-An-Sa's wagon and rode away to the north, leaving behind the asses and the wagon we had stolen from the people of Ish-Ra-El. While I sat in a corner of the wagon, wondering about the fate of Samson and his men, I watched Nala and Kho-An-Sa talking. Nala spoke breathlessly, mentioning my name several times, often gesturing and glancing my way. Kho-An-Sa nodded frequently, apparently pleased with what she told him. Finally, he raised his hand for Nala to be silent and spoke to me.

"It seems Nala is very pleased by your actions, young panther," he said. "I am pleased also that you accomplished your first task so well."

I grunted and looked away. As the wagon rolled on through the night, I

SHADES OF MEMNON

drifted off to a dreamless sleep.

I awoke hours later as the rays of Aten touched my face and saw that we were on the streets of a very large city. Within moments I recognized the familiar language of the people of Canaan and knew we had at last reached Gaza. Winding our way through throngs of people from many different lands, we took in the early morning sounds and sights of a major seaport: the cries of merchants as they sold their wares, musicians playing for food and shekels on the streets and the spicy, sweet and pungent odors of early morning meals being cooked in a thousand pots.

At last tall sails loomed ahead of us and we came to a stop at the seaport of Gaza. Kho-An-Sa got down from the wagon and disappeared inside a small building on the edge of the docks. Nala looked at me very strangely as she offered me dried fruit and water to break the night's fast.

"How was your rest, Memnon?" she asked.

Something about her voice made me look into her eyes. I found a passion there that I had never noticed in a woman before.

"It was...bearable," I said, taking the fruit. "Thank you."

As I popped the morsels into my mouth, Nala lifted a flask to my lips and poured the cool liquid down my throat. I swallowed vigorously until she stopped and pulled the flask away.

"Memnon..." she said. "I have been assigned to teach many men the things I am to teach you, but I have never taught one quite like you."

Wiping the water from my lips with the back of my hand, I took another bite of the fruit.

"What do you mean?" I asked.

"You are young, but there is something about you," Nala replied. "You have strength beyond your years...you are handsome. . .you are. . .desirable."

I was about to ask her to go on, but Kho-An-Sa appeared.

"Out! All out!" he cried. "We will board the ship now," he bellowed, then turned toward Nala and I.

"Come, we will sail immediately. Memnon, bring the Baa en pet."

I seized the sack containing the sky-metal and followed behind him. Nala carried her own bags beside me, and we boarded a large vessel of the type known in most ports as a "Blybos ship," named after the great Caananite city of shipbuilders. It was perhaps 350 cubits long and 80 cubits wide, with huge sails and storage space for a trip of two dozen moons or more. Warriors and sailors swarmed all around us, shouting and swearing as they prepared for our departure.

Looking around closely, I saw that the vessel had been outfitted for conflict. There were wooden shelves near the sides of the boat, which I recognized as archery platforms. Small bronze bowls containing pitch, used to light flame arrows, sat in wooden frames, while large urns for the water used to put out fires sat nearby. Spears and javelins were also strapped to the sides of the ship. Wherever our journey would take us, I reasoned, it surely must be fraught with danger.

Kho-An-Sa took the Baa en pet from me and directed Nala and I to a structure built onto the deck of the ship. Upon walking inside we found it was a sleeping room, modestly furnished with a large bed and a small couch. Nala seemed to like it very much and tossed her bags happily to the floor. She plopped down upon the couch, bouncing up and down playfully.

"This is your sleeping quarters, Memnon," Kho-An-Sa said. "And Nala's."

Nala looked at me with a big wicked smile and a gleam in her eyes. Kho-An-Sa looked at us both and grinned knowingly.

"I will interrupt you very little during this journey, young panther. You have much to learn," he said, then disappeared through the exit, closing the door behind him.

As soon as he was gone, Nala stood up and walked seductively towards me. I stood with my hands at my sides, not knowing what to do as she circled me, giggling like a small girl. She moved just close enough to reach up and gently touch my face.

"Memnon," she began. "I need time to prepare. Why don't you go and look around the ship. Come back when Aten passes nearly to night."

I knew little of the ways of women, and I had no idea what she needed to prepare for, but at that moment I would have done anything she asked.

As I walked out of our quarters, the ship was leaving port, sails blown full with air, heading north across the Great Green Sea. As a child growing up I had seen many ships and had always been fascinated with the sailing of large vessels. So I watched the sailors pull and tie the huge billowing sheets of cloth and work the rudder that steered the ship. I watched the captain, a burly, dark brown Kushite from Canaan with a slight limp, lick his finger to test the wind and shout orders to his crew.

As I strolled across the deck, I noticed that the quarters for the warriors and crew were also bustling with activity. Standing near the doorway, I watched arguments over sleeping arrangements, proximity to the exit and other pettiness common when men live closely.

But one warrior among them received no argument. Conversations ceased as Cronn walked past me and entered. The giant Tamahu strolled in among them, claimed the space of his choice and cast down his huge sword, sleeping blankets and other belongings.

There had been no contact between us since I humiliated him before

SHADES OF MEMNON

the assembly in Petra. Since then he avoided me at all times, walking the other way when I came near or leaving any room when I entered it. Despite having beaten him, I was still cautious near Cronn. I knew he hated me for his defeat and humiliation, and I knew that if he took me unawares I would surely die.

I remained on deck for hours, watching the port of Gaza disappear in the distance. Finally the time came to go back to the sleeping chamber...and Nala. Walking in, I immediately smelled the scent of sandalwood, the fragrance of Het-Heru, the perfume of passion. The windows were covered with cloth and the room was totally dark. Suddenly two candles on the floor near the bed flamed to light. Standing between them was Nala. Sheer garments of light green and yellow were wrapped tightly around her body and draped about her face, making her golden eyes stand out in the candle light.

Slowly she began to dance, with lingering, sensuously delicate moments that entranced me further into the room. When she flicked her hands, a light chiming sound filled all the space between us, keeping time to her graceful movements.

She came closer and began to dance around me, teasingly chiming near my ears and tossing the corners of her sheer garments into my face. I tried to embrace her, but she was too quick, snatching her hips away before I could close my grasp. I was shaking with desire and breathing heavily when she finally stopped near the bed. Suddenly she began casting off the sheer garments piece by piece.

Taking a deep breath, I gazed at her small dark body, oiled and glistening in the candlelight. In my passion I leapt forward and tried to embrace her, but she stepped aside and I landed on the bed, frustrated and confused. Then I felt her soft hands on my back and the heat in my body rose. Turning over, I found her beautiful eyes looking deeply into mine. I opened my mouth to speak, but she placed a hand over my lips and said softly, "Shush, Memnon. You are too fast. You must be gentle."

She then slid her flawless body down onto mine, covering my lips with a kiss. It was then that my lessons truly began.

During the long voyage I was educated by the throes of ecstasy, and Nala's most enthusiastic method of teaching. I learned that the force of Rau runs just like wind and wave between man and woman and that the source of passion and power are the same. After repeated unions with Nala, I learned self control, and the tricky technique of retaining my seed in order to build up this Rau power.

Nala told me that the treatments I received from Sung Li allowed me to feel my Rau to a greater degree than most men; and that I could increase my Rau greatly by tapping into this power generated between us when united. She also said that in order to stay strong I must practice this Kula Yoga for the rest of my life.

Soon we could remain embraced for whole days or nights, with the Rau force traveling back and forth between us. Circulating like blood, it was cool one minute and hot the next. If I retained my seed throughout a session, I came away bursting with vigor and had to run several times around the ship to burn it off.

But there was one other consequence of the techniques Nala taught me that was not pleasant. I first noticed it one day during a run around the ship. Feeling irritable for no reason I could understand, I found myself running under the noon-day heat of Aten. The ship was full of activity as warriors practiced their sword and spearplay and sailors tended to the needs of the vessel. I ran past a group of sailors and warriors who, taking a break from their duties, were grouped together in a circle. Their backs were bent, and their vigorous shouts and oaths indicated they were engaged in a bit of gambling. Running by, I heard one of them laugh and stopped suddenly. I had the distinct feeling that one of them was laughing at me.

"Who laughed?" I asked angrily, turning toward them.

They stopped their game and looked up. There were six of them, four Tamahu warriors and two Kushite sailors from Canaan. I did not think they could understand me, but my anger would not abate. I stepped closer to the group of men, shaking with uncommon rage.

"Who finds me amusing!" I screamed, pointing at a sailor. "Is it you?" I growled at another man. "Or is it you?" I shouted, pointing rudely close to a man's face.

The warrior's complexion turned red and he slapped my hand away. I knew that my reputation struck fear into them due to my defeat of Cronn, but the warrior stood his ground and even took a step closer. Without hesitation, I swung my fist into his jaw and watched him crumble to the deck. As I turned to threaten another man, the sailor I had first confronted leaped upon my back. Then two more leaped forward and the fight was on. Warriors and sailors from all over the deck came over, forming a big ring around us as they watched.

The four of us went tumbling back and forth, cursing and spitting. Around and around we surged as the men hit and kicked me until I would seize ahold of one and throw him to the deck. For long minutes we brawled, and the men fighting against me were as surprised as I was that I did not seem to tire.

Stepping back to catch their breath, they huffed and puffed as they circled me. Blood poured down from my lip and somewhere near my eye, but I did not care. "Come," I shouted, shaking my fist, "who is next? Who wants more!"

The men around us began whistling. Shekels and notes changed hands as bets were laid on the fight. The sailor and the two warriors circled me like

SHADES OF MEMNON

cats. I did not know who would leap next, so I prepared myself for an attack by any or all of them. Suddenly I heard the sailor who had circled behind me scrape his foot upon the deck and ducked low. Looking up, I saw him sailing over my head, directly into the belly of the warrior facing me. The crowd roared with laughter as the men tumbled to the deck.

The face of the remaining warrior became livid with rage. Reaching into his boot, he pulled out a knife and lunged toward me. Leaning backwards as the blade slashed inches from my face, I seized his outstretched arm and yanked him to me, slamming my fist into his belly. He doubled over, the knife slipped from his hand and I stepped on it. Then with the other foot I kicked him savagely in his side. Howling painfully, he dropped to the deck, defeated.

There the four men lay before me, writhing and moaning. Blood dripped down my face as I stood there, but still the rage and power in me did not lessen. Just then the crowd grew silent. The men parted and the giant Cronn appeared. An evil joy swept through me and I smiled, anticipating more fighting, but then Cronn stepped aside and Kho-An-Sa was there.

"Cease, young panther," he said. "You have fought enough for now."

Ignoring Kho-An-Sa's words, I fixed my gaze upon Cronn. Feeling an urge to fight that would not be denied, I lifted my foot and picked up the knife. As I walked towards the Tamahu giant, Kho-An-Sa's voice rose in a chant, his hands made signs in the air and suddenly I felt like sleeping. I took two more heavy steps, struggling to fight the drowsiness, but it was no use. The knife fell from my hands and I fell into the arms of my giant enemy.

I awoke in our sleeping quarters to find Nala massaging my body with fragrant oils and singing a soothing melody. The irritable feeling was gone and at last I felt at peace.

"Nala," I asked, "what happened to me?"

Reaching up, she touched my lip lightly and I winced from the pain. "You've been fighting," she answered matter-of-factly.

I sat up and immediately felt dizzy. My body ached and throbbed from head to foot. Groaning from the pain, I pressed Nala for an explanation.

"But why?" I asked urgently. "Why did I feel that way? I wanted to hurt those men, and I don't know why..."

Nala lit a stalk of incense with a candle and handed it to me.

"Here, smell this."

I took a deep breath and a wonderful tingling feeling came over me.

"You were flowing with too much Rau. You have been building it up too much lately without spending it. We have to take it slower."

"But I know about the extra Rau," I replied. "That is the reason that I must run so much. But why did I want to hurt those men?"

Nala shook her head. "I told you, Memnon. You have been flowing with too much."

"But...I don't...."

"Hush, Memnon. Rest now. Go to sleep."

I slipped off into a slumber, but not with my mind at peace. I did not pursue the matter further, but throughout the journey I would often feel angry for no apparent reason, and I could not help thinking that there was something Nala was not telling me.

The voyage lasted a full moon. During this time Kho-An-Sa told us many times about the dangers we might face in the land of our destination. As a place saturated with the force of the Reckoning, any force of nature could be perverted. I thought of this when we finally saw land and sailed into a deep bay offshore.

Kho-An-Sa chose 20 warriors besides myself and Cronn for the journey. Then he prepared some of his strange flasks and vases for transport and gave each of us a necklace that he said would help protect us—all of us, I noted, except Cronn. After stocking weapons and provisions for the trip, we boarded three small boats and rowed to shore.

We disembarked and I looked at the northern land we had come to. Directly before us was a range of hills covered with thick green forests. Tall grasses and trees I had never seen before stretched in all directions and though it felt warm, there was something in the air, a chill of a sort that I had never experienced. I knew this was indeed a strange and different land.

Kho-An-Sa seemed unusually cautious. Instructing us to be wary at all times, he insisted we report anything unusual immediately. Only Cronn seemed to be at ease as we set off through the unknown wilderness. There almost seemed to be a spring to his step as he led us along, picking out the best routes through areas that seemed never to have been trodden before. I observed him carefully, noticing how he would stop periodically, sniff the air, and change directions.

We walked for hours over hills and flatlands covered with thick endless forests. At times the trees were so close that little light came through, causing the men to walk closer together, peering cautiously all around, jumping at any strange sound or motion. We finally emerged into a clearing as Aten slipped down beneath the horizon. There we built a fire and settled down for the night.

After setting up a defensive system of shields and lances around the camp, four men were posted for the first watch. As we sat around the large campfire, under a full and luminous moon, we noticed other strange things about this land. There were none of the familiar sounds of a forest at night, like insects chirping, night birds signaling their kin or animals dashing on nocturnal hunts.

SHADES OF MEMNON

And besides our anxiety over the lack of these familiar things, somehow we felt we were being watched. Even Cronn grew agitated as he sat near Kho-An-Sa, arms folded across his huge chest, eyes roaming the darkness beyond the light.

Suddenly a loud, long howl pierced the night air. All of us leapt to our feet, brandishing weapons and uttering prayers or curses.

"Calm down," commanded Kho-An-Sa. "It will do no good to panic. Be seated."

We sat back down and Kho-An-Sa turned to Cronn. They made eye contact and the giant rose to his feet. He left the light of the fire, leaving his weapons behind, and walked out into the night toward the direction of the howl. For long minutes we all waited breathlessly, wondering why Cronn would dare to venture forth, alone and weaponless into this strange forest. But he soon reappeared, walked rapidly back into camp and straight towards Kho-An-Sa.

After he whispered into the magician's ear, Kho-An-Sa stood up immediately and cried, "Break camp! We must leave now! Break camp! Now!"

The men started stuffing bags and rolling bedding with great haste motivated by fear.

"It will be dangerous to move about at night," Kho-An-Sa said. "But it will be more dangerous to stay here. There are creatures about that should not be faced under a full moon."

Several men lit torches and handed one to Kho-An-Sa. Then the magician reached into a pouch, pulling out a small vase covered with leather and bound shut with a cord. After placing it on the ground near the fire, he then reached into a larger bag and pulled out a small black cat. It was only a kitten, but it struggled and writhed fiercely to free itself. Kho-An-Sa held it close to his face and spoke into its ear. Immediately the cat closed its eyes and went to sleep.

All the men watched curiously as Kho-An-Sa placed the kitten next to the vase, untied the cord around it and pulled back the leather. A red mist rose from it as Kho-An-Sa began chanting and working a series of hand signs in the air.

The mist swirled above the cat, forming a circle in the air above its motionless body which I recognized immediately. It was what Kam-Atef called a gateway to the Taut, the major tool for the spread of the Reckoning. Most occurred spontaneously, but some magicians could call them forth at will.

A bright flash of red light leaped from the portal, enveloping the feline, and then the portal disappeared. The cat leapt to its feet, emitting a cry as if its heart were being torn out. Its color changed from black to blood red, while crackling noises like the sound of burning wood, emitted from its quivering body.

Then to our astonishment, the cat started to grow. We gasped in disbelief as it swelled to the size of a jackal. Men stepped back when it grew to the size of a panther, and as it grew bigger still, the warriors pointed their weapons at it fearfully.

"Do not be afraid," Kho-An-Sa said forcefully. "It is here to assist us. Make no sudden moves."

Finally, at nearly twice the size of a full grown lion, the cat creature ceased growing. Glancing around at the men assembled, it walked up to Kho-An-Sa, lowering its head obediently.

Kho-An-Sa smiled and spoke to it with authority. "Go forth creature of Herukhuti. Kill those fiends who would hunt us! Kill the wolf-creatures who hunt in the night. Go! Now!"

The huge feline nodded before Kho-An-Sa, then turned obediently and bounded off into the forest.

Kho-An-Sa spoke to us all, pointing in the direction the cat-creature had gone. "My servant will not be able to kill all the beasts that hunt us, but it will keep them busy enough for us to gain some distance. In the morning, when it is safe, we will rest. Now, let us depart."

We traveled through the night with torch bearers on either side, out front and at the rear of the company. The going was slow and we stumbled often, but no one relished the idea of meeting these "wolf-creatures" who hunted us, especially if they posed a danger to the fearsome Herukhuti-cat created by Kho-An-Sa. Cronn led us once again, but this time even he seemed to be disturbed.

I asked Kho-An-Sa to explain our situation and he shook his head sadly. "I had no idea it had gone this far. Nothing is as it should be."

"Will we make it to the workshop of the blacksmith?" I asked.

The look on Kho-An-Sa's face was grave. He looked around at the warriors, then answered me softly.

"Some of us may, young panther...most, perhaps all, will not."

I looked at the three warriors who carried the vases filled with spirits. Kho-An-Sa noticed and pointed at them. "I don't know that these will be enough," he said.

"The big cat...won't he come back to protect us?" I asked.

"Even if the Herukhuti-cat survives his battle with the nighthunters, these conjured creatures can only be asked one task. Afterwards, the creature is free to do its own bidding."

When the rays of Aten broke out over the land, we stood atop a hill overlooking a lush green valley. At its center a strong river churned, flowing from a high mountain in the distance.

"That is our destination," said Kho-An-Sa, pointing to the mountain. "It is there that we will meet the great blacksmith. We must first cross over this

SHADES OF MEMNON

river, though, and then we will stop to rest."

As we made our way down the hill I saw signs of animal life for the first time. Small creatures with stripes on their backs ran to and fro, hiding in the grass and behind the rocks on the hill. Birds flew above the valley and I could see fish jumping and thrashing near the surface of the river. We all felt better as we descended into the valley, noticing its bountiful, vibrant life.

Kho-An-Sa, however, did not share our enthusiasm. "Remain careful," he said cautiously. "Do not be fooled by appearances."

As we approached the shore of the river, two warriors prepared to cross it, extending their spear butts to probe the bottom.

"Hold!" Kho-An-Sa shouted. "You know not what lies beneath the surface of that lake."

He walked forward and waved the warriors back. I looked at the river carefully. Though it swept along strongly, it seemed a normal body of water. But I knew nothing was as it seemed in this land saturated by the Reckoning.

Kho-An-Sa walked forward and stood on the bank, his hands stretched out over the roiling surface of the water. Closing his eyes, he waved his arms and moved his lips for a few moments. Finally, he lowered his hands and turned towards us. "It is safe to cross," he said. "There is nothing to harm us in this river."

Another warrior and I took our spears and waded in. The current was strong and we stumbled slightly as we planted our spear-butts for support. As the other warriors splashed in I kept my head down, probing with the spear for holes or drop-offs. Just then I heard fearful cries behind me. Turning around, I saw them all, including Kho-An-Sa and Cronn, bending low over the river and pointing to the sky.

I felt a rush of air overhead as a dark shadow flew by. Ducking low, I extended my spear upright, confused by the frightened cries of the men behind me. Then a horrified scream rang out and I turned toward the warrior who had waded out with me.

My eyes widened as I saw him struggling in the clutches of a gigantic bird. Flapping its wings a few cubits above the river, it held him in its claws as a falcon would a rabbit, and would have taken off immediately if not for the warrior's valiant struggles.

Screaming in pain and terror, he stabbed into the bird's huge breast with his spear, causing the creature to emit an ear-splitting screech each time it was struck. Water splashed as the beast beat its wings, attempting to fly away. I looked behind to find several warriors holding spears aloft, poised to throw, but afraid to for the sake of the struggling warrior.

I was nearly close enough to thrust my spear at the creature, but the tremendous wings blew enormous gusts of wind, keeping me off balance. Determined to help though, I braced my spear on the rocky bottom of the river, slowly straining toward the hovering creature. I was nearly in position to attack when the giant claws around the warrior tightened and I heard a loud snap.

Suddenly the spear dropped from the warrior's hand and his body grew limp. Immediately I lunged, but it was too late. Beating its huge wings rapidly, it swept up from the surface of the river, bearing its dead prey into the early morning sky.

As I stood watching the huge bird fly away, another roar went up from the warriors behind me, and Kho-An-Sa was shouting the loudest.

"Memnon! " he cried. "Young panther, look to the sky! Look to your right!"

Too late, I brandished my spear and swiveled to my right. But I was struck so swiftly and with such force that all I could only see were stars and a huge, white feathery breast. Then giant claws seized me and shook me violently, squeezing the breath from my body. Gulping for air, I thrust my spear into this new bird, causing it to screech in pain and anger. Jerking and kicking, I thrust deeper, but its claws only wrapped around me tighter.

Looking up at its huge legs and body, I realized fearfully that this creature was larger than the other. As I struggled desperately, I heard Kho-An-Sa shouting to the others.

"Throw!" he cried. "Cut the creature down, now!"

Eighteen spears sliced through the air. A few hit the bird, causing it to screech terribly, but still it did not fall. Gripping my spear again, I thrust until I felt the point hit bone, but it still would not let go. Then I felt a jerking motion, and the surface of the river fell away. The huge wings flapped harder and suddenly I found myself high above the trees, watching Kho-An-Sa and his men becoming specks in the distance.

Higher and higher we climbed, the huge wings gliding on strong gusts of wind. I had no doubt about my fate and struggled on, preferring the quick end of a fall over being eaten by this beast and others who awaited in it's nest. But then its talons tightened around me again, shooting terrible pain throughout my body, especially my back. Resolving not to cry out, I clenched my teeth in bitter defiance, awaiting the awful snap that would surely seal my doom.

SHADES OF MEMNON

SHADES OF MEMNON

CHAPTER 8: THE WOLF CREATURES"

I passed each moment, in agonizing pain, awaiting the sound of my back bones breaking. But as the pressure increased and it did not happen, I remembered the words of my trainer Sung Li, that my bones had been strengthened by Rau and could not be broken. As this realization came over me, I let go of the spear and went limp. Immediately the bird's grip loosened and the crushing pressure disappeared. Thinking its prey now subdued, the creature rose on a gust of wind, gliding towards its destination.

But I was not subdued. Now that I could catch my breath, I knew what to do. Closing my eyes, I breathed deeply, murmuring a litany of chants from the Book of Knowing the Creatures of the Taut. After several attempts, I hit upon one that worked, and the effect of its power was immediate.

Shuddering, the bird became disoriented and released me. Reaching up quickly, I managed to seize a leg to keep from plunging to my doom. I held on tightly, chanting louder, since I could see it was making the bird fly even more erratically. Soon the bird's head drooped low, blood ran from its beak, and it's large golden eyes struggled to stay open. Moments later it's huge wings ceased flapping and trust out rigidly. Then we slowly descended towards the ground.

Just above the tops of the trees, I looked to the east. There was the white-capped mountain that Kho-An-Sa said was our destination. Much closer and to the north there was a small village, which would be my first stop, if I could only get to the ground alive. I knew the landing would be hard, but I had no choice but to let go of the bird's leg just a few cubits above the ground.

Tumbling head over heels, I landed roughly atop thick bushes without much injury. Pulling free from the vegetation, I looked up, just in time to observe the bird's violent landing. After crashing through a stand of bushes, it flipped violently end over end, before finally smashing against the trunk of a huge tree. Raising it's head once, it gave a sharp, piercing cry, and then fell silent forever.

I managed to get to my feet, but only very slowly, my back aching from the bird's grasp and the fall. I then made my way over to the creature to retrieve my spear. But upon close inspection I found the tip of my weapon poking from it's feathery back, driven completely through from the impact of the fall.

Hesitating momentarily, I pulled two other spears from its breast that had been thrown there by the other warriors. After wiping the blood from the blades upon its white feathery chest, I settled down beneath a nearby tree. There I sat for quite a while, staring at the giant bird and contemplating the strangeness of this land.

SHADES OF MEMNON

When Aten rose to midday, the pain in my back subsided and I set out for the village. Remembering Kho-An-Sa words, that nothing was as it should be, I held one spear poised to throw and carried the other over my shoulder. I had no way of knowing what strange beasts I would encounter, but I wanted to be ready.

After a brief trek, I stepped from the forest into the fields surrounding the village. I found it much smaller than it had seemed from above. Perhaps five dozen small thatched huts were the whole of it. A well-worn road led into the village from the west, then stretched on to the east, marking this place as a major stopping point for those journeying to the great mountain.

But as I observed the area and I could sense there was something wrong. The fields were covered with the husks of unharvested crops that were blown over with sandy, parched earth. I saw no people in the village nor travelers on the road. Indeed the site before me was as still and as silent as death.

Walking cautiously into the village, I immediately noticed the carcass of an ass, its bones poking through a leathery hide that looked as if it had been shredded by tremendous claws. Nearby I spied a pile of clothing and poked it with my spear. When I felt the bones inside and heard the dry clacking as they knocked together, I knew it was the remains of a man.

I took a look around at the dwellings and noticed signs that some great violence had befallen the place. The doors of the huts had been torn down, while deep cuts marred the window sills and walls. Fences had been trampled to the ground and tools and other items were scattered about. Animal and human remains were everywhere.

As I continued through the village, the grim truth became apparent: Something had attacked this place and killed every living thing, and from the chewed and twisted state of most of the remains, it seemed likely that the population had been devoured.

Turning on my heels, I rapidly headed back the way I had come, intending to leave this place of death. But on the outskirts of the village my rumbling empty gut forced a thought upon me; if this place had been destroyed as rapidly as the evidence indicated, then there might be some food left. Food which the dead villagers no longer needed, but which I needed desperately.

With this in mind I turned back to begin my search, looking around cautiously for signs of movement. The first hut I came to had gruesome splashes of blood on the walls, but in a corner I found a bag of grain. From a nearby dwelling I scrounged a sack of dried fruit and nuts. I drew water from a well in the middle of the village, then settled down in the cooking area of another dwelling to prepare a stew.

As the light of Aten waned, I sat cross-legged before the pot and a small fire, stirring my stew with a wooden spoon. Suddenly I heard the sound of footsteps from outside. Seizing a spear, I crept quietly to the window and drew aside the curtain. There stood a small Tamahu boy. His eyes closed and his nostrils flared, he was apparently enticed by the smell of the stew. He was dirty and tattered, with long filthy hair the color of straw and so thin he must have been near to starving.

I was happy to see that someone had escaped the carnage that had overtaken the village, and, without thinking, tapped the window sill to get his attention. Startled, the boy looked up quickly and our eyes met. I smiled warmly, but he turned on his heels and ran.

"Wait!" I cried.

Darting from the hut, I shouted again, but the boy was gone. Then I heard the sound of rapid feet to the left and ran in that direction. Soon I saw him, running amazingly fast, darting between huts and fences.

I realized then that I had been a fool. There was no way to know the state of the child's mind after witnessing the death of his people. Besides that, he had probably never seen a Kushite before. From my brief look at him, he seemed to be no more than 10 years old; and I, a very tall man, chased after him holding a spear. There was no reason for the child not to be terrified.

With the boy still a good distance ahead, I stopped running and tossed down my spear. "Child, wait," I said in the most gentle voice I could muster. "Please stop."

The boy looked over his shoulder, then stopped and turned hesitantly. He gazed at me briefly with a confused expression, then took off again, disappearing behind a nearby hut. Leaving my weapon behind, I walked toward the dwelling with my hands outstretched. Since the doorway faced me, and the boy had not emerged from the other side, I walked around the hut expecting to see the child there, cowering in fear.

But nothing was there but an empty water trough, once used by the now-dead animals. I was puzzled. After walking around the hut several more times, I finally accepted that the child had disappeared.

Picking up my spear, I walked back to the hut for my stew, wondering all the while where the child had gone. I poured some stew into a bowl and placed it outside near the doorway, then sat inside the hut, eating silently. I hoped the child would take the food, but I heard nothing.

By the time I finished eating, the village was in total darkness and I thought about how I should proceed. I did not feel safe here, but I had no wish to travel in the dark, alone and in unknown territory.

With great trepidation I decided to bed down there for the night, but not before taking precautions. First I propped the door that had been knocked down back into place, pushing a table and several stools against it. Then I

SHADES OF MEMNON

took a mound of bedding and skins that were heaped into a corner and spread them atop my body for concealment. Placing my spears close by, I tried to appear as much like a mound of clothing as I could before drifting off to sleep. I think later this tactic saved my life.

After an undetermined period of fitful sleep, I awoke to the sound of loud slurping noises. Smiling, I thought of the child finding the stew, perhaps eating his first cooked meal since the death of his people. Then I heard loud scraping and sniffing noises, followed by a low growl.

Peeking through the cloth and skin, I found the light of the full moon streaming through the window, and the night air being pierced by a loud, bone-chilling howl. My blood ran cold. The wolf creatures! I thought about the fate of the villagers, and suddenly it all made sense.

Peering up at the window again, this time I saw two red eyes staring in. Then a long, dog-like snout poked past the curtain, sniffing at the air and growling dangerously. When the eyes and snout disappeared, my mind raced in a near panic to come up with a plan.

As I wondered what I should do, a loud crash resounded, the table and stools flew back and the door crashed to the floor. The sniffing grew louder as two large clawed hands wrapped slowly around the doorway. Then my heart stood still as a pair of huge, wolf-like beasts crept into the room. Each of them was silver-gray, a full cubit taller than me, and stood upright like a man. Their stooped backs and strangely shaped legs were poised as if to spring, and it was clear that they were hunting. I knew they were hunting for me.

The creatures lumbered through the hut until they were standing above the pot of stew. Snatching it up, one of them pulled the pot to its snout and began slurping. The other tried to snatch it away and they growled and snapped momentarily. Then, after a few more guzzles, the waiting creature snatched the pot to finish what was left.

Continuing to peek through the cloth, I watched them eat the stew, terrified and fascinated by these strange creatures. Finally, they tossed the pot to the floor and headed for the doorway. But before they stepped through, one sniffed the air again. The other raised its nose also, and then they looked at each other, growling as if in agreement. Slowly they turned and shuffled toward me.

I had positioned my arm so that I could seize my nearby spear. Though I did not expect to win a battle against these creatures, I was prepared to defend myself rather than die like a sheep at the slaughter. I could hear their raspy breathing as they came closer, teeth bared and claws extended. My fingers were already gripping the shaft of the spear and I steadied myself to plunge it into the body of the one that got to me first.

But just as they hovered right above me, a thundering roar came from outside, shaking the very walls of the hut with its ferociousness. Immediately it was followed by several howls and the growls of other wolf-creatures. The two monsters before me raised their heads to the ceiling, howling in unison as they returned the call of their companions. Turning away from me, they leapt to the doorway, stopping only briefly to look back my way. One creature curled its clawed hand into a fist and shook it at me, and then they both bounded away.

Moments later I heard the sound of a tremendous battle. Tossing off the cloth and skins, I seized a spear and ran to peek outside. Another heavy roar shook the air as my eyes focused in the moonlight. There in the distance was Kho-An-Sa's Herukhuti cat, locked in a furious struggle with the wolf-creatures. Several of them lay dead at the cat's feet, while it shook another in its huge jaws.

Leaping up and down around it, the wolf-creatures were obviously afraid of the huge beast, which was three times as large as any one of them. Though eight of them surrounded the feline, they hesitated, growling furiously and howling in frustration.

Suddenly a crunching sound ripped through the air and, the cat tossed its latest victim aside. The body landed several cubits away, broken and still. Four of the wolves rushed over, howling mournfully. Angered by the death of their companion, they circled the giant cat until one of them found the nerve to jump astride its back. Biting and pawing furiously, the wolf beast tore at fur and flesh until the cat finally threw it off. An instant later the attacker was dead, gutted by the lightning-fast claws of the feline.

Then the remaining wolf-creatures leaped forward to attack, including the four mourners who left their dead companion and joined the onslaught. There was a furious flurry of activity as the creatures rolled around under the moonlight, howling and growling, pawing and scratching. One wolf-creature was thrown from the melee and limped out of sight.

Though I hoped the cat would be victorious, it was clear that it was gravely hurt. There were now three more wolf-creatures dead at its feet, but blood dripped from terrible wounds on the cat's sides. Yet still it stood, roaring defiantly.

Circling warily, the remaining wolf creatures searched for an opening. The giant cat stumbled, causing one of the wolves to leap boldly, only to be snatched by a claw as quick as a flash, then dragged in to the powerful jaws and brutally decapitated.

There were only three wolf-creatures left, and I knew it was only a matter of time for them. But then I saw that the wolf creatures were more formidable than I had suspected. My eyes widened as the one who had limped away suddenly reappeared, carrying a long bow and a quiver of arrows.

SHADES OF MEMNON

Howling to signal the others, it notched an arrow, and let it fly as soon as they moved away. The missile landed in the huge cat's side and it roared in pain. This caused the other wolf-creatures to howl gleefully, jumping up and down in delight.

Looking on in horror, I knew I could not let them kill the cat, because then they would turn on me. Springing quickly from the hut, I ran forward with my spear poised, intending to kill the wolf creature with the bow before he could notch another arrow.

"Ho, monster!" I cried. "Look this way!"

The creature turned toward me and looked quickly, then howled towards its companions. I was poised to throw the spear, but one of them had detached itself from the battle and was bounding toward me. Throwing my weapon now would leave me defenseless, so I held on to it, readying myself to fight.

The archer notched another arrow and pointed it at the giant cat as its companion came upon me. Growling menacingly, it tensed itself to spring, while I held my spear low and gripped it firmly.

After eyeing me for a long moment, he finally pounced, coming down upon me as a dog does a cornered rabbit. But I brought the point of the spear up with all my strength, piercing its hairy chest in midair.

Yelping in pain, it tried to grasp me with its long, sharp claws. But as the blade entered the monster's hairy chest, I planted the butt of the spear in the ground and rolled aside. The beast came down hard, forcing the blade clear through its back. It broke off with loud snap as the beast hit the ground.

Seizing the broken shaft, I smashed it upon the creature's head until its struggles finally ceased. There I stood above the dead beast, breathing heavily, holding the bloody shaft of the spear. My body shook terribly from the shock of what I had done and, I could scarcely believe that I survived the attack of such a creature.

But there was no time to gloat, as an arrow shot past me, then another, forcing me to dive to the ground. More arrows came close and I scurried for cover behind a broken wagon. Peeking from behind it, I looked on as the monstrous archer turned back and shot arrow after arrow into the giant cat. When its back and chest were bristling with arrows, the valiant feline finally fell as the three remaining wolf-creatures leapt to extract their revenge.

As I watched the wolf-creatures tearing at the giant beast, I wondered what I should do. They would surely come after me next and there was no place to run where they could not find me. Suddenly, I heard a whistle. Looking over my shoulder, I spied the young boy who had run away earlier. Crouching low beside a nearby hut, he beckoned me to follow. Taking a quick glance back at the wolf-creatures, I saw them tearing the cat to pieces and rolling around in its blood. Keeping low, I slowly made my way toward the boy.

Quietly he led me through the village, towards the hut where I had lost him earlier. Every few cubits he would stop, reach into a bag hanging at his waist, and toss a handful of powder over our footprints. I recognized the smell of the strong spice, for we used something similar in the rituals of Kamit. The boy was tossing crushed red pepper to cover our scents.

Slinking low behind the hut, he led me to the long animal trough I had noticed earlier. Shoving it to the side, he revealed a large hole in the ground and gestured for me to jump in. As I did, he took a branch, swept away our footprints for a few cubits, then spread more of the crushed pepper on the ground. Pulling a formidable knife from his belt, he leaped in beside me. I helped him pull the trough back over the hole and we settled down quietly.

It was not long before we heard the wolf-creatures. Howling and growling for more blood, they were trying to sniff out my trail. We sat silently in the dark, listening to them shuffling and sniffing, then sneezing and wheezing as they inhaled the hot red pepper.

Several times the sounds came quite close and I could feel the boy's body tense and tremble. Reaching out in the darkness to touch his hand, I found it clutched tightly around his knife. After an hour or so the wolf-creatures gave up the search and the boy and I drifted off to sleep.

Hours later I awoke to see the rays of Aten slipping through the cracks in the trough. The boy stirred also and we listened for a while for sounds. When we were satisfied that none of the creatures still lingered, we pushed the trough aside and emerged.

Looking around cautiously, I stretched my limbs. The child slipped the knife back into his belt and did the same. Then I beckoned him to follow and we cautiously went back through the village. There we saw the remains of the huge cat that the wolf creatures had taken their terrible revenge upon. No part of its red hide was not scored by clawmarks and its entrails lay scattered for many cubits around. I tried to cover the child's eyes and turn him away, but he pushed my hand aside and stood where he was.

As we pressed on, I looked down at the boy, amazed at his strength, ingenuity and his will to live. He had knowledge beyond his years and much toughness. I thought then that we should be introduced, and after bending down so that my eyes were level with his, I pointed to myself. "Memna-un," I said. "My name is Mem-na-un."

The child simply looked at me.

"Memna-un," I repeated, thumping my chest with my knuckles.

The child's expression remained blank, but he nodded as if he understood. I pointed at his chest. "What is your name?" I asked.

He continued to look at me blankly, so I pointed first at my mouth and

SHADES OF MEMNON

then at his and asked, "Can you speak?"

The child did not respond. After several more attempts I finally gave up and we made our way back to the hut where I had first encountered the wolf-creatures. I made us another pot of stew and the boy ate ravenously. Noting his hunger, I made another and he ate it also. Then he stretched out on the floor without a word and went to sleep.

As he lay there, I contemplated the situation. The only option that seemed reasonable was to go to the mountain and hope to meet up with Kho-An-Sa and his men there. I had no doubt that the magician thought me dead, but, having come so far and endured so much, perhaps he would have the weapons created regardless.

Looking at the child lying near me, I considered his fate. I could not bring myself to leave him alone in this village. For despite his cleverness, it was only a matter of time before the monsters would catch him. The boy would have to go along with me. As he lay there asleep, I gathered the provisions I had found the day before, stuffed them into a sack and prepared to leave. Then I shook the boy and he immediately sat up, eyes clear and alert. I motioned for him to follow and we left the hut.

Soon we arrived at the outskirts of the village, near the road leading to the mountain. But when he saw my intentions, the boy shook his head and pulled my arm, pointing back instead to the village. He seemed very fearful of leaving, repeatedly pointing towards the hole that was his refuge. Shaking my head, I pointed towards the road, and then up towards the mountain.

The child let go of my hand and stood still. I walked a few steps further, then turned to beckon to him. He only shook his head again. The giant dead cat was within sight and I pointed to it. After he looked at it, then back at me, I raised my hands in a claw-like gesture, baring my teeth to mimic the wolf-creatures. The boy's eyes grew wide and he looked back at the dead cat again. Turning around, I headed for the road, smiling slightly. After a moment or two, I heard the boy's footsteps as he ran to catch up with me.

The boy and I traveled down the road for many days, during which he proved himself as resourceful as he had been in the village. He seemed to know the surrounding country well, pointing out stopping points for water and food like an experienced guide. He made snares for small game and foraged for wild edible plants with ease. But most of all he knew how to avoid the strange creatures that lurked in this strange land.

During the day he sensed when the giant birds soared overhead in search of prey, pulling me off the road many times as a large shadow swept over us. It was due to his insistence that we slept in trees at night, after he had spread more of the crushed pepper over our tracks. There we would lie, high among the branches, tied to them tightly so as not to fall. Below us were the wolf-creatures and other beasts, prowling for prey during the night. If not for this mysterious child, I would never have survived the trip to the mountain.

Looking up one day, about three-quarters of a moon into the trip, I found the mountain filling the landscape before us. Our destination was perhaps a day's travel away but I and the boy were both road-weary. We sat down at midday to lunch, I eating nuts and roots found for me by the boy, and he eating a small bird he had roasted on a fire. The child was hungrily biting into the meat when he suddenly stopped and looked up the road alongside us.

Handing me his food, he walked over to the road, dropped to his knees and put his ear to the ground. After several moments, he jumped to his feet and trotted towards the forest, gesturing for me to follow. He had saved us too many times for me to question him, so I kicked dirt over the small fire and followed him into the brush. There we crouched for long moments, looking down the road expectantly.

Soon I felt rumblings coming from the ground, and then I heard the unmistakable sound of galloping four-legged beasts. In the distance a large group of creatures appeared, kicking up dust as their thundering hooves rapidly pounded the road. I could make out no chariots, so at first I thought it a large contingent of horse riders, rare in Kamit due to the scarcity of large northern horses. Then they came closer I was astonished to see what they really were.

As they ran past us, I gazed up from their pounding hooves to their thickly muscled horse bodies, to the stout human torsos and heads atop them. The creatures were half horse and half man. All of them carried clubs and looked very fierce, with large bushy eyebrows and thick beards of brown, yellow or gray. Their long manes, starting out as human hair on their heads, stretched down their human necks, down their human and horse torsos and ended in a normal horse's tail. A few wore protective leather helmets and vests over broad muscular chests.

There were dozens of them and I was totally breathless as they ran by. I had heard of such creatures in legends and had always dismissed them as myths. But since meeting Kam-Atef and coming to this strange land, I had already begun to rethink what was real and what was not.

My immediate concern, however was that they seemed to be heading for our destination, the mountain, and that they did not seem friendly at all. The boy was insisting that we not get back on the road, so we traveled instead through the nearby forest for the rest of the day. After bedding down for the night, we gazed down from the trees, observing a strange and fascinating sight.

Many more of the horse-men ran by in the darkness. Carrying torches, they galloped through the night in an eerie display of light and sound. They seemed to be in a hurry, and for some reason this worried me. I hoped that

SHADES OF MEMNON

their business would not interfere with my own.

Walking through the forest the next day, we spotted a group of men in the distance camped in a clearing. The boy noticed them first and pulled me into the bushes. Moments went by as we listened and watched. Then I saw a warrior patrolling the area who seemed familiar to me. After recognizing familiar voices, I realized that this was the group I had come to this land with. It took much coaxing, but I finally convinced the boy that it was safe to emerge and we approached the guard.

At first the man jumped back, startled, brandishing his spear, until he recognized me.

"Memnon!" he cried, calling me by the name the northerners preferred. He shouted again and more men came running. Surrounding us, they touched me and swore many oaths while escorting us into the camp. There Kho-An-Sa greeted me with a nod, smiling broadly as I approached him.

"Young panther," he said. "My...devices said you still lived."

"Indeed?" I replied.

Kho-An-Sa looked me up and down. "But they could not tell me your condition. Tell me, young panther, are you sound?"

I thumped my chest with my fist. "I am in one piece."

Kho-An-Sa smiled broadly again. "Excellent! Excellent, for we have much work to do. But first tell me, what happened after you were swept away from us?"

We sat down and I told Kho-An-Sa what had transpired. He nodded as I recounted the tale and seemed greatly impressed by the way I had handled myself. He was also interested in the boy after I told of his part in the story.

"Very good, Memnon," he said. "It seems my investment has been worth while."

He then gave the boy a curious look. "Interesting child," he said. "Very interesting."

The boy squirmed under Kho-An-Sa's gaze. It was clear he did not like the magician and I could not blame him, for the look the magician gave him was akin to a herder appraising livestock.

Then Kho-An-Sa stood up abruptly, saying, "I will reward the child later, Memnon. But now we have other matters to attend to. You and I must go up the mountain to take the sky-metal to the great blacksmith. There he shall forge you weapons like no others. But there is a problem."

"And what is this problem?" I asked.

Kho-An-Sa motioned for me to follow and we walked away from the camp. The boy stayed behind, ravenously eating a bowl of food given to him by the men. Soon we caught up with Cronn, who was patrolling the area like a great stalking beast. He showed no emotion at the sight of me, merely nodding a quick greeting. Then we continued on until we came to the edge of the forest.

Ahead the huge mountain loomed above a huge grassy plain. Movement attracted my eye to the far right, and there, hundreds of the horse-men we had seen earlier were milling about a large armed camp. Some jousted with their clubs while others ran in formation under commanders wearing helmets and leather jackets.

Kho-An-Sa tapped my shoulder, then pointed to the other side of the plain. There hundreds of other strange creatures moved about. They were tall and manlike, but had curling horns jutting from their heads. Shaggy hair covered their bodies and pointed beards jutted from their chins. Their legs, strangely bent, yet well muscled, were also hooved. I was looking at a contingent of goat-men.

These creatures jousted with one another also, but with spears, throwing javelins and slings. Just like the creatures they resembled, they were very agile, often jumping high into the air from a standing start. All wore leather corselets and kilts, with knives strapped to their sides. Wondering what was going on, I turned to Kho-An-Sa for answers.

"Memnon, what you see are preparations for war," Kho-An-Sa said.

"Why?" I asked. "Why are these creatures at war?"

Kho-An-Sa shook his head.

"That I do not know, young panther. I only know that neither will allow the other access to the trail up the mountain, which runs up from the middle of this plain. Nor will they allow any others access."

"Perhaps we could wait until after their war is over..." I started. Kho-An-Sa threw up his hands.

"No, young panther, that will not do. Our business must be taken care of within the next few days, during this, the month of Sekmet. We must go up this mountain today."

I shrugged my shoulders. "How are we to do this?"

"My devices can shield us from their sight for a few moments, long enough to get through their defenses and out of their sight. Come, let us return to camp and prepare."

We went back to the camp, where Kho-An-Sa told his men to wait for us and to avoid contact with any of the creatures. Gathering up some of his small vases and instruments, he put them into a sack, which he slung over his back. I carried the sky-metal and some other provisions in my bag. Then we both slipped into long, thick cloaks to withstand the cold of the higher parts of the mountain.

Before we left I tried to explain to the boy that he had to stay behind, but he either did not understand or had no wish to comply. Kho-An-Sa and I tried to leave several times, but the boy refused to stay behind. Finally, we had two warriors restrain him as we left. At the edge of the forest, Kho-An-Sa

SHADES OF MEMNON

explained to me what we were to do.

"I shall make us invisible. It will only last a few moments but it should be enough, Memnon," he said. "You and I will not be able to see each other when it takes effect, so you must hold on to my arm. Walk carefully and quickly and we will pass through these creatures without their ever knowing."

Kho-An-Sa reached into his bag, pulling out a handful of yellow, sweet smelling herbs. After crushing them into his mouth, he closed his eyes and began to chant. Suddenly, as I held onto his arm, he disappeared. Then I watched as the effect crept up my arm also, overtaking my chest, torso and legs. When I could no longer see myself, Kho-An-Sa's voice came from the air near me.

"Hold tight, Memnon," he said. "We go now."

Strolling out from among the trees, we started across the middle of the plain towards our destination. Guarding the path up the mountain, a line of horse-men stood a few cubits across from a line of goat-men. They gestured menacingly at each other, their mutual hatred apparent.

"Soon we will be between their lines Memnon," Kho-An-Sa whispered, "Walk very quietly."

Suddenly the field was in an uproar as the creatures cursed and snarled at something behind us. With a feeling of dread, I turned to look. There I saw my young friend, bursting from the protection of the forest. He began running across the field, stopping suddenly when he spied the field full of monsters. He then tried to turn back, but several creatures rushed to cut him off. I looked on with grave concern for the boy who had saved my life. He must have heard us speak of going up the mountain and somehow escaped the men in the camp. Now, determined to catch up with me, he had ran out to his doom.

As the child stood in breathless fear, a horse-man detached himself from the line, moving towards him with a huge club. Then a goat-man leapt forward to intercept him with a javelin. Feeling the tension in my body, Kho-An-Sa blurted out his orders. "Memnon, do not let go!" he hissed. "Keep going! Leave the child..."

Ignoring his orders, I let go of the magician's arm and dashed toward the boy.

"Memnon, no!" Kho-An-Sa shrieked.

Another roar went up as I materialized before the creatures in the field. They hesitated in surprise for a moment, which was all I needed to rush forward and scoop the child into my arms. Realizing what I had done, I looked around desperately for an escape route. But the forest was too far away and the field ahead was filled with hostile monsters.

On my right the horse-man galloped forward again, swinging his huge club, uttering a fearsome cry. On my left the goat-man bounded towards us, the point of his javelin aimed at my chest. Shoving the child to the ground, I crouched defensively above him, preparing to fight for our lives.

SHADES OF MEMNON

CHAPTER 9: "THIS IS THE SMITHY OF DAEDALUS"

My mind was racing, trying to find a strategy to fend off the terrible creatures, when suddenly an invisible hand pressed against my shoulder and the child and I both disappeared. As Kho-An-Sa yanked us away, our bestial attackers swept by without striking a blow.

Cries of surprise and frustration went up from both sides of the field as the magician's voice hissed into my ear. "Memnon, you fool!" he said. "Were you not so valuable, I would leave you to these creatures. Come! And stay close to me!"

"I will not leave the boy," I replied.

"Very well then, the boy comes also! Let us depart, now!"

Kho-An-Sa pressed himself between the child and I as we walked across the field toward the path up the mountain. The throngs of half-human creatures milled about in a state of confusion, wondering what had happened to us.

Within moments, however, their attention turned towards each other as both groups cast suspicious looks at the other. Shouts and curses flew forth between them, then a javelin from among the goat-men sailed into the midst of the horse-men. By the time we reached the path leading up the mountain, the creatures were fully engaged in a furious battle.

It was a strange thing, seeing creatures such as these exchanging blows. I had been informed by Kam-Atef that these things would occur, but still it did not prepare me for the awesome sight.

Leaping nimbly, the goat creatures dodged the clubs and hooves of the horse-men, deftly poking, thrusting and drawing much blood with their javelins. The horse-men were much slower, but when they did strike one of the goat-men with their huge clubs or powerful hooves, most did not rise again.

Shouting out cries of terrible bloodlust, they seemed bent not only on winning the field, but on each other's total slaughter.

Kho-An-Sa, the child and I kept close as we walked up the rocky path, the sound of the battle fading as we climbed higher and higher. Moments later I noticed the form of the magician flickering back into view. When I could finally see him clearly walking next to me, the boy and I also became visible and Kho-An-Sa released his grip upon us.

Perspiration dripped from the magician's face, and for a moment he seemed weak and dizzy. But he quickly composed himself, gazing at me with a bitter scowl.

"Young panther," he began venemously, "your disobedience jeopardized our entire enterprise and very nearly cost us out lives."

I looked down at the boy. His arms were wrapped around my waist and

SHADES OF MEMNON

159

he stared up at Kho-An-Sa in utter terror. I opened my mouth to speak, but the magician threw up his hand to silence me.

"I care not what you have to say," he continued. "I am the master here. Remember that the life of your sister is in my hands. Disobey me again and you will be punished. I will start by taking the heart of this child that you seem to care so much for. Is that clear?"

I looked away and said nothing.

"Is that clear young panther?"

"Yes," I answered. "Yes, it is clear."

We walked up the mountain path for hours. At first there was much vegetation in the form of small trees, bushes and thick green grasses. But as we climbed higher, the greenery gave way to rocks and brown grasses, while the air became colder and harder to breathe.

The cold winds blew stronger, causing Kho-An-Sa to pull his cloak tight. After noticing the boy shivering, I lifted him into my arms, drawing my cloak around us both to share the warmth. Soon we found ourselves enveloped in a thick white mist that clung to our clothing and made it impossible to see more than a few cubits ahead. We kept going slowly, picking our way carefully up the rocky path, peering ahead into the mist to keep our footing.

At one point I noticed movement in the dimness ahead, but it disappeared quickly and I said nothing. But as we plodded on, I glimpsed the dark figure again. This time it was much clearer, and I knew we were not alone on the path. I glanced at Kho-An-Sa and he nodded. He had seen it also.

"Do not be alarmed, young panther," the magician said. "They are merely the messengers of the blacksmith."

Walking on, I noticed one of the dark figures standing ahead of us. As we came closer, I saw that it was about the half the size of the boy. Though the mist still shrouded the figure, I could see that its body was round and shapeless, like a lump of unmolded clay. Its eyes were like large silver dishes and it seemed to have no feet. When we stopped a few cubits before it, a limb emerged from its shapeless body and formed into a hand.

Kho-An-Sa stepped forward and raised his hand in a gesture of greeting, and they began talking in a language that I had never heard. After a brief exchange, the creature's body melted like hot wax, directly into the ground without a trace. Moments later it rose from where it had disappeared, extending an arm again to beckon us onward. Kho-An-Sa nodded and we followed the creature up the path.

After a short while we emerged from the mist to find ourselves at the bottom of a sheer high cliff. We could go no further and I looked inquisitively at Kho-An-Sa. The magician gestured for patience as the small creature plodded up to the face of the cliff and touched the rocky surface.

A loud grinding noise pierced the air as a square slab of the cliff's face shook and receded. After grinding back a cubit, it slid to the side, revealing a long tunnel lit by strange flameless lights. We followed the creature inside as the opening closed ominously behind us.

Again we walked for a long time, following the endless lights along the walls, deep into the heart of the mountain, only to emerge in a huge cave filled with large spikes hanging from the ceiling and jutting up from the floor. We came to a halt in the middle of the cave, facing another smaller tunnel on the other side.

Suddenly a tapping sound echoed all around us. Peering down the tunnel ahead, we saw the shadowy figure of a man walking slowly toward us. He was hunched over, supported by a stout cane, which was the source of the tapping as it touched the floor of the cave. As he came closer I noticed he was surrounded by a dozen or more of the shapeless little beings, who scampered around his feet like well trained pets. He walked right up to us, his cane continuing to tap, until he came face to face with Kho-An-Sa.

"Greetings, magician," he said in perfect Kamitian.

"Greetings, great blacksmith," Kho-An-Sa replied.

"I will do the work if you can pay the fee," the blacksmith said. "Can you pay my fee?"

"That we shall see, great Daedalus," Kho-An-Sa answered. "That we shall see."

"Follow me," Daedalus said.

Daedalus turned back to the tunnel he'd come from and we followed closely. I observed him carefully in the dim light. He was an aged Tamahu with olive skin and small, piercing blue eyes. Never blinking, they flickered to and fro as he talked. A shiny bald head topped a broad torso equipped with hugely muscled arms and large hands.

He wore a long sleeveless garment of thick leather that reached below his knees, with boots to match and bracelets of the same leathery material. His skin was darkened in patches, no doubt from years before the heat of the forge. I noticed also that one of his legs was shorter than the other. Even so, he walked with a strong, sure-footed rhythm, punctuated by the tapping of his cane.

I wondered about the little creatures that followed him, happily milling about his feet. Some rubbed against our legs, giving off a strange, cool dampness. They seemed especially drawn to the boy, who kicked at them nervously, trying to shoo them away. Noticing this, Daedalus looked at the boy strangely, then spoke a sharp word, causing the creatures to melt into the floor and disappear.

"Excuse my friends, please," Daedalus begged. "Earth elementals can be very...touchy."

We continued down the tunnel until we emerged into a large chamber.

SHADES OF MEMNON

It was very hot, filled with the sounds of metal striking metal, and the little black creatures were scampering everywhere. Daedalus turned towards us, and with a sweeping motion of his hand, guided our eyes across the room.

"Welcome to my domain," he said. "This is the smithy of Daedalus."

The smell of melting ore filled the air and metal contraptions of many shapes and sizes were all around. From the ceiling hung a replica of a human skeleton, made of pure shining silver. One table contained swords and weapons of all kinds, all wondrously crafted with keen and flawless edges.

On another large table there were tiny metal animals made of bronze, moving about in small metal cages as if alive. A tiny metallic replica of a lion lurked near the cages as if standing guard, roaring a tiny roar as it paced jerkily back and forth.

A nearby wall had several holes bored into it, all glowing with different kinds of hot metals. A long trough on tall legs stood over the holes, its bottom glowing red hot. Tubes from different sections of the trough led to the opening of each hole, each dripping with flowing hot metal. There was also a large bellows poking into a tube along the side of the trough. Several of the elemental creatures jumped up and down upon it, causing air to enter the tube with a loud hissing sound. The bottom of the trough glowed bright red and yellow-white as more hot metal poured down into the holes.

Never had I seen such devices, not even in the metal shops of Kamit. Daedalus, leaning upon his cane, grinned proudly as he watched the looks of wonder upon our faces. The boy seemed especially taken by the goings-on in the shop, his face lighting up with the first smile I had seen as he gazed at the wondrous contraptions.

Kho-An-Sa let out a loud whistle, bowing low before the blacksmith. "Truly, it is as they say. The wonders of the shop of Daedalus are like the workings of the Neters."

"I can do the work if you can pay the fee," replied Daedalus. "What is the work?"

Kho-An-Sa gestured toward me and I stepped forward. Reaching into the sack on my back, he pulled out the sky-metal and handed it to the blacksmith.

"Ah, Sky-metal!" Daedalus cried, turning the rock over several times in his hands. "Very pure. Where did you get it?"

Kho-An-Sa shifted a little, rubbing his chin for a moment before reluctantly opening his mouth to speak, but Daedalus held up his hand to interrupt him.

"Never mind," Daedalus said sharply. "It is not my business where you acquired the ore. I only asked because it is the purest I have ever seen. What is it you wish?"

"Weapons," Kho-An-Sa said. "Weapons of a most wondrous sort. Weapons to conduct the life force in a way that will allow its bearer to defeat any foe, man, beast or monster."

Leaning upon his cane, Daedalus stared at the ore for long moments then said, "It is true that sky-metal, forged properly can be a conductor of life force, but who is to wield these weapons?"

Kho-An-Sa pointed to me.

"He is to wield them." Daedalus looked at me incredulously. "But he is a mere youth. The bearer of such weapons would have to be trained to channel such power, and trained in the ancient tradition of the greatest warriors and kings. He would surely die otherwise."

Kho-An-Sa smiled. "He has received this training," he replied. "And he is the son of the Great Memnon of Troy."

Daedalus leaned forward on his cane, looking at me closely. "Yes! Yes I see it now!" he exclaimed. "The son of the great Memnon of Troy!"

Then he looked at Kho-An-Sa suspiciously.

"But why would you, a Servant of the Serpents, want to arm the son of your greatest enemy with weapons such as this?"

Kho-An-Sa looked at the blacksmith gravely.

"I have my reasons, which you need not concern yourself with.... Can you do the work?"

Daedalus raised the sky-metal to his eyes and asked, "Can you pay the fee?"

"What is the fee?" asked Kho-An-Sa.

"Come," replied the blacksmith, "let us enjoy a meal and we will discuss it."

Daedalus led us to another torch-lit chamber containing a large table and several chairs. Two young women emerged from an adjacent chamber. Daedalus spoke to them briefly, and they scampered back the way they had come. They were young and pretty Tamahu women, and I was surprised to see them in the company of the crippled old blacksmith.

Moments later they came back with several platters of food and mugs of drink. My plate had only vegetables and nuts, while the others dined on small birds. Daedalus looked at us and shook his head.

"I hope that these meager offerings satisfy your hunger, my friends," he said, "my stores are growing light, due to the situation at the foot of my mountain. I might not be able to offer you much more than this."

"You mean the war between the monsters," I replied.

"Indeed," the blacksmith answered. "It is a grave situation."

"Tell me, blacksmith, why do they war?" Kho-An-Sa asked.

"It is part of the madness that has overtaken this land," sighed Daedalus.

SHADES OF MEMNON

"Those creatures were normal men a short time ago. The goat-men, called Satyrs, were common herders who dwelled near the foot of the mountain. The horse-men, called Centaurs, were mounted nomads who habitually raided them."

"It is the Reckoning," said Kho-An-Sa.

"Yes," answered Daedalus. "The Reckoning. I have seen them come and go over many thousands of years. Mankind likes to forget about them, never learning the lessons they are intended to teach, choosing instead to push these dark times into the realm of myth and folktale. But it is real, and it will keep happening until mankind changes its ways, or is destroyed."

"Or until the proper powers take control," added Kho-An-Sa.

Daedalus looked at him and suddenly there was strong tension between them. Then the blacksmith shook his head sadly.

"I have seen many attempts similar to the one your coalition plans, Kho-An-Sa. They always end in disaster."

"This time we will succeed," retorted Kho-An-Sa angrily.

"That remains to be seen, magician," the blacksmith shot back.

Both men glowered, until I spoke up to stop their argument. "How have you seen the Reckoning manifested over the years, great blacksmith?" I asked.

Taking the chance I offered, Daedalus leaned back in his seat before answering me. "When the negative forces of the Taut overwhelm a land, it changes those who are spiritually unprepared, bringing the animal nature within them to flesh. It changes their bodies to match their thoughts. Then they fight endlessly, savagely, compelled by their lusts, greed and pettiness."

"Unless they are shaped and molded by men of power," quipped Kho-An-Sa.

Ignoring the magician's comment, Daedalus took a bite of his food and continued. "Some, like the Wolven, those terrible wolf-creatures who dwell to the east, make actual pacts with the dark forces. They then become what Kamitians call Sebau fiends, knowing servants of Set. Eaters of human flesh and drinkers of human blood. Fortunately, there are less Wolven than there are of the others, for they are surely the most fearsome."

"I have had some dealings with them," I reported grimly.

"Then you are fortunate to be among the living," replied the blacksmith. "My concerns now lie primarily with the hooved beings. These creatures, when they were men, brought me food and other items in exchange for my services. If their war continues much longer, I shall starve here in my mountain."

"What do you plan to do?" asked Kho-An-Sa.

"This is the fee that you must pay for my work," the blacksmith replied.

"One of the groups must win this war, so that some trade can resume."

"And what would you have us do?" I asked.

"Simple." Daedalus replied, tapping his finger on the table. "In exchange for my forging your weapons, you must align yourselves with the Satyrs, who are far less savage than the Centaurs. Make certain that they win this war and gain control over the area."

Kho-An-Sa and I looked at each other.

"We will do this," the magician said.

"And one other thing," Daedalus said, pointing to the boy. "Who does this child belong to?"

I placed my hand on the child's head, jostling his golden hair. "His people were killed by the Wolven, he is under my protection."

Daedalus stared into the child's face. "I sense something special about him. I have need of an apprentice. Leave me the child, that I might teach him the craft, and your debt to me will be paid."

"Surely," replied Kho-An-Sa.

"No!" I cried.

Kho-An-Sa looked at me menacingly.

"Do not challenge me on this, Memnon..."

Daedalus looked at us both, then pointed to the boy. "Let us see what the boy has to say." He then addressed the child in the local Tamahu language. At first the boy was distraught and seized my arm, looking fearfully at the two older men. But as Daedalus kept talking, the fear changed to a look of curiosity.

Finally the blacksmith reached into a pocket of his garment and brought forth a tiny golden replica of a panther. After placing the tiny feline on the table, he tapped its back with the tip of his finger and the panther's head reared back, letting out a tiny roar, and then it ran toward the boy. The child caught it as it leapt from the table and looked up with his eyes beaming with joy. Daedalus spoke to him again and the boy nodded happily.

"It is settled," the blacksmith said. "While I forge your weapons the child will learn to construct wonders such as the toy he holds. If at the end of your time here he would learn more, he will stay. It will be his choice."

I observed the boy carefully. Looking into his eyes, I could see the happiness he felt. Kho-An-Sa looked satisfied and Daedalus grinned triumphantly.

"Then it is done," said the blacksmith. "I have had my women prepare chambers for your rest. Let us retire now. Tomorrow, the forging begins."

The next day we stood before the ore-melting device of Daedalus, marveling at his skill and precision. First he pulverized the rock and melted the sky-metal away from the refuse. Then he poured the pure metal back into the trough for the final phase of heating. Kho-An-Sa had told me what I was to do at this stage, and I stepped up to the trough and held my hand over it. The magician took a small knife and sliced my palm. I ground my teeth in pain as the blood flowed into the metal, hissing loudly.

After long moments, the blacksmith released the first portion of the metal onto a slab of rock and put it to the side. Three more portions flowed from the trough until all the metal was released. After letting it cool, he placed each piece atop a large slab of metal and struck them with a huge hammer. Over and over again he pounded them, until the pieces took on elongated shapes. Then the blacksmith stepped back. It was now up to Kho-An-Sa to empower the metal.

The magician stepped up to the slab. Closing his eyes, he waved his hands over it and rocked back and forth. Resting his head in the world of the spirits, he then began to chant. At first it was low, but gradually it grew louder and fiercer in intensity.

"Fire lover," Kho-An-Sa cried, "fierce one, lover of slaughterings, devoted lady who comes in the guise of Sekmet, slaughterer of Sebau fiends at eventide. By force of the might of Ra, make all fiends burn to dust."

As the magician continued to chant, the already hot air in the chamber grew hotter, and after long minutes, his face was covered in perspiration and his clothing was soaked through. Kho-An-Sa continued on, until after a full hour of chanting, the chamber suddenly turned cooler. Looking closely at the space before the magician, I saw the reason why. The heat had gathered before him in the form of a red swirling mist as he continued to chant.

"Fire lover, fierce one, lover of slaughterings..."

The blacksmith and I stepped back as the red mist coalesced into a large human-like form. Then my eyes widened as a lion's head appeared upon the figure. I feared for all of our lives, for Kho-An-Sa had dared invoke one of the most terrible forces in creation—Uachet, the heat of creation, in her guise as the war Neter Sekmet.

The hot mist thickened and Sekmet's head became more defined. Then her womanly body solidified, emphasizing her full, round breasts, voluptuous hips and finally her thickly muscled legs. She threw her head back, emitting a terrible roar that shook the entire chamber. Kho-An-Sa ceased chanting and looked at me. I remembered his instructions, but hesitated.

"Memnon!" Kho-An-Sa shrieked. "I cannot hold her for long. Give her the blood, now!"

Still I hesitated. In awe of the fearsome image, I could not move.

"Memnon, now!" he cried again. "She must have the blood, or she will kill us all!"

I stepped forward as Sekmet roared again, raising her claws to strike Kho-An-Sa. But I thrust my arm forward and offered my hand, still dripping with blood. Her fiery eyes veered from the magician to me, and she seized my hand in her burning grasp.

Bringing my hand up to her mouth, she opened her huge maw as if to bite it off. But then she saw the trickle of crimson and hastily licked the wound with a tongue of hot blue flame. A flash of heat rushed through my body and I momentarily lost my senses.

When I opened my eyes again I was on the floor. Looking up, I saw Kho-An-Sa chanting once more, as the great Neter Sekmet danced before him. It was the Kamitian war dance, and though she floated in the air, she was bobbing and stepping around the room as if on solid ground. She danced all the moves for long minutes, until Kho-An-Sa gestured toward the four pieces of metal.

Sekmet then stopped, bowed her head obediently and changed back into red mist. Kho-An-Sa gestured again and the mist separated into four streams, sweeping down to the metal and enveloping all the pieces. Suddenly the metal turned bright red and shook violently. Kho-An-Sa stood proudly as he gazed down upon them.

Then the wizard stepped back and Daedalus took his place at the forging slab once again. Lowering his head, he spoke a word I could not hear and made a sign in the air. Immediately the metal stopped shaking and the red color faded. He then seized the pieces with his tools and resumed pounding them. Each time the hammer came down, I heard a low growl as Sekmet was being tempered and forged into the very essence of the weapons.

We watched the smith at work for hours that day and for days afterwards as he crafted the weapons with all the skill at his command. During the forging process, he imbedded the colorful jewels of the eight great Neteru into the hilt of each blade, so that they would conduct all the vibrations of the life force. Then he turned his attention to the edges of the weapons.

Daedalus went to a corner of his smithy, returning with a small glowing stone of an intensely yellow hue. With great care and reverence, the blacksmith ground the blades of the four weapons against it for hours on end, checking them carefully after each stroke. Though Kho-An-Sa and I inspected the blades and deemed them finished several times, still they were not good enough for the smith.

"No," Daedalus insisted, " these blades must slice the very breeze from the air, the heat from the flame, the breath from the lips that breathe it."

It was difficult to tell time in the heart of the mountain, where neither the rays of Aten nor the beams of the moon penetrated. But we slept and awakened 15 times before the day came that Daedalus pronounced the weapons ready.

Kho-An-Sa and I rushed into the blacksmith's workroom, after being summoned from our resting chambers by one of his strange servants. There

SHADES OF MEMNON

upon a large table lay the weapons—a long sword, a short sword, a dagger and a small throwing knife. All gleamed with the brilliance of polished white silver, the color of the forged sky-metal. The jewels in the hilt of each weapon shined brightly in the torchlight and beside each weapon lay a finely crafted scabbard of rich leather. Daedalus stood beside the table with a satisfied smile.

"These weapons are quite possibly my finest work. The purity of the sky-metal allowed me to hone them to a precision unknown even in my experience."

"Yes, you have done well, blacksmith," replied Kho-An-Sa. "These weapons will be feared and revered by many."

"Yes they shall, provided the bearer can provide them with the proper force," replied Daedalus. "Are you sure that this young panther, even though he is son of the Memnon who fought at Troy, is prepared to wield such powerful arms?"

Gazing at me from head to toe, Kho-An-Sa answered the blacksmith. "He has proven himself a great fighter, especially since coming to these lands, blacksmith. I have had a master of the Short Path to the Knowledge of Rau temper him as you did these weapons. They are imbued with his own blood and are therefore a part of him. He is, I assure you, ready to wield these weapons.

Daedalus nodded.

"Very well. Young Memnon, step forward."

I took two long strides and stood before the blacksmith. He then lifted the long sword, holding it inches away from my outstretched hands. Suddenly I felt a strange tug upon my body as my whole being cried out to hold the weapon. Daedalus noticed this and nodded again.

"Yes, yes," he cried enthusiastically. "These are indeed your weapons, young Memnon. Forged with your own blood, they are a part of you now."

The sword seemed more beautiful than anything I had ever seen. My mouth grew dry and I reached for it, but the blacksmith jerked it back.

"But beware," he said. "Never have there been weapons such as these. As receptacles of such power, they are a grave responsibility. Do you understand this?"

I swallowed hard. At that point, I would say anything to possess the weapons.

"Yes." I cried.

"Good," replied the blacksmith. "These are the very Claws of Sekmet, empowered with the ka of she who lives to slaughter. The jewels will tell you what power drives your enemy, so that you will know how to fight it. Again, are you sure you are ready for such power?"

"Yes, give them to me!" I cried.

The smith passed the hilt of the blade into my eager hands and as soon as the sword touched my fingers, the Rau rose from my center, near the bottom of my belly. Flowing up through my body, it passed into the sword and back again into me, circulating like blood, pulsating like the very heart within me.

When I first grasped the weapon, I felt that its weight was of medium heft for a weapon of this size. But as the Rau rushed through me, the swords weight disappeared. I could scarcely believe what I was feeling. Waving the weapon before me as I gripped its hilt, it felt like one of my own limbs. Daedalus and Kho-An-Sa both smiled, looking on approvingly.

"Can you feel it?" the blacksmith asked. "Can you feel that it is a part of you?"

"Yes," I answered. "Yes!"

"Focus your Rau, young panther," Kho-An-Sa said. "Focus it into the sword."

This time I consciously pushed the life force from my body into the sword, and the weapon pulsated. Looking at it carefully, I saw no movement, yet it throbbed like the blood in my veins. The blacksmith handed me the short sword and the same thing happened. Grasping the two weapons, I felt no weight as they seemed to meld into my hands, becoming part of my flesh, one with my bones.

SHADES OF MEMNON

Lifting my head, I tilted it back and my mouth opening in a silent scream of ecstasy. My life force now pulsated from the tip of my toes, to the top of my head and into the very tip of each weapon. I could feel the razor sharp edges the way I felt the tips of my own fingers and toes and I could feel the rumble of a low growl emerging from them. Only then did I know for certain that what the blacksmith had said was true: These weapons were indeed a part of me and they were empowered with a ka of mighty power. I had at my service the spirit of retribution feared by all men and beasts; I possessed the very Claws of Sekmet.

And as I stood there holding the Claws, the pulse of the Rau running through me, I felt a familiar sensation, not unlike what I had felt that day on the deck of the ship. This time the feeling was even more intense, and I was both strangely elated and unsettled.

Compelled to feel them in motion, I began whirling the weapons in defensive patterns, only to discover another intoxicating aspect of the blades: As they cut through the air the growl transformed into a high pitched scream that echoed throughout the chamber. This was Sekmet's scream for blood.

Suddenly I wanted to run down the mountain and single-handedly slay all the creatures who threatened the well-being of the blacksmith. I knew it was not right, but my will could not fight the compulsion. With these new, deadly weapons in my grasp, the Rau pulsating within me and the urgency of Sekmet's scream, I felt a strong urge to make war.

SHADES OF MEMNON

CHAPTER 10: "SHOW NO MERCY"

For the next several days, Kho-An-Sa, Daedalus and I discussed ideas for ending the war between the creatures at the foot of the mountain. After consulting with many of his elemental servants, Daedalus hit upon a daring plan that would allow us to repay him for the forging of my weapons. On the morning of our last day with the blacksmith, we sat around a table in his smithy, finalizing the plans for the bold actions we intended to take.

"Then it is agreed," Daedalus said, leaning forward over the table, "that these are the steps that must be taken to put an end to the conflict. Kho-An-Sa and I nodded as Daedalus went on, repeating the plan once again.

"My servants tell me that the wife and child of the leader of the Satyrs were taken by Wolven two nights ago. In order to ingratiate yourselves with them, you, Memnon, must go into the town of the Wolven and get them out, provided they still live."

"Understood," I said. "And it must be done during the day, when the Wolven are at their weakest."

"Correct," replied the blacksmith. "And you, Kho-An-Sa, will use your powers to cause a distraction in the town of the Wolven to assist Memnon, and, if you can, you should capture their leader for the next phase of the plan."

"Yes," said Kho-An-Sa. "I will bind and hold him until nearly nightfall, then turn him over to the Centaurs. The Wolven will track their leader and attack the horse-men during the night. Then we attack at daybreak with the Satyrs. With their forces surely weakened by their battle with the Wolven, the Centaurs will be defeated and your troubles resolved."

"Yes," replied the blacksmith. "If this works, I am sure my woes will be alleviated. When the battle is done, return here and I will give the weapons their final component, the gift of Infinite Return."

I fingered the hilts of my weapons, which were now strapped at my side. In the days since they were given to me, my whole being had been flowing with Rau, with the swords acting as a strong focus for my life force. What else, I wondered, could the blacksmith bestow upon them?

"Infinite Return," I asked, "what is that?"

"You will find out after this task is over, young Memnon," replied Daedalus. "For now, you need know only this: it is a gift I have bestowed upon only two other warriors over the centuries. It is a gift all warriors dream of having. It is a gift that will be yours if you complete this task successfully."

"Then let us be about it," declared Kho-An-Sa, as we rose to begin preparations.

SHADES OF MEMNON

As we strolled from the chamber, I noticed my young friend at a table, working intensely. Looking up briefly, he smiled, then went back to tinkering with his small, crudely shaped models of animals. They were far from the polished, lifelike specimens of the blacksmith, but were remarkably well done. I thought briefly of bidding him farewell. Then, thinking better of it, I simply left him to his work.

After we gathered our essentials, Daedalus led us to a tunnel that we had not noticed before. One of his little servants stood before the entrance, holding a torch in its inky black hand.

"This tunnel ends near your camp," the blacksmith said. "After you have completed your tasks, come back to the entrance and knock four times. My servant will open it and lead you back to me. Farewell for now."

Kho-An-Sa and I bowed to the blacksmith, then followed his servant into the tunnel. We walked for two or three hours, following the torch held by the creature ahead. Finally, the light stopped and the little creature pushed against a wall, causing a section of rock to pull back. There before us was a shallow cave, light streaming in through its entrance. Kho-An-Sa and I stepped through, and the hole closed silently behind us.

We emerged from the cave with our hands over our eyes, for the light of Aten, after so many days in the dimness of the mountain, was dazzling. Looking around, I found that the blacksmith was correct. We were indeed quite near the camp. In fact, I could hear the familiar voices of some of Kho-An-Sa's men.

We walked toward them, and within moments spotted a guard patrolling the area. He greeted us reverently, looking at my weapons with great interest.

Inside the camp Kho-An-Sa gathered his warriors before him, shouting orders in the Tamahu language. Several men went away rapidly, returning moments later bearing ten leather cases. As they carefully undid the straps, my eyes widened. The cases concealed 10 composite bows.

I had not known that Kho-An-Sa's men were in possession of such weapons. I had only seen one bow in this entire land, and it was only a simple one, made perhaps of sapling wood. These composite bows, with their sophisticated melding of bone and hard and soft woods, would be accurate and deadly in the hands of a competent archer. They alone could kill dozens of unwary enemies before they knew what had hit them.

The camp was alive with movement and sound as the warriors made preparations for battle. Cronn seemed especially eager at the prospect of fighting and, after speaking to the magician, sat down to sharpen his huge blade with a large flat stone. Shouting orders to his men, Kho-An-Sa packed his pouch and changed his clothing while I discarded my cloak and donned a long brown tunic, padded for war. As I strapped on my weapons Kho-An-Sa beckoned me towards him.

"Come, young panther," he said as I joined him. "It is time to repay the blacksmith."

Cronn joined us and we walked away from the camp, heading east toward the town of the Wolven. After a while we happened upon a well-worn path, covered with the footprints of the wolf creatures. There were also human footprints, signs of struggle and blood.

We followed the path until midday, when the town finally loomed into view. The settlement, perched atop a broad hill, was surrounded by a tall, spike-topped wall. The tops of dozens of dwellings could be seen with smoke rising from the fires burning inside. Toward the middle of the settlement, towering over all the rest, stood a large structure of solid black, painted with blood-red symbols.

The hill itself was dotted with wooden stakes, well sharpened and positioned to impede a mass attack. Because of this, the only safe way up was the small path on which we walked, which ended before a large wooden door. It was of the type controlled by ropes and pulleys, and now stood raised for the day's comings and goings.

Two guards stood near this opening, holding spears and scanning the area diligently. I was surprised that they seemed to be normal men. "Kho-An-Sa," I asked. "Why are the guards not Wolven?"

"Oh they are, young panther," the magician replied. "Remember, some of those who make pacts with Set gain the ability to change at will. Subterfuge is one of Set's greatest gifts, as I shall now demonstrate."

The magician then reached into his bag, pulling out a handful of the herbs he had used before to become invisible. "When you see the guards fall, young panther, come to the gate. When the fires start, go in and find the female Satyr and her child. You may be heavily opposed. Show no mercy if you wish to come out of this alive."

With that, Kho-An-Sa crushed the herbs into his mouth and disappeared. Then Cronn, who had been holding onto his arm, also dissolved before my eyes.

I observed the guards in the distance for a few moments. Suddenly one of them dropped his spear, seizing his chest in pain. He then fell to the ground, a pool of blood forming around him. When the other guard bent over to assist him, there was a loud chopping sound and his head went rolling down the hill.

Taking this as my signal, I ran to the gate and peered in. There the townspeople went about their business, oblivious to the fate of the guards. Suddenly a terrible odor assailed my senses and I nearly retched. I had never smelled anything like it, and if not for my assigned task I would have fled with all haste away from it.

As I shook my head to clear my distressed nostrils, a loud cry went up in

SHADES OF MEMNON

the village. Peeking in again, I saw people running towards the far side of the town, where a huge flame had erupted, engulfing several structures.

Taking advantage of this distraction, I ran through the gate, reaching for my Claws as I went. As soon as my hand touched the hilts of the weapons, Rau rushed from my body to the sword and I was filled by an intense bloodlust.

I then scanned the area, for the location of the prisoners. Suddenly I heard a terrible scream and ran in its direction. The scream rang out several more times, drawing me to a long wooden building a short distance away. As I neared it a man stepped forward menacingly, brandishing a spear and shouting at me. I tried to ignore him and keep going, but he lifted the spear as if to throw and I was forced to turn and face him.

With a terrible howl he then sprang toward me, his face elongating and his limbs becoming hairy with each stride. He stopped a few cubits short of me, growling fearsomely and looking exactly like the beasts from the doomed village. But this time I was not afraid.

Stepping forward boldly, I cut the blade of his spear away with one swift stroke. When he pulled the shaft back in surprise, I lunged, plunging my blade through his belly. He opened his mouth to cry out, but I flicked my short Claw across his hairy throat and he only made a painful gurgling sound. I was running toward the building as his body hit the ground.

As I neared the building I heard the horrified scream again. Then I kicked the door open, to be met by an intense blast of that terrible odor. My eyes watered profusely, and when I finally blinked them clear I saw the most horrible sight. There before me was a dim, torch-lit chamber. A very large, surprised man hovered over a table, holding a huge carving knife. He wore a gray apron that was soaked in blood, and upon the table before him lay a small Satyr child. Its mouth bound tightly with cloth, tears streamed from its eyes and blood spurted in torrents from its four severed limbs. The child was being butchered alive.

Looking around quickly I saw a cage filled with crying, whimpering Satyr children, and my blood fairly boiled with rage. I stared at the butcher, amazed at the cruelty displayed before me, as he smiled malevolently and seized another knife. Then he walked slowly toward me, transforming into the largest Wolven I had yet seen. He was so tall that he had to bend down to keep from hitting his head against the ceiling, and his arms were extremely long. An evil snarl rumbled across his lips as he began slashing the knives at me.

As I blocked his strokes I observed well his blade technique. His quick, precise moves indicated that his work gave him considerable skill with the blades, but my weapons were longer, and I struck back faster, cutting him in several places. Intense moments went by, during which I wounded him many times. But for some reason he did not call out. Instead he kept on coming, despite the pain and injuries I inflicted upon him.

Finally, in a desperate attempt to overcome me, he rushed in with his long arms flailing. My swords now screaming, I blocked the knives rapidly, sending sparks flying in every direction. Then I sidestepped quickly, and with one whirling stroke, sliced both claw-like hands from his arms. His weapons clattered to the floor, black blood spurted from his wounds and his head shot back in a howl of shock and pain. I flicked my short Claw once again, slicing his throat as I had his comrade, cutting short his painful cries. His heavy body hit the floor and I stepped over it toward the table. Sheathing my weapons, I bent to examine the child, but found it was too late. The poor thing lay still and cold, dead from the blood loss and the shock.

Footsteps approached the building and I stepped back into the shadows beside the door. A Wolven entered the room, looking around and sniffing in canine fashion. Seeing his dead companion, he bent to examine him, whimpering and moaning in grief. His pointed ears perked to attention just as I stole upon him from behind, but before he could move my blade came down and he joined his cruel companion.

Striding across the room, I sliced the bars of the wooden cage open. As the children crawled out I called the name of the female I had come to retrieve. "Dila?" I called anxiously "Dila?"

A small child stepped forward, tears streaming down its face, pointing to a door on the far side of the room. I walked over and kicked it open to find another room lit by a single torch, where a female Satyr was tied to a post. As she looked up fearfully I lowered my weapons.

"Dila?" I asked in a low voice.

She nodded and I cut her loose. Then the little Satyr that led me to her ran into her arms. I had found my prizes.

Putting a finger to my lips, I signaled for silence and helped her to her hooved feet. Then we gathered the others and headed for the door. Passing the butchering table on the way, Dila ran over to it, weeping and crying over the body of the dead Satyr child. I was forced to pull her away so that we could go on.

We peered out into the village to find shouting and bustling in all directions. The people ran with pots of water towards flames that now engulfed half the town. Kho-An-Sa and Cronn had done their work well. We now had the diversion we needed.

I hustled Dila and the kids out, planning to sneak them from building to building towards the gate. But several men spotted us and threw down their pots. Howling terribly, they transformed into Wolven as they ran towards us. We were still well away from the gate, so I pushed Dila and the children towards it.

SHADES OF MEMNON

"Run!" I cried. "Don't look back, just run!"

As they took off for the gate, I glanced at the hilt of my weapons. Anger and bloodlust had distracted me from noticing before, but the emerald gem was gleaming brightly, identifying the Wolven as negative aspects of the Neter Sebek. As several of them rushed towards me, I recited the proper chant from The Book of Knowing the Creatures of the Taut and the effects were instantaneous.

The creatures became disoriented, stumbling and slipping against each other. I then pulled Rau from my center, pushed it into my blades, then hacked away at the confused monsters as the voice of Sekmet screamed.

Two fell before me, then three, four and five, until only one creature was left standing. Injured and astonished, he took several steps back, howling for assistance. Others in the distance now ran to assist him, calling for more help as they came.

Despite the strength of the chants, I knew their greater numbers spelled my doom, so I turned and ran for the still-open gate. But another Wolven had seen me and ran to the gate first. Immediately he began unwinding the rope from the pulley, trying to drop the gate and lock me inside. I knew if he succeeded my fate would indeed be sealed.

Running as fast as I could, I leaped upon him just in time, plunging my long Claw through his side and seizing the final bit of rope. Kicking the dead creature aside, I peered through the gateway. In the distance I saw Dila and the children, disappearing into the forest to safety.

Satisfied that they were out of danger, I glanced behind me to find hordes of Wolven closing in. Spears poised and claws extended, they were eager to avenge their friends and dine upon a meal of Memnon. Sheathing my long blades, I pulled out my dagger as a spear shot past my head. Then I seized the rope attached to the pulley, yanked it tight and slashed it with the blade.

The huge gate came plunging down and I shot straight up to the top of the gate, just as the Wolven pounced on the spot where I'd been standing. Pausing briefly to cut the rope from the gate, I leapt over amidst a hail of spears. Landing safely on the other side, I took off for the forest, a satisfied smile upon my face.

I caught up with Dila and the children on the path. Shortly thereafter, we came upon Kho-An-Sa and the giant Cronn, who held a struggling figure, wrapped in a thick cloth over his shoulder. Kho-An-Sa looked very pleased.

"Well done, Memnon," he said. "Let us be away quickly before they give pursuit."

"It will be a while before they can," I replied. "The fire still rages, and I extracted the rope from their gate."

Kho-An-Sa nodded. "Very well done, indeed."

SHADES OF MEMNON

We made haste down the path, looking behind frequently for signs of pursuit, which never came. Soon we arrived back at the camp, where Cronn threw his struggling burden down, placing his foot upon it triumphantly. The other warriors gathered around, intensely interested in the struggling bundle. After giving Dila and the children water and food, I came over to investigate the prisoner myself.

"He is their leader," Kho-An-Sa said. "We took him directly from his great hall as he directed the firefighting efforts. His Wolven brethren will surely try to retrieve him tonight."

"What will we do with him until then?" I asked, watching the bound figure writhe upon the ground.

"Cronn will watch over him until nearly nightfall, when he will be delivered to the Centaurs. They have reason to hate the Wolven themselves, and will be glad to receive him. Time now to return Dila and the Satyr children."

Our party split into two groups, with half the warriors going with Kho-An-Sa and I to bring the goat-creatures back to their people and the other half staying with Cronn to deliver the prisoner to the Centaurs.

As we approached their camp, several Satyrs rushed towards us with javelins leveled, but Dila and the children ran forward and they lowered their weapons. Kho-An-Sa and I waited at the edge of the camp as they entered amid loud cheers and happy greetings.

Moments later Dila and two Satyr men came forth, beckoning us to follow them. We were led to the middle of the camp, where a large Satyr sat before a fire, playing with Dila's young child. He put the child down as we were led before him and stood up. Raising a hairy hand, he greeted us graciously.

Kho-An-Sa answered him and I bowed. He then walked over to us, placing one large hand on each of our shoulders. Then he gestured for us to join him by his fire.

Kho-An-Sa, who understood his language with some difficulty, introduced him as Ladin, leader of the Satyrs. He was much like the rest of his comrades: golden hair, a barrel chest, curled horns jutting from his forehead and a pointed beard. But by his regal bearing and intelligence one could tell that he was their leader.

He and Kho-An-Sa talked for some time, with my name coming up frequently as well as the name of Daedalus. At one point Kho-An-Sa pointed to the edge of the camp, where the rest of his warriors waited. Ladin immediately dispatched an assistant, who came back moments later, leading the magician's men.

Kho-An-Sa shouted an order and some of them stepped forward, bearing the leather pouches that contained the composite bows. They untied the straps and pulled them out amid low whistles and cries of surprise from the

Satyrs. Ladin's eyes grew large as a bow was handed to him. He turned the weapon over several times, plucking the string and flexing the wood. Kho-An-Sa made galloping gestures with his hands, then feigned being hit by arrows, causing the Satyrs close by to burst out laughing. Then, after another brief exchange, the two leaders shook hands vigorously. The alliance had been made.

For the rest of the day Ladin and the magician made preparations for the attack against the Centaurs. Arrows were soaked in pitch for setting fires, Satyrs sparred with Kho-An-Sa's warriors and even practiced shooting the composite bows.

I sat in the shade observing the goat-people with great interest. They seemed an easy-going, fun-loving lot when not fighting, with a penchant for jokes and mischief. And their women and children were given much respect and not abused, always the mark of a civilized people. I also noticed that they ate no meat—only grains, fruit and vegetables, which suited me just fine. Why the Taut would take such good-natured people I did not know, but I was glad to help them oppose the evil beings who threatened them. When the orb of Aten glided toward the horizon and the shadows lengthened, Cronn joined us at the camp with the rest of the warriors. He had successfully given the leader of the Wolven over to the Centaurs. Now we had only to wait.

We sat around the campfire for hours, waiting for signs of the attack. Finally, when the quarter-moon was high overhead, we heard the first shouts. Moments later the air was pierced with awful howls and terrified screams as the Wolven leaped from the shadows upon the horse-men.

From across the field we saw torches moving to and fro as the Centaurs fought desperately against the savage night beasts. All through the night sounds of the battle raged on, causing much pleasure among the Satyrs around us. I, however, found no joy in the thought of anyone facing the Wolven hordes, especially at night.

At one point a screaming Centaur came running over to our side of the field. Shouting hysterically, he seemed out of his mind with fright. The Satyrs immediately surrounded him, their javelins poised. His entire body covered with blood and horrible wounds, the Centaur seemed unmindful of the imminent danger as he whimpered and wailed for sanctuary. Getting down on his horse knees, the creature begged pitifully for help, but the Satyrs only gazed at him coldly. Finally, Ladin gave the signal and javelins pierced his throat and heart. His wailing ceased as he fell down dead upon the field.

Several other Centaurs galloped over during the night, only to receive the same treatment. After a while I could not bear to see any more and excused myself to the far side of the camp. Sitting quietly against a stack of supplies, my chin tucked into the palm of my hand, I had the distinct feeling

SHADES OF MEMNON

that what I was involved in was very wrong. The idea came to me to try to contact Kam-Atef for advice.

Slowing my breathing, I closed my eyes, thinking the name and recalling the image of the great serpent. Over and over again I called, but there was no answer. Finally I gave up and drifted off to sleep.

I was shaken awake to find the rays of Aten washing over the landscape. Kho-An-Sa stood over me, pointing across the field. "Come, Memnon," he said "the battle begins."

We hastened across the field just in time to see the Satyrs meet the first line of Centaurs. After clashing viciously for several minutes, the goat-men fell back and Kho-An-Sa's archers rose up with notched arrows. After one volley from the powerful composite bows, several Centaurs fell, clutching at chests and necks pierced through. Another volley cut into them they wavered. Then a third hit them and their line fell completely apart.

The Satyrs then swarmed into the enemy camp shouting victoriously as they stabbed and threw their javelins. The Centaurs, weakened and injured from the night-long battle with the Wolven, went down quickly before their fresh opponents. Meanwhile the archers picked off Centaurs at will, while Cronn waded into the midst of the carnage, hacking and slashing with his huge sword.

Groups of female Centaurs and their young huddled together as the battle raged around them, crying and shaking in fear as the rout quickly changed into a slaughter. Feeling sorry for the innocents, I turned away from the carnage and walked off the field. Kho-An-Sa watched as I left.

"Memnon, where are you going?" he asked.

"To the cave where we are to meet Daedalus' servant," I answered. "You don't need me here."

The magician said nothing as I walked into the forest. Soon I was back at the mouth of the cave. Seating myself before it, I listened to the sounds of the battle. Suddenly I heard the galloping of hooves close by and a Centaur stumbled into view.

Leaning weakly against the trunk of a large tree, he was cut and bleeding from many small wounds. Looking up, he spotted me and raised his huge club menacingly. I was about to pull my Claws to defend myself, when the creature moaned loudly and the club fell from his shaking hands. Then he toppled over and hit the ground heavily.

I walked over cautiously for a closer look and found that he had a deep, heavily bleeding cut on his left rear thigh, impossible for him to reach with his human hands. Tearing a piece of cloth from the lining of my tunic, I bound the wound tightly. Then he opened his eyes and looked up into mine, confused and very afraid.

"Do not worry," I said, gently patting the wound. "I won't harm you.

SHADES OF MEMNON

There has been enough fighting and death today..."

He opened his mouth to speak when suddenly his eyes widened at something behind me. Turning to see what it was, I was just in time to see a huge club descending toward my head. Ducking quickly, I rolled away and sprang to my feet. There before me stood another Centaur, whirling his club menacingly, a mad look in his eyes.

The one I had just assisted threw up a weak hand, saying something to the attacker, who shot hostile words back, pointing at me accusingly. They argued for a few moments until the second Centaur finally shouted him down. Then, before I could act, the intruding Centaur raised his club and brought it smashing down upon the head of his injured comrade. The sickening sound of crushing bones echoed throughout the forest.

There was nothing else to do now but reach for my weapons, but when I did, they felt strange. As I pulled them out they seemed heavier than normal, and when I tried to push Rau into them, none came forth.

The mad Centaur rushed upon me, swinging his club in a sweeping arc. This time the weapon struck my shoulder, knocking me from my feet. Though the pain was terrible, I clutched my blades tightly as I hit the ground, hoping they would soon come to life. Then as I struggled to get to my feet, I noticed a new peril: the strength in my limbs was also leaving. Still I rose, weapons raised in defiance, as the merciless Centaur came in for another pass.

Noticing my faltering arms, he grinned hatefully and closed in, bringing his club down against my shoulder once again. This time the blow sent me tumbling head over heels through tall grasses and bushes. Struggling to my knees, I weighed my options, reluctantly deciding to flee. With my weapons still stubbornly clutched in my hands, I crawled through the vegetation in an effort to find an escape route. But a glance behind me revealed the cruel Centaur hovering nearby, tauntingly switching his club from one hand to the other.

I pulled free of the bushes and tried to run back toward the field of battle, but my assailant caught me quickly and struck another blow squarely in the middle of my back. Pain shot all the way to my feet and I fell to my knees, while the Centaur pranced around me. I tried to crawl the other way, back toward the mouth of the cave, but soon his hooved feet blocked that path also.

Then the Centaur gazed into my eyes, searching for signs of fear. Seeing none, he became irritated and smashed his club down upon my head. Blood flowed down into my eyes and my face landed hard in the dust.

SHADES OF MEMNON

*"He Was Dark As Ebony, But The Handsomest Man Alive
And Like Achilles Wore Arms Forged By Hephaestus"*

Arctinos of Miletos, 700 BC

CHAPTER 11: "I FORGED FOR YOUR PA"

I felt my body being carried along and opened my pain-filled eyes to see what was happening to me. Dense darkness surrounded me and I could see nothing, but I knew I was being carried downward from the angle of my body. I soon recognized the cold dampness pressed against my limbs, and realized I was being taken by Daedalus' strange servants back into the recesses of the mountain. But I could not speak, my head throbbed painfully and my eyes would not stay open.

I awoke later to the feeling of a cool, wet cloth being applied to my head. Opening my eyes, I saw before me one of Daedalus' women. Smiling gently, she greeted me with a friendly nod. Behind her stood the blacksmith himself, leaning on his cane and peering down upon me. He said something in the northern language and the woman rose and left the room. Then the blacksmith stepped forward.

"Young one, you are lucky to be alive," he said sharply.

"I know," I replied, remembering the blow I had taken from the Centaur.

"If your bones had not been strengthened during your prior conditioning, that creature would have split your skull. Even so, when my servants arrived, he was preparing to strike you again, which would have surely killed you regardless. They are truly a craven race of creatures, those Centaur..."

"What happened?" I asked.

"Luckily for you I sent several of my servants to observe the progress of the battle," Daedalus replied. "The Centaur feared them and ran away in fright. Then they brought you back here."

"Thank your servants for me, Daedalus. Now I must get up from here..."

I tried to rise, my head throbbed violently and dizziness overcame me. Daedalus shook his head as I fell back onto the bed. "You are still too weak. You must have more rest. Now that you are awake, though, there are things we must discuss."

I lay back and prepared myself to listen. Daedalus sat down on the edge of the bed, his cane between his legs, his hands perched atop it. He looked around the chamber cautiously, then peered deeply into my eyes.

"Know this, young Memnon: I have existed for many centuries, peacefully working metals here in my mountain, forging for any who could pay my fees. Having few earthly needs, it has been easy to remain apart from the affairs of the world."

I tried to pay attention, but the pain and ringing in my head distracted me. Daedalus noticed and rubbed my brow gently. The pain subsided and I could hear him better.

"But this time..." he continued, shaking his head sadly. "Never before

SHADES OF MEMNON

have the affairs of the world threatened my way of life, so I must do what is necessary to maintain it. It seems, therefore, that I must break my code of neutrality to assist you."

"Assist me?" I asked. "How? Why?"

"Listen to me," said the blacksmith. "There are things you are not being told by Kho-An-Sa. Things you need to know."

"What do you mean?" I asked.

"Young Memnon, you are being deceived. I sense things about your spirit...the woman you have been given..."

"Nala?" I asked.

Daedalus nodded. "She is beautiful, is she not. A true mistress of pleasure...and power?"

"Why, yes," I replied with a smile.

Daedalus shook his head grimly. "She is a viper! She is using her skills to cloud your mind and change your nature."

"But she empowers me. After I am with her I feel as if I could do anything..."

"Yes," said Daedalus, poking a finger into my chest. "Yes, you are empowered, but do you not feel something else?"

I thought for a moment. "Why...sometimes...at times I have felt more warlike. Ready to fight...but...I..."

"You are being manipulated," the blacksmith continued. "It is Kho-An-Sa's wish that you become a killer with no remorse, and Nala is his instrument. When you are joined she attracts negative forces. Then, working her magical arts, she seals them to your spirit."

It all made sense to me now. Kho-An-Sa knew that I would never willingly be as he wanted me to be. So he gave me this woman, seeking to use her skills to change me. I lowered my head, ashamed that I had been so easily fooled. Daedalus placed his hand upon my shoulder.

"Be not ashamed, Memnon. For you are young and know nothing of these things. It is Kho-An-Sa's wish that you become dependent upon this woman, for only a warrior who combines his life force with that of a woman of power can manipulate the forces that have been set free within you. You have been away from her for a long while, and that is why your strength and weapons failed you."

"What should I do? I asked.

Daedalus rubbed his chin.

"There are other women who have such talents. Temple women, priestesses, others. Until you find a mate with the required skills, these are the women you must seek out. For now, take my advice: do not go near this Nala again. Refuse her. Reject her."

"But ...what shall I tell Kho-An-Sa?" I asked.

Daedalus tightened his grip upon my shoulder.

"I am sure you will think of something. I tell you this because you play a large part in Kho-An-Sa's plans."

"You know his goals?" I asked.

"I can see where he is going. I have seen this coming for some time," the blacksmith replied sadly. "He and his coalition, the People of the Sea and other Servants of the Serpents, wish to take control of the force of the Reckoning and twist it to their own ends. They wish to recover the riches and the dominion they once possessed."

"What do you mean?" I asked.

Daedalus held up both his arms, nodding towards the metal bands upon each of his wrists. One band shone a lustrous yellowish-brown; the other was polished just as highly, but had a dark, coal-black sheen.

"This is the metal of the past," he said, pushing the bronze band toward me. "And this, the metal of the future."

I looked closely at the darker band as he held it close.

"Iron," the blacksmith said grimly. "The time of iron is upon us and the world will run red with blood."

"But why?"

"The People of the Sea wrested control of the trade in bronze and held it for many years. Your pa's Kushite coalition, who started this trade long ago, took it back, rendering the Sea Kings to the status of couriers. But now that iron is coming into general use, their share of the profits are shrinking..."

"And so... ?"

"And so, the Sea Kings have lost their fortunes. At first they took to piracy and highway robbery. But the taking of two strategic cities, Troy in the north and Petra in the south, shows that their ambitions are much more serious now. This, I think, is where you are involved, young Memnon."

"How so?"

"Your pa was once their main opponent, combating them in all lands, upon all seas. It would please them greatly if you, his son, would be their warrior and assassin."

"Do you know my pa?"

The blacksmith leaned forward, smiling. "I forged for your pa."

My mouth fell open in surprise and my mind reeled with many questions. But just then we heard footsteps and Daedalus placed a finger to his lips. We passed a moment in silence, then Kho-An-Sa strolled into the room.

"Ah, young panther! You are finally awake. I feared you would not wake up after the many days you lay there."

"Many days ... how long was I asleep?"

Kho-An-Sa and the blacksmith looked at each other.

"You were severely injured, Memnon." replied Kho-An-Sa. "You have been here for 14 days."

SHADES OF MEMNON

I sat up and shook my head even though the pain of moving went through my every limb. Kho-An-Sa stepped toward the bed, holding a small wooden box in one hand and an object I did not immediately recognize in the other.

"You performed better than I expected in this last venture, Kho-An-Sa said with a satisfied smile. "So I have decided to reward you."

He placed the box in my hand and opened it. Inside was the ring given to me by the Anu prince on the Island of the Ka.

"My ring," I cried, snatching it from the box.

It was shining in all its obsidian glory, the torchlight bouncing off the contours of the feline carvings. But I noticed that the special mark was not there.

"I can detect nothing more than an ornamental use for that ring," said Kho-An-Sa, "and so I return it to you."

"Thank you," I replied, pulling the ring onto the middle finger of my right hand. As I positioned it there, the feline face moved and the symbol of leadership re-appeared upon its brow. I covered it discreetly to conceal these things from Kho-An-Sa.

"And this," the magician said, offering me the other object.

My mouth fell open as I recognized an object I thought I would never see again: It was a leather helm with a lustrous ring of carved bronze circling the crown.

"Yes," Kho-An-Sa said. "It belonged to your pa."

My eyes widened. Here before me was the very helm worn by my sire as he battled his way across the world. Tighter fitting and different from the protective headgear worn by the native warriors of Kamit, the helm made my pa stand out from all others and added to the legends about him. "Brazen crested Memnon" he was often called. He had told me the helm was from his homeland.

"This will help to protect your head the next time some creature takes a swing at it," Kho-An-Sa said. "Why do you hesitate? Take it! "

Many questions ran through my mind. Where had he acquired my pa's helm? What did he know about his fate? And why was he giving it to me now? In light of the conversation I had just had with the blacksmith the answer to the last question became immediately clear—the magician wanted me to be the image of my pa, to continue the legend of Memnon, but as a servant loyal to his evil purposes. Little did he know that his plans to change me had been discovered. Pushing my questions aside for the time being, I reached out and took my pa's helm. Turning it over in my hands, I vowed that the legend would go on, but not in the way the magician expected.

"Good, good," Kho-An-Sa exclaimed. "Your next gift will be time with Nala. She will help to bring you back to full strength—and bring you much pleasure."

"I no longer want Nala," I replied.

"What?" cried Kho-An-Sa.

"I no longer want her," I shot back. "She no longer pleases me."

Kho-An-Sa shook his head in disbelief. "What do you mean? Nala is one of the most beautiful women in creation. Stop this foolish talk."

"I mean it. I no longer want her. I want," I began, but had to stop and think for a moment. "I want a Tamahu woman," I lied. "That's it. Get me a Tamahu."

Kho-An-Sa was taken aback. He looked at Daedalus, but the blacksmith only shrugged his shoulders.

"Who can fathom the lusts of youth?" the blacksmith said dryly.

"A Tamahu," said Kho-An-Sa, shaking his head. "You want a Tamahu?"

"Yes," I said. "Like Daedalus' women who took care of me. And I want two of them, just like Daedalus has."

Kho-An-Sa's mouth dropped open. "You want...two of them?"

"Yes. Two of them. I prefer one with yellow hair and one with red. Just like Daedalus' women. I admire his taste."

Kho-An-Sa looked at the blacksmith again. Daedalus shrugged once more, turning toward the doorway.

"Perhaps we should let him rest now. Tomorrow he will receive the final gift for what he has done for me. Kho-An-Sa, we should let him sleep."

The magician nodded in agreement, the incredulous look still upon his face. I turned over in bed, clutching my pa's helm to my breast. Then I laughed silently and drifted off to sleep.

This time my slumber was tortured by anguished dreams of my family and images of Kam-Atef, all cascading before me in a deluge of confused images. They were mercifully interrupted when a tug at the covers of my bed woke me with a start. Rousing from my fitful dreams, I rolled over to find one of Daedalus' elemental servants standing nearby. As I rose, washed myself and dressed, the lingering image of the great serpent remained. I knew I had to contact him soon.

Daedalus' servant led me down a long corridor, identical to hundreds in the domain of the blacksmith. Soon we emerged into the familiar hall and were greeted by the smoke, sounds and odors of the great workshop. There, next to a large table, stood Daedalus and Kho-An-Sa. On the floor nearby I saw the boy I had brought. Upon seeing me, he leapt to his feet and ran into my arms. I hugged him affectionately.

"Greetings, Memnon," said Daedalus. "Today you will receive my final gift as payment for what you have done for me in this land."

I stepped forward and bowed to the blacksmith, then nodded at Kho-An-Sa.

SHADES OF MEMNON

The boy then tugged at my arm, leading me to the floor where he had been playing. There I saw numerous metal objects, including crude replicas of animals, tools and other implements. Looking closely, I noticed some slight movements among the animal replicas. The blacksmith leaned towards us.

"I was correct, Memnon, in choosing this child as my apprentice," he said.

"It seems so, great blacksmith," I replied.

The boy walked to Daedalus and stood next to him. Kho-An-Sa stood nearby, silently nodding, rubbing his chin.

"The child certainly is gifted," the magician said.

"He is much more than gifted, Kho-An-Sa," replied the blacksmith. "This boy is chosen. He is attuned to the elements of the earth, as I suspected by the love my servants have shown him. He will be a master blacksmith."

I looked carefully at the child. He seemed happy and quite proud of himself, and I was glad he had found something to give his life meaning, after what had happened to his people.

"He still has not uttered a word," said Daedalus. "So I don't know what he was named at birth. I call him Phastos - he seems to like it."

"Hail, Phastos," I said, bowing to the boy. "Great smith in training."

Kho-An-Sa stepped forward.

"Ahem," he cleared his throat. "I think now it is time to be about the real business of the day. We must be gone from here soon."

"Quite true," replied the blacksmith. "Memnon, approach the table, please."

I walked up to the large table to find my long and short swords, dagger and throwing knife lying upon it. The weapons had been shined and polished to a sparkle. Next to them sat a large tub of water. Daedalus waved his hand over the tub and spoke a word. Suddenly the water began to smoke and bubble.

"Memnon," said the blacksmith. "How much do you want these weapons?"

I looked at the him curiously.

"Very much," I replied. "I want them very, very much, Daedalus."

"Good," he said. "Soon you shall have a chance to prove it."

The blacksmith clapped his hands and four of his little servants appeared. They leapt upon the table, and each sat upon one of my weapons. Daedalus said another word that I could not understand and their little bodies began to dissolve. Sinking down slowly, they were absorbed into the very metal of my weapons. Each blade shook violently as a creature became one with it. I looked at the blacksmith in astonishment.

"Fear not, younger Memnon," he said. "Here is your first test."

He clapped his hands once again and suddenly each weapon stood upon its own handle. Then one by one the blades hopped to the tub and leapt into the bubbling water.

"Now, Memnon," said Daedalus, "retrieve your weapons."

I looked at the blacksmith as if he had taken leave of his senses. More smoke was rising from the tub and it bubbled more violently.

"Do as he says, Memnon," Kho-An-Sa ordered.

I had no doubt that my hands would be scalded severely, but I stepped up to the tub nevertheless. The water bubbled so violently that I could not see the weapons, but I steadied myself and plunged my hands into it. To my surprise and relief, the water was cool to the touch.

Immediately the long and short swords placed themselves into my hands and I brought them out. After laying them to the side, I plunged my hands back in for the others. They too leapt into my grasp and I pulled them from the water. I placed them all on the table, then turned to face Daedalus and Kho-An-Sa.

"Very good, Memnon," said the magician.

"You have passed the first test," said Daedalus. "Your weapons have been bonded with earth spirits. And because you have proven to them that they are wanted, by rescuing them from apparent danger, they are forever bonded to you. But now comes an even more difficult test: you must harmonize the earth spirits with the ka of Sekmet."

"How do I do that?"

"You must convince the lady of vengeance to accept the other spirits," Daedalus replied. "It will be dangerous, for the only way is to trick her into devouring them. You must go inside yourself, to your place of power, where you and these weapons are one. Once there, you must taunt Sekmet into eating the spirits. Then, at the correct time, you must embrace her so that you are all one."

I thought for a moment of the terrible figure of the Neter Sekmet. During the forging of my weapons she had drunk my blood. Though she was the fighting spirit of my weapons, I had no wish to meet her face to face again.

"Are you sure this is necessary?" I asked Kho-An-Sa.

"It is," replied the magician. "Do it, young panther. She does not harm those she has become bound to. At least, not much."

I nodded and proceeded to sit cross-legged upon the floor. Kho-An-Sa stood over me, moving his hands in strange patterns over my head.

"Do not let her catch you until all the spirits have been devoured," he said. "It is then that she must be embraced. Good luck, young panther."

I closed my eyes while Kho-An-Sa continued to wave his hands over me, now murmuring potent words of power. Suddenly there was a flash of light in my mind.

SHADES OF MEMNON

I opened my eyes to find myself standing before a huge red temple. The walls of the structure were covered with paintings and carvings of me battling all the creatures and men I had faced thus far in combat, from the men I had killed in my first encounter with Kho-An-Sa, to the Wolven creatures from the land of Daedalus. In all the encounters I held the Claws of Sekmet, even in situations where I had yet to possess them.

Two giant statues stood outside the walls on high pedestals. One was an exact likeness of Sekmet as I had encountered her during the forging of my blades. The other statue was of me, standing tall and holding my weapons. There was another pedestal which stood empty. Instinctively I knew it was the one I had come to fill.

As I approached the steps of the temple I noticed one of the earth spirits sitting there. When I stopped to have a closer look, it transformed itself into a plump, juicy black pig. Continuing up the stairs, I approached the entrance, where there was another earth spirit sitting patiently. As I walked by, it transformed itself into a fat monkey. Continuing on, I stepped into the temple and started down a long hall. In the distance there were three silver thrones. A bright red creature with the body of a woman and the head of a lioness sat in one of them. It was Sekmet.

I looked around for the other earth spirits and saw one sitting halfway down the hall, right in the middle of the floor. As I passed by, it lifted its shapeless black body and transformed into a black sheep. I kept going towards the thrones, looking for the last of the earth spirits. When I came near, I found Sekmet asleep, her head slumping to the side. The last earth spirit sat right before her. It looked up at me before changing into a small black deer.

I stood before the throne, gazing up at the sleeping deity. Deciding to take the direct approach, I seized the black deer and tossed it into her lap. Sekmet's eyes blinked open at once, and her fiery stare bore right through me. Then her jaws opened to impossible proportions, and her roar shook the entire temple. I swallowed nervously, praying I had taken the right approach, as she looked down into her lap.

I watched in amazement as she lunged without hesitation, seizing the disguised earth spirit. Smacking her lips hungrily, she lifted it to her gaping jaws and slid it down her throat. Then she stood up looking at me, the hungry look still in her eyes. Turning on my heels, I ran down the hall, with Sekmet close behind. As we ran, I came to the little black sheep, bent down and scooped it up. Then I turned quickly and tossed it to the deity. She caught it deftly in her claws, looked it over and tossed it into her mouth. She was chewing loudly as I headed for the entrance.

Just outside the other spirit awaited calmly for its turn to be devoured. I scooped it up and tossed Sekmet this latest morsel. The monkey disappeared just as quickly as the others, but this time I could see a visible lump in

Sekmet's belly. Nevertheless, she came at me again as I ran down the stairs of the temple. At the bottom stood the first earth spirit in its pig guise. I bent down to scoop it up, but when I turned Sekmet was upon me. Knocking me down to the ground, she raised her sharp claws and opened her razor-toothed maw. The heat of her breath scorched my face as I pushed the pig into her mouth.

Her jaws slammed shut like a trap and she swallowed again. This time her belly bulged to huge proportions and she stepped back from me. To my great relief, the hunger in her eyes subsided, a gentle purr arose from her throat and she took on a peaceful demeanor. Sensing that the danger was over, I extended my arms to embrace her.

When we touched, the lump in Sekmet's belly pushed into me and I felt the stirrings of the creatures she'd just devoured. I also felt an overwhelming sense of security and strength, as if nothing could ever harm me. Peering over her shoulder toward the temple, I gazed at the last pedestal. It was occupied now by the statue of an earth spirit. Hugging the deity tightly, I closed my eyes and smiled.

Then the voice of Kho-An-Sa aroused me.

"Memnon! Memnon, awake!"

I opened my eyes to find the magician and blacksmith standing before me with satisfied smiles. They nodded to each other triumphantly, and Daedalus pointed to my weapons.

"Memnon, you have harmonized the forces of your blades. Sekmet has accepted the earth spirits, making it possible for them to do what they must do. Never will you have to worry about losing these weapons: they will always make their way back to you. Throw the dagger as you will, plunge the blades as you must. The Gift of Infinite Return is yours."

I lifted my long sword and held it up high. Immediately the familiar rush of Rau from my middle, through my arms and into the weapon. Its weight disappeared as the powers of the Rau force washed over me and I smiled. Then suddenly the feeling was gone. I lowered the heavy blade carefully, so that Kho-An-Sa would not detect how weak the force was within me.

"Thank you, great blacksmith," I said. "This is a gift without price."

"Thank you, Memnon, for what you have done for me," Daedalus replied. "May these weapons serve you well."

Kho-An-Sa stepped forward and bowed to the blacksmith.

"Great Daedalus," he pronounced graciously, "I will see to it that your name is known in the four corners of the world for what you have done. We thank you for your work. Now we must be gone."

I embraced Phastos warmly as we stood before the long tunnel that would take Kho-An-Sa and I back to the camp. The boy still had no voice, but the tears in his eyes told me he was greatly saddened by my departure.

SHADES OF MEMNON

Though I had grown fond of him also, I thought it best to leave him with the blacksmith. As I looked down into his sea-green eyes, he handed me a small panther made of silver.

"Thank you, Phastos," I said. "One day, my little friend, we shall meet again."

"He will be well taken care of here," said Daedalus. "He has a destiny to fulfill and I will see him through it."

The blacksmith assigned another of his little servants to lead us back to the camp. From there we were to follow the creature back into the tunnels with all the men. It would then lead us to another tunnel that would take us back to our ship, avoiding entirely any hostile confrontations like those we had encountered coming here.

As we walked along through the tunnel, I noticed that Kho-An-Sa seemed especially preoccupied and irritated. Lost in thought, his face contorted into expressions of anger and worry, and he glanced at me many times before he spoke.

"Memnon," he began slowly, "there is a task to be done."

"What sort of task?" I asked.

"A task I had hoped to avoid..."

"What is it?"

The magician shifted the torch he was carrying from his left to his right hand, then stopped walking and turned to me. "Do you know of Minos?" he asked.

I thought for a moment.

"You are speaking of the king?" I asked. "Mad king Minos of Keftui?"

"The same," replied Kho-An-Sa, as we commenced walking.

"What about him?"

"He and his sires before him have been valuable allies in our coalition, especially since they took the Island of Keftui and opened it for our purposes. But madness has always run in their bloodline, none worse than the current king, Minos the fourth."

"And so?" I asked.

"And so he is no longer of any use to us. He also refuses to give back a valuable tool I loaned him. As you lay recovering from your wounds, Daedalus informed me of the mad king's latest misdeeds."

"Daedalus knows him?"

"Daedalus forged for him. It was the only time the blacksmith left his mountain home to do his work. Minos repaid him by trying to enslave him and caused the death of the smith's only son; this is why the blacksmith longed so for an apprentice. There is no love between the great blacksmith and mad King Minos, I assure you."

Suddenly it occurred to me what the task might be, but I decided to ask regardless. "What do you plan to do?"

"Something that has never been done in the history of our coalition. You, Memnon, must go to the court of Minos. First you must find my property...."

"And then?"

"And then you must relieve the mad king of his pathetic life."

When we arrived at the camp, the men greeted us with loud cheers and questions about our journey. They were very curious about my pa's helm and our strange guide, but cautiously kept their distance from it. Only Cronn, who stood off to the side, leaning upon his huge sword, seemed unconcerned with our presence. Kho-An-Sa joined the giant and they talked for a while. Then he barked orders at his warriors to break camp. As we hurriedly packed, I asked Kho-An-Sa about this new urgency.

"Though it is no affair of yours, Memnon," said the magician, "we are very late in departing from this land. Cronn and I have pressing business in the far northern regions he calls home. We must get back to the ship quickly."

We broke camp and followed the little creature to a large cave on the side of a nearby hill. Inside was a long dark tunnel leading down into the ground. Some of the warriors were reluctant to go in, but after a few threats from Kho-An-Sa and Cronn, torches were lit and we descended.

We walked for many miles for what seemed to be several days, stopping periodically for brief rests. Finally, we emerged from the tunnel just before daybreak, onto the sands of a beach. Our strange little guide bowed once, then slipped back into the tunnel and disappeared.

As the rays of Aten brightened the landscape, we saw our ship moored nearby and set out for it. When we came within signaling distance, Kho-An-Sa lit a large torch and waved it in a special pattern for several moments. The pattern was repeated on the deck of the ship, and soon three small boats were sent in to retrieve us.

As we rowed back to the vessel, I took one last look at the land that had given me so much but had nearly taken my life. When we were climbing aboard the ship, I wondered if I would ever see Daedalus or Phastos again. And, remembering what the blacksmith had said, I wondered when my pa had come this way.

The sailors and warriors rushed to greet us, embracing friends and, in some cases, mourning those who had not come back. Pushing through that crowd and heading right for me was Nala. I looked for a way to avoid her, but it was too late.

She threw her arms around me, smothering my face with kisses "Oh, Memnon," she said, "I knew you would come back to me. Come to our room. Please, please come."

She was as beautiful as ever and her perfume was invigorating, but I pushed all that out of mind, then pushed her away too.

SHADES OF MEMNON

"Memnon, what is wrong?" she asked.

"Nala," I began, "there have been...changes since we parted..."

"Changes? What changes?", she snapped, finally sensing my mood.

"Changes," I said with finality.

As I walked away, Kho-An-Sa appeared and began talking to her. I headed for the warriors' quarters to find myself a space to sleep, but before I stepped inside I turned to look at Kho-An-Sa and Nala. He was gesturing vigorously, shaking his head and tossing both hands into the air. Suddenly there was a long pause, and then Nala turned and looked at me, her beautiful face twisted into a bitter mask of pure hatred. With a petulant flip of her hair, she stormed off to her quarters.

The ship immediately set sail, rapidly putting distance between us and this strange land with its strange creatures. After watching the shore disappear, I spent the entire day observing the warriors in their quarters and polishing my weapons. Several times I saw Nala peeking through the window, but I ignored her. When night fell the other warriors engaged in games of chance and the sharing of tales, but I sat in a corner alone. Ignoring all that was going on around me, I quieted my mind and slowed my breathing. It was time for me to contact Kam-Atef.

I rested my head for long moments, concentrating on the image of the great serpent. Finally I heard his voice.

"Greetings, Memna-un!"

"Greetings, Kam-Atef," I answered. "It is so good to speak to you again. So much has happened..."

I told the great serpent what had taken place since I last had spoken to him. He was proud of the way I had handled the various challenges, but he scolded me harshly about my hesitation to contact him.

"I'm sorry, great one. I won't hesitate next time."

"You should not have been ashamed of what you had to do to save your lives," said Kam-Atef. "No one forced through torture and threats is expected to keep his word."

"But let us continue," Kam-Atef said. "I have tried a number of times to send you messages, but some force has prevented it."

I thought for a moment. "I too have tried to contact you. Could the influence of Nala have blocked our communications?"

"Hmmm," he replied thoughtfully. "That is highly probable. Even now, it is more difficult than it should be. Daedalus was correct, you must not go near this woman again."

I then told Kam-Atef about the latest assignment I had received to kill King Minos and retrieve some mysterious "tool" from the kingdom of the mad monarch.

"The kingdom of Minos..." sighed the great serpent. "Hold, Memna-un. I must contact another."

A few moments later, Kam-Atef's voice was with me again. "Go to the court of Minos, Memna-un. There you will find someone who can help you. But first you must assist him."

"But what about King Minos?"

"My friend at Minos' court says that political intrigue will be the king's undoing very soon. You will not have to kill him."

"I am relieved, great one. I will not kill for Kho-An-Sa."

"I know you wouldn't, Memna-un. Contact me again after my friend has made you stronger."

"But wait, great serpent. How will I know this friend at the court of Minos? How will I know how to help him?"

"You will know what he needs when you meet him," Kam-Atef replied. "And fear not. He will know you."

SHADES OF MEMNON

SHADES OF MEMNON

MEMNON'S LYRICS
BANG MASTER D OF THE BLACK PIRATE MILITIA

SHADES OF MEMNON

Ova da horizons past Aten my sight can see
I crave to be immortal for eternity
Knowledge be
Cubed like Rubiks
Ship sail 60 wide, long 250 cubits
Wherever our journey took us
I knew it would be danger
C.E., Mo-therapy, Serious Anga,
JahBangJah
Warriors, Sailors practice Maat
It just might save ya
Have no fear my sista
I'm comin ta gitcha
The oracles told me to hook-up wit
Tha *Black Pirate Militia*
Ra boosted, heads flew off
I knew I had to do it
Spies -n- perpetreacherous foes executed
My Shepsu by my side
Amen Ra as my guide
Veggie fed, child of Geb
Images of Kam-Atef all up in my head
My best bet Ausar Auset
Vainglorious battle cries
My claws of Sekmet
Yo' last breath met
I'm not cho' prey, all Vipers I slay
Beast or man, any opponent that stand
in my way
Herukhuti walkin' among U in tha flesh
Sky-metal forged blades put yo' ass to rest
I'm blessed
Shades of Memnon

Chorus:
Dark like the shade of no other
Dark like the shade of my father
and my mother
Dark like the shade of my sister and
my brother
Dark like the shade of his color
The shade of Memnon

Keep yo' weapons close to heart
Whole world caved in
Everything fell apart
But it's my destiny to take this trip
Hra-Twa spirit my sister from the ship
Terrible vengeance descended on my
adversaries tip
Memnon, the dark shade

Noble and great possessing all my
Daddies traits
Determined to save my sister from an
ill fate
But wait, so many serpents and demons
My swords screamin'
Kho-An-Sa steadily schemin'
Fo' his blood I'm feignin'
Why in tha' hell you wanna barter
I'm ready to slaughter
For defacing my momma's only daughter
I'm choppin' off tokens of yo' manhood
Sending a warnin' to the masses
So I'm overstood
In this game of life U just a pawn
At the crack of dawn
I had to take out Cronn
Somebody please
Tell me what's goin' on
As a warrior I'm made like Teflon
Shades of Memnon

Chorus:
Dark like the shade of no other
Dark like the shade of my father
and my mother
Dark like the shade of my sister and
my brother
Dark like the shade of his color
The shade of Memnon

Be Proud of where U come from!
-N-yo melanin can absorb 246
vitamins from the sun
U betta recognize!
Black Man!
U gotta elevate and rise to your
highest level!

To be a man U got to see a man
M-E-M-N-O-N and
U being brought up on charges
It's impossible to stop this
Deep in the labyrinth
My life was spared by a inch
Still I refuse to flinch
Repugnant smells of the creature's
stench
All in my face
Hanging out all day
With the Medjay
Learning my lessons

As a young scribe
Never ever havin' loyalty
To the otha' side
My ancestors died
For the cause
Forever I'm a revolutionary
With no pause
I'm talking to all ya'll
I ain't no servant of Set
My swords of Sekmet
About to get U wet
Kho-An-Sa
U gon' regret we ever met
It's mandatory
I gotta come gitcha
Even it I have to come
With the whole Black Pirate Milita
Evil doers heads I see decapitated
No tears
No fears
No love
No hate
Death is yo' fate
And I can't wait
To uplift and elevate
First I check em'
In the name of Shekem Ur Shekem
I fought like hell spawn
Last man standin'
Bang Master D ya'll
Bang Master D ya'll
Shades of Memnon

Chorus:
Dark like the shade of no other
Dark like the shade of my father
and my mother
Dark like the shade of my sister and
my brother
Dark like the shade of his color
The shade of Memnon

Fresh for tha' 2G's
This is JahBangJah Khali
All I can say is
Black Man U gotta elevate and rise!
And yo' Melanocytes inside yo'
Black dark skin U gotta recognize
We gotta remember how to build
tha' pyramids
All it takes is two people to remember
Know what I'm sayin'
700,000

As a modern day Memnon, I am fighting for the mental liberation of my people. Of my grandmother's mother's mother and all of our ancestors who were slaughtered and sold during the Atlantic slave trade and who were killed during the wars with the imperial powers. Today my battleground is modern day urban America and my sword is my tongue. I have not come here of my own accord, but have been delivered by the most high to awaken the third eye of the masses. I give thanks and praises to the most high, and much love to Brother G for making this book possible and reminding us of our glory as kings and queens.

Bang Master D of the Black Pirate Militia

SHADES OF MEMNON

SHADES OF MEMNON

BOOK TWO PREVIEW!

Behind me I heard shouts and curses as the Medjay holding the gate tower came under attack. Focusing on the task at hand, I urged the men on to greater speed as we ran down the road. Within moments we were rushing upon the first gate, taking the warriors manning it completely by surprise.

Because it was designed to ward off attack from without, Medjay archers cut down many before they knew what had hit them. Then we swarmed over the building, killed those inside and raised the heavy door. Once again we left a force to hold what we had taken, then rushed on to take the next gate.

I noted that the forces of Kamit were already starting their siege, exchanging arrows with the gate's defenders. Preoccupied, these gate protectors would be taken unawares also, leaving the opening for the Kamitic forces free and clear. But as we neared this final obstacle, a shadow fell across our path.

Looking up, the warriors around me gasped in astonishment.
"A skyboat!" someone exclaimed. Indeed it was a skyboat, similar in design to the one I had seen on the Island of the Ka. However, something told me that it did not contain friendly Anu.

As I and the rest of the Medjay stood in awe, a familiar voice rang out near me. It was Hra-Twa. "Memna-un," said my little Anu friend desperately, "you cannot stand against the occupants of that vessel. Stop standing there and take the other gate. The Shekem is your only hope."

I was totally surprised. Hra-Twa had never come to me on the field of battle. Something very dire was about to take place. "Half you men take that gate," I shouted, "go, go, go!" I was left with perhaps 40 warriors, including Ka-Sah and Pa-Sah, who stood ever by my side. The sky-boat landed before us and the door began to open.

"Memna-un," cried Hra-Twa, "don't do it." "I have no choice my friend," I replied coolly. "I cannot allow them to attack us from the rear. Better to face them now."

Hra-Twa stepped into a shadow and was gone, as the door to the sky-boat completely opened. Out stepped several Tamahu warriors wearing attire I had never seen before. Their silver corselets wrapped in black sashes immediately caught my eye, along with their strange headgear topped by stiff, upright horsehair. All of them carried exquisite long swords of very fine workmanship and brightly colored, thick round shields.

A column of 50 or so emerged, placing themselves into battle formation to the left and right of the sky-boat. Then out stepped two strange Tamahus unlike any I had ever seen. Both were as tall as I, unarmed and wearing long white robes and elegant jewelry. With green wreaths wrapped around their heads, they stood with a haughty, arrogant air. But the most striking thing was their golden colored hair and strangely glowing complexions.

As these two stood motionless, from behind them stepped a man that I did recognize. It was the yellow-haired warrior that I had seen when I last visited Petra. The one who had wanted my head. Dressed similar to the two shining ones beside him, he was armed with a long gleaming spear and two swords.

His eyes swept the scene for a moment, finally settling upon me. Then he handed the spear to one of the shining ones and strode toward me, a bitter sneer spreading across his face. "Greetings, Memnon the younger," he said in broken Kamitic. "Who are you?" I asked, stepping forward myself. "Who am I?" he answered with an evil grin. "Why, I am your death, man. I am Aias, son of Achilles."

SHADES OF MEMNON

Printed in the United States
47860LVS00005B/370-390